JASMINE

THE KINGS OF GUARDIAN, BOOK 6

KRIS MICHAELS

D1603605

DISCLAIMER

This story is a work of fiction. All of the characters
mentioned, organizations described, and events
detailed in this novel are either products of the
author's imagination or used fictitiously.

CHAPTER 1

*J*asmine King scanned the writhing crowd from her concealed vantage point. Seventy-four thousand over-heated, drunk, high, and generally obnoxious people sang, danced, chanted, and pumped their fists in rhythm with the beat of the blaring country music anthem. *Country Music*'s 'Voice of the Century,' *Demure Magazine*'s 'America's Sexiest Man Alive,' and for the fifth year in a row, country music's reigning entertainer of the year, Chad Nelson, the man, the myth, and—if you believed his press—the legend, released his unending energy into the Georgia Dome crowd. The man sang, danced, and showed his skill at playing multiple instruments all while pouring his brand of music out to his faithful followers. At one point during a ballad, he stopped singing, and the crowd's voice lifted to fill the void in the dome. The melody of thousands of voices echoed in a surreal testament to the man's impact on literally millions of lives. It was probably a performance to remember— if not for one minor detail. At least one of the super-star's rabidly loyal fans was off-the-deep-end, batshit crazy. The question was, who in the thou-sands in attendance wanted Nelson dead?

Jasmine assumed Nelson's label had hired Guardian Security when the usual type of weirdness associated with the fans of the famous singer esca-lated from run-of-the mill threats to stalker-psycho insane. Someone had placed a mutilated picture of Chad with a hand-scrawled note attached to it on his tour bus. According to the message she'd received when she was diverted to take this case, two things had converged to freak out the suits that handled the superstar. First, the picture of Chad wasn't a publicity shot. It was a candid shot taken when he wasn't touring, although the star's people couldn't figure out exactly *where* or *when* it had been taken. Second, the tour bus had been locked in a secure, guarded parking area. Meaning, the person who had put the picture on the bus could be someone within his inner circle.

The headliner was currently in Atlanta performing a sold-out, three-night show that culminated his Back-2-Me tour. Jasmine King glanced at the performer briefly before she scanned the crowd —again. The musical number the band was playing was the final song of the second encore, and it would be the last, at least according to the road manager who'd briefed Guardian's security team when they'd arrived. She'd been late to arrive at the Dome and hoped the information passed on to her from the team already in place hadn't changed.

Jazz stood just inside the right-wing entrance to the stage. She had an unobstructed view of the stage and the crowd. Nelson's gorgeous muscled back, sans shirt most of the last encore, glistened with sweat. In the last two hours, she'd been a firsthand witness to why promoters lauded the sexy singer as the hottest act in the nation. The background she'd hurriedly read revealed that with the exception of the rock god, Lucifer Cross, Nelson outsold all artists of any genre in music sales, downloads and concert attendance.

Her earpiece and radio were rendered useless by the deafening thrum of the amplified music and screaming crowd. She hadn't heard a single transmission since the concert had started. She systematically scanned the crowd looking for possible threats. The ground-level stage security was in full force beneath Chad and his band. There were barriers keeping the crowd out of a cleared buffer zone in front of the stage. Venue security stood shoulder to shoulder in the area, keeping people from rushing the stage. Guardian had a small presence strategically placed in various locations. They weren't here to control the crowd. Guardian assets were looking for a needle in a drunk, surging, swaying haystack. *That* was something she was going to talk to Jared about. Nothing about this detail was normal, from her last-second diversion to Atlanta, the lack of time and coordination on the venue security, to the caliber of Guardian's high-profile private security officers who currently dotted the Dome. Two and two didn't equal four, but she'd get to her brother and ask her questions after the job was done.

The music peaked, and pyrotechnics flamed, erupting in twenty-foot spews of sparks and smoke that dramatically ended the show. *Thank God they warned us about the fireworks.* Jazz purposely looked away from the flames and focused on the crowd. She glanced momentarily at an interlinked mesh of neon-yellow-clad event staff as they stopped fans from rushing the stage to get closer to the superstar.

The faces smiled, screamed and looked adoringly toward the media and fan-appointed demigod who bowed to his fanatical, surging audience.

The house lights came up, and she identified her subject just as the realization that the concert was over rippled through the crowd. He was a big, burly man with a wild mop of brown hair and a long, thick beard. He had his eyes focused on the stage like everyone else, but he wasn't partying, laughing or reacting like the crowd around him. A quick glance toward the front of the stage confirmed that assistance from the ground-level security detail or other Guardian personal security officers was out of the question. Feral fans pushed forward in a vain attempt at getting to their idol. The Georgia Dome's security team had their hands full, and other Guardian assets weren't close enough to help. The deafening roar of the audience negated any chance of radio communication.

Jasmine could see both men, her charge and her target, in her peripheral vision. The performer started walking toward her at the same time the man in the crowd made his move. The front-line security didn't see her suspect effortlessly vault the barrier near the right wing of the stage. He launched up onto the platform in two bounding steps.

Jazz moved from the shadows and bolted between the country singer and the crazed bear of a man heading his way. The performer, some of his band, and one or two stage crew stopped short as she bolted in front of him.

"Get out of here. Now!" Pushing the startled star backward, she turned on her heel. Luckily, the focused rage of the man charging the stage blinded him to all but his intended target. With the man's size, that would be her only edge. She assessed and acted. Concentrating every ounce of athleticism she could muster—she clotheslined the bastard.

The hit to the man's throat did absolutely nothing except spin him toward Jasmine and deflect his rage to her, which, hey, worked for her. *Protect the client at all costs. Mission accomplished.* The man hunched forward. His reactionary jab deflected, Jazz countered his move. She didn't anticipate the curved hunting knife in his hand, but countless hours of training had formed muscle memory patterns. She reacted, instinctively grabbed the man's wrist as he lunged, and used his momentum against him. The movement controlled the knife and allowed his body to go forward while she twisted his arm, swinging it behind his back. Her speed and his weight worked in her favor. He flipped forward and landed on his face.

Jazz followed the man down and landed with her elbow in his kidneys. The blow would have taken out most normal men. But it didn't faze the crazed behemoth. Whatever extreme emotion or mind-altering drug the man was flying high on kept him going and blinded him to the pain Jasmine knew she had inflicted. He threw her off and launched forward.

Jazz followed him up, positioning herself between where Nelson had been and the lunatic. She shifted to the balls of her feet. The psycho still grasped the knife in his hand and brandished it at her. He sliced using quick, unpredictable thrusts. Shifting her weight, she feigned to his left, dodging the knife as it passed her arm. Grabbing his wrist with both hands, she pulled him into her body. The knife and his arm shot past her. Jasmine once again used his momentum and her speed to pull him off balance. She stomped on the arch of his foot with all of her might, grinding her boot heel into his foot. He bellowed out an enraged cry and loosened his grip slightly as he opened his stance to try to get to her.

Jazz moved instinctively, jerking her knee up and forward with as much force as she could gather. She felt his cock and balls compressed into nothing under the impact of her blow. Though she winced in pain, Jasmine felt nothing but relief when her knee connected with his pubic bone. *That* dropped the son of a bitch to his knees and then to his side, where he curled into the fetal position, retching. Using her body weight to slam him forward onto his face, she ground her knee into his neck and braced her shin on his lower back while she handcuffed the beast of a man. When she released him, his body once again curled instinctively in on itself in agony.

The man wheezed a high-pitched, "Fucking cu—"

Jasmine dropped down and slammed her hand against his chin, stilling his venomous words, and hissed, "This was supposed to be an easy assignment. You have no idea the day I've had. Shut up and save us all some pain." Jazz dropped her hand from the man's face and lifted his arm about two inches. The shoulder joint hinged just at the popping point. "Give me a reason to dislocate your shoulder. Just one. That's all I need. It has been a *really* bad day."

The fucker still struggled, but she'd done her job. Her cuffs secured his meaty wrists behind his back. With each breath, his insults got louder, stronger and more inventive. Whatever, at least the bastard was in custody. Barely.

The entire confrontation had taken mere seconds. Personal security was ninety-nine percent preparation and one percent *'oh shit'*. Tonight that one percent of effort had taken everything she had to give. Jazz pulled in ragged breaths as her chest heaved. Looking down at the bear squirming on the ground, she saw a widening pool of blood on the man's back. Her mind and body chose that moment to sync up, and she felt a sharp burn along her forearm.

A quick glance confirmed a cut on her arm dripped blood onto the man's shirt. "Honestly? This is just what I didn't need." She lifted her gaze and swept the immediate area. A swarm of neon-yellow t-shirts was headed her way. It took less than twenty seconds for the stadium's security detail, along with two Guardian personal security officers, to respond and take control of the bull of a man. Jasmine stood as they grabbed him and carried the maniac away.

Her body thrummed from the adrenaline rush that amped her system. The throb radiating from her arm drew her attention downward and she caught her first good look at the slash on her forearm.

"Awesome." Blood dripped down through her fingers and pooled on the stage.

She raised her injured forearm higher than her heart. Holding the cut closed with her other hand, she headed away from the stage area, looking for something to stem the blood loss. At least ten roadies scurried around pulling cables and moving equipment. She wondered if they even realized their meal ticket had been in danger. Probably not. In her experience, people mimicked sheep. Most of the time they were blissfully ignorant of the wolves in their midst.

Jazz cast a quick look at the expanse of the backstage. With the house lights up everything seemed smaller. Less impressive. What *would* impress her would be a way to stop the slice in her arm from bleeding. Was it too much to ask for a bathroom? Where had she seen it? The map she'd burned into her mind seemed to be misfiled, because, for the life of her, she had no idea which way to turn. *Lord, the nonpublic area of this facility could be used as a Halloween maze.* The feel of blood leaving a warm trail down her arm pulled her eyes toward her injury again. Dark crimson slowly ran from the slice on her forearm down to her elbow and dripped onto the floor. *Yep. Awesome.* Jazz cast around looking for an ad hoc bandage. A few paper napkins left on a stack of chairs in the outer wing of the stage caught her attention.

She took two steps toward the chairs and yelled,

"What in the hell!" Unable to keep her balance, she stumbled backward. White cloth blocked her vision for a second, then her elbow was grabbed and material wrapped around her arm. Jazz pulled back violently, dropped to the balls of her feet and crouched, ready to fight.

"Hey, hey... it's all right. You need to apply pressure to the wound." A man bent down slowly, cradled her arm, and tightened the material around her cut. Her medic slash attacker was quick, she'd give him that, and he wasn't gentle.

"Ouch! Stop it! That hurts, you freaking gorilla..."

Jasmine yelled at the chest and shoulders in front of her and pushed against the solid wall of muscle that had plastered itself all up inside her personal space.

"Sorry, darlin', but you have to get that bleeding stopped."

Jasmine stilled instantly. She recognized that voice. She'd heard it for the last two hours. She tipped her head back and her gaze traveled up from a gorgeous chest and shoulders to the chiseled chin, high cheekbones, strong straight nose and vivid blue eyes of country superstar Chad Nelson. His black hair was wet with sweat from the physical exertion of his show. *He was still standing in the wings of the stage.* And *that* fact pissed her off.

"Didn't I tell you to get out of here? What were you thinking other than, 'Oh, hey! I'll be an idiot today?'"

His famous and well-documented sexy smile made an appearance. White teeth flashed as his dimples deepened. "Well, let's see, in the scant one minute since you pushed me backward into a stack of chairs, my band came off stage, formed a human shield around me and almost prevented me from watching you kick some serious ass. Impressive, by the way. You've got some moves. I saw your arm and knew you needed to stop the bleeding. I was in the Army for six years, and I know a thing or two about treating wounds. Now, we could stand here while you bleed, or we could go to my dressing room and get you some medical attention. If you haven't noticed, blood has already soaked through my shirt."

Jasmine dropped her eyes to her arm and grimaced at the drenched fabric. No, she hadn't noticed until he mentioned it. But she could tell her adrenaline rush was starting to subside. The dull throb of her heartbeat in her forearm and the ache from the wound were becoming pronounced. She took a deep breath, counted to five, and exhaled. This day just wouldn't end.

She shook her head, turned to look down the black-painted hallways behind the stage, and sighed. "This probably needs stitches. My people are busy with your psycho stalker. Event security is busy with your rabid fans. I need to call in and get a ride to the emergency room." That wasn't a call she relished making. Getting injured on the job meant paperwork that her brothers would see. Maybe it wasn't as bad as she assumed. She glanced down at the soaked t-shirt. *Yeah. Right.*

The man put his hands on his hips, catching Jasmine's eyes with the movement. So her gaze happened to linger over the prominent lines of his Adonis belt formed by the very well defined abdominal muscles he flaunted. It wasn't her fault. She was hyper-aware after the fight. That was her alibi, and she planned on using it.

"The stadium has a doctor on staff. Come with me and we'll get him to take a look at that for you."

Well, that would eliminate the paperwork. One less thing for her brothers to fuss about, right? She could hear Jason going on and on and on in her mind. She loved her brothers, but they smothered both her and her sister Jewell. *No, definitely best they don't find out.* Jazz nodded to herself and pulled her shoulders back. His soft chuckle brought her gaze back up to his amused expression. She lifted an eyebrow and waited.

"Sorry, watching the wheels turn in your head just now was interesting. You have very expressive eyes." He turned on his heel and started down one of the hallways. His jeans clung to his muscled thighs and hugged his perfect ass. He stopped and glanced over his shoulder at her. He cocked his head in question.

The pain in her arm had dulled her senses. Yep, that was it. Muddled senses. Fractured thinking kept her following those massive shoulders. Brain damage forced her down the stage's access ramp to the labyrinth of the stadium's belly. Shock. She was in shock, and it had nothing to do with that man— not a thing.

Jazz caught up with him and glanced around. It was an involuntary habit carved into her everyday existence from years of training and working security. She cast a quick look around the facility, taking in the door positions, and located adjacent hallways while sweeping the area for threats. She was still on the clock, and the job always came first. Jared had sent her down here to play bodyguard to Mr. Howdy

Doody. What she'd done to piss off her brother enough to be assigned to this grunt detail escaped her. She'd checked in the day she left Italy to communicate that her assignment with a world-famous opera singer had ended. There'd been no hiccups or problems with the principal, but at the last minute she was detoured from the final leg of her flight home and instructed to board the first plane to Atlanta. Of course, her luggage didn't get the message to deviate. Last time she'd checked, the bags were flying to Dulles. Naturally.

The short walk to the dressing room resembled a rush hour traffic accident or a logjam. Roadies, event staff, tour crew members and what appeared to be an excessive amount of fans made it impossible to walk down the corridors. Jazz started detailing faces as a distraction to keep her mind off the blood-soaked shirt around her arm. Women of all shapes and sizes lined the hallway. Jasmine glanced at scores of beautiful women while they all ogled the still shirtless singer. Why? Jasmine glanced at the t-shirt on her arm. *Oh.* She was using his clean shirt as a bandage. She held back a completely inappropriate bubble of laughter. Well, at least she'd done her part to enhance the fan experience. If she wasn't bleed-ing, this portion of the show might have been entertaining. Every last one of the female groupies positioned themselves to present a seductive display to the band members scattered down the hallway. Once the crowd registered Nelson's presence, the corridor shrank with an immediate press of people.

Nelson put his arm around her shoulder, shielding her injured arm from the jostling crowd, protecting her with his body. When the heat of his arm surrounded her, she realized she was cold. The obvious after-effects of the fight and adrenaline. She shrugged off his arm and pulled away from his side. She wasn't a shrinking violet who needed a male to play caveman. She had enough overprotective testosterone in her life, thank you very much.

The crowd surged, and Jasmine winced when someone hit her arm. Chad reached for her and tugged her against him again. *Oh, this right here? This is not happening.* Who in the hell was he to protect her when she'd been sent to save his ass? She couldn't allow this Neanderthal thing the man had going on to continue. If her brothers or coworkers had tried it, she'd have taken out a few knees or broken some fingers. Jasmine pulled away again and stepped back into personal security mode, her new course of action decided: One, get the client to his dressing room. Two, get the hell out of this place.

Three, suck it up and go to the hospital for some stitches, and four, clock out. Oh, and five, find her damn luggage. The job was done, and so was she. What a day.

Her shaking from the cold worsened, and she felt thirsty and dizzy. Had she lost more blood than she'd realized? It didn't matter. She needed to get the hell out of Dodge. She took a quick inventory of the sea of cowboy hats lining the hallway. Another ill-timed bubble of mirth forced its way up. She gave a small smile. Get the hell out of Dodge wasn't just a figurative statement tonight. With this many cowboys, she could rebuild Dodge City. She gave a small snort and shook her head. Damn, she needed to focus.

Nelson filled his lungs and yelled, "Kirk, clear this damn place! Get a doctor to my dressing room now!" A few members of the Dome's security team, band members, and road crew scurried at his demand and worked to part a way for them through the crowd.

The dressing room he led her into was surprisingly small. A loveseat and a recliner sat a comfortable distance from each other opposite a minuscule area that could be used for makeup and hair. A single comb, deodorant, toothpaste and covered toothbrush lay on the vanity by the tiny sink. A large clothing rack held two shirts and a pair of jeans. Jasmine gave a mental tick in the man's favor. Chad Nelson didn't appear to be a prima donna, unless this wasn't his dressing room. So far that was the one and only mark in the 'good' column she'd admit to giving the singer. Well, that and the protector thing, but that really didn't count because it pissed her off. One good mark. Eight or nine bad marks, starting with 'doesn't listen to directions' and ending with 'legendary womanizer.' She'd learned her lesson the hard way when it came to wandering eyes and cheating men. Unfortunately for her, the hard way seemed to be the normal method of tutelage if you were a King.

Chad motioned for her to sit down on the couch. He grabbed a clean hand towel from the bathroom and returned quickly, dropping on his knees in front of her. He lifted her injured arm. Jasmine started to pull the blood-soaked shirt off the wound.

"No, don't take that off. If the blood has started to coagulate, we don't want to disturb it and get it bleeding again. I am just going to wrap this over the top to soak up the blood." Jasmine held out her arm as he carefully snugged it over his t-shirt.

The man was so close when he leaned in, his

body forced her legs open. *Oh crap.* She could smell his cologne. It was spicy and rich, and his musk entangled in the aroma. Heavenly. His bare chest and shoulders were directly at eye level. And good God, what an eyeful they were. No wonder he was on every magazine cover in the free world. He could be immortalized in stone and forever be looked upon as the perfect male form.

No, no, no, no... more bad marks than good. You are not interested. Jazz closed her eyes as his long fingers tucked the end of the towel close to her wrist. The technique secured the edge to prevent it from unwrapping. When his fingers ghosted over her wrist, she shivered because it was cold in the room—no other reason.

He lifted her left hand and lightly pinched the nail bed of each finger of the injured arm. "You have good capillary refill. Can you feel me touch you?"

Only with every nerve ending in my body. He was so close there were only inches between them. Jasmine looked up into his eyes and hitched a breath. The intensity of those riveting blue eyes turned her entire body into a molten mess. Closing her eyes, she inhaled and purposefully exhaled in one long, deep breath, clearing her senses. "Yes, I can feel you."

He continued his ministrations. "Clench your hand into a fist gently around my fingers."

Slowly, her fingers clenched and released.

"That's good. Doesn't look like the idiot damaged too much." He lifted her chin, and his sea-blue eyes seemed to look through her again.

His scent and touch wreaked havoc with her normal, rational sensibilities. Desperate to find space to breathe, she pulled away. Her mouth felt lined with cotton batting. She squirmed backward again, leaning deeper into the loveseat cushion to create a wider space between them. She croaked, "May I have a drink of water, please?"

His hand dropped from her chin as his eyes searched hers before he spoke. "Yeah, it is rather hot in here, isn't it?"

He lifted his hand and tucked a strand of her hair back behind her ear before he rocked effortlessly back on his heels and stood, giving her a perfect view of the sizable bulge behind the button-up fly of his 501s. *Oh, holy hanging hammocks,* her mind fritzed like a static-filled screen. She immediately lost focus on whatever the hell it was they were talking about. Jasmine blinked twice to reboot her brain and then closed her eyes tightly. God, she'd lost too much blood, that was the only explanation for her delayed responses. She'd worked and lived around good-looking men her entire life. Nobody had affected her like this. It had to be blood loss. Shock. She was in shock. There was no other explanation. Thankfully, he added distance when he walked across the room to the small refrigerator and pulled out two bottles of generic labeled water.

Handing her one after he opened it, he asked, "So do I keep calling you darlin', or are you going to tell me your name?"

His voice curled around her in a slow southern drawl that she was sure every woman in the stadium would love to hear one-on-one. Jazz pulled a tight smile as she took the water. Distance was the way out of this very confusing situation. When he'd asked her name, he'd handed her an advantage that she'd use. Jazz leaned back, and for the first time tonight, she relaxed, before she plastered on a subtle smirk. "Whoever hired my company should be able to find out for you. They're paying us, after all. Ask them."

An eyebrow rose before he asked, "So you're a security specialist?"

Jasmine batted her eyes and shook her head. "Oh no. You see, I won a local radio contest. I was the fifth caller, and I got a backstage pass." She put the bottle down and muttered, "They grow them smart down here, don't they?"

"Okay, fair enough, I earned that one. But seriously, what's with the secrecy? I mean, I just want to know who to thank."

Jasmine saw the devilish light in his eyes and upped the ante. The distraction from the ache of her arm was more than welcome. Her natural southern accent lilted as she bantered, "Why, you would thank me! So there you have it, I am me, and you are you, and there is absolutely no need for any other introductions."

"Well, as I believe you might happen to know my name, I don't think we're even." He laughed as he placed the water to his lips and took a drink.

Jazz waited until he started drinking and quipped, "See, that's what the problem is. I don't like to be even. I prefer to be on top."

The country star choked, spewing out the gulp of water. Chad wiped his mouth and stared at her from across the room. His deep voice sounded like liquid sex as he raised an eyebrow and drawled, "Really, I had you pegged as someone who would want her man to be the one in control."

Jasmine suppressed a shiver induced by his natural timbre and forced a chuckle. "Isn't that rather overdone these days? I seem to recall I just kicked some serious ass without any help from..." Jasmine lifted her uninjured arm and made quotes in the air with her fingers, "...a man. Why on earth would I need a man to lord over me?"

He leaned back in his chair, his stare disturbingly direct. "Such a spitfire. I bet you're in control of everything, every minute of every day. Don't you ever want to be able to let go, even for a few moments?"

"No." The response was emphatic and honest. "No, I don't." Jazz held his gaze. Losing control meant getting hurt. Been there, done that and had the unused wedding invitations and the bridal planning book to prove it. This cowboy had stepped over a line that she allowed no one to cross. Even though the sexual tension between them was palpable, she wouldn't back down. She'd be damned if she'd let this man play games with her head. She had five brothers to do that job. Jazz knew only too well the cost of losing control, and she wouldn't pay it, not again. They both swung their attention to the door as a tall blond man walked into the room and stopped. He stared at his boots while he held a phone to his ear.

The guy wasn't as tall as Chad but was cut from the

same cloth. Heavy muscles, bright eyes and that 'good ol' boy' feel. His nose had been broken a time or two, and he wasn't as genuinely handsome as the singer, but he was good looking in a more rugged, less perfect way.

He stood with his hand on his hip as he surveyed the dressing room briefly before he stared blankly at the wall on the far side of the room. "Well, how long will it take?" He looked down at the floor and then at Chad. "Thirty minutes?" The pause was pregnant. "Yeah, keep me posted."

He spoke to Chad as if Jasmine wasn't in the room. "The doctor is dealing with a cardiac arrest in the mezzanine." He turned toward the door. "We cleared the backstage area; you're good to leave the dressing room to do whatever you want."

"Great." She muttered under her breath as Chad stood and pulled a t-shirt from a hanger of his very limited wardrobe. The man must think she was one of Chad's conquests, because he seemed disinclined to give her the time of day. Obviously, the man had seen this scenario too many times. Jasmine stood and walked out of the dressing room door, leaving the sexy singer in the small room. She got her bearings and headed toward the rear exit before she glanced in Chad's direction. "Thank you for the triage. I believe you've stopped the bleeding. I'll be fine."

Chad caught up with her. He fell into step, pulling his shirt on as they walked down the hallway. "I'll drive you to the hospital."

She stopped in the hallway and looked up into those brilliant, probing blue eyes. "Mr. Singer Dude, you need to listen to me. I'm leaving, you're not. You need to stay with your band's normal security team. You're not welcome to come with me, but thank you for your hospitality."

He fell into step with her as she walked down the hall. "You're covered in blood."

Tired of the day that just would not end, she stopped again and pegged him with a stare. The pain in her arm was obnoxious and throbbing. She was tired, dressed in blood-soaked clothes, had no idea what hotel she was checked into, *and* as far as she knew, didn't have a toothbrush to use before she fell into a heap at said mystery hotel. Enough was enough. "Contrary to your assumption in the dressing room, I don't need you or anyone else's protection or company. I'm a big girl. I take care of myself. I've been doing it very well without your help for many years, and I'll continue to do so when you get on that big bus and drive away. Go play your games somewhere else."

She'd reached the limits of her tolerance—granted, they were never very high—and her voice lost all emotion. "I hope you enjoy your life. Goodnight and goodbye, Mr. Nelson." Jasmine turned on her heel and walked away.

CHAD LEANED against the wall and watched that peculiar woman walk away. He'd never met anyone who was simultaneously so damn willful and yet selfless. Hell, the woman wouldn't even tell him her name. That alone earned his curiosity. He thought it was some ploy at first, but it appeared she honestly didn't want to give him her name. And that was… odd. He was used to the adoration and the games the groupies played. This one? Well, she had his interest, all right. Leaning against the wall, he breathed deeply, mentally reviewing the events of the evening. He'd noticed her several times in the wings. Nondescript, or at least she tried damn hard to be, although it was rather like putting a thimble over a searchlight. Didn't stop the damn thing from shining brightly. She'd never looked at him and had purposefully moved away from him when he stood next to her while he waited to go back on stage after his break. He didn't have time during his performance to wonder who or what she was. He figured she had something to do with the Dome. But security, who'd have believed it?

She reminded him of a colt he once owned. All legs and spirit. With those boots on she could nearly look straight into his eyes. He decided he liked the heels on those boots and smiled to himself. She was more striking than pretty. Take your breath away striking. The expression in those big green eyes told him she'd seen a lot of life. She didn't wear any makeup, and the dark circles under her eyes became more pronounced as the evening had worn on. Or maybe he'd just noticed her more as the evening progressed. Not a designer clothes person, either. She wore inexpensive black jeans that fit loose and a simple white shirt. She'd buttoned it up to the top button when he noticed her earlier in the evening. She must have popped open a couple when she wrestled the brick shithouse of a man to the floor. And damned if he didn't enjoy the cleavage the fight had exposed.

With her black hair pulled back and pinned up in an unflattering bun, he'd normally pass her by without a second look. But he had looked, and he'd liked what he'd seen. The woman was all natural. She had looked up at him as he wrapped his t-shirt around her wound... those eyes. He could only describe them as deep mossy green, and they held emotion that spoke straight to his soul. Exactly what that emotion was eluded him, but there was a vulnerable softness behind that frosty exterior, and it called to him.

Chad drew a deep breath. God, he should have been more of a gentleman. His mom would tan his ever-loving hide if she'd known what an ass he'd been to his mystery woman when she was hurting. But hell, what type of man could have resisted propositioning her? Well, a better man than him, that was for sure.

He'd sensed she wanted him. He'd felt it during the split second she'd molded into him when he pressed his body against hers in the hall. Even if that tiny surrender only lasted a second, he'd felt it. Damned if that moment hadn't stoked his desire. He wanted her. Imagined his kick-ass-and-take-names mystery woman soft and compliant under him, surrendering herself. Well, that thought sent a jolt straight to his dick. He could still smell her. Cinnamon, with some other light fragrance he couldn't place. She was a live wire with a quick wit. *Radio show winner.* Huh, the girl had spunk. *And she wants nothing to do with you.*

He would've pushed himself off the wall and walked to his dressing room as soon as she'd left, but his body was in no condition to move. For no apparent reason, that woman did it for him. Chad chuckled to himself. Maybe he should say did it to him. It had been a long time since he'd wanted to be involved with a woman for more than a one-night event or a scene that lasted a couple of hours... a long time. Damn. He shifted his rock-hard cock in his jeans and pulled away from the plaster that was holding him up.

Well, if the mountain won't come to Mohammad... Ol' Mo was fixing on doing some hiking. He laughed at his joke and busted out in an old John Denver song. A little sunshine on his shoulders would definitely make him happy. Life for his mystery woman was about to get interesting. Kirk, his road manager, needed to get his chief of security on the phone. He wanted a name.

CHAPTER 2

*J*asmine listened for footsteps. Thank goodness the hall remained eerily quiet. Tired and sore, she didn't want to deal with anyone, especially the self-absorbed performer. She pulled her cell from her pocket, called in and did the walk of shame toward the secure rear entrance of the Dome. She asked for a transport to meet her there. God only knew where the others on her detail had ended up. She should have gone with them, but nooo, she ended up with that crooning cowboy. Lord, she was going to get a rash of shit from the others if they found out.

Jet lagged and hurting, she waited in the shadows of the building until a Guardian vehicle pulled up. The distinctive blacked-out SUV with multiple

antennas, bulletproof glass and tires, and undercar-
riage that could withstand a bomb blast was hard to
miss. Subtle differences about this particular vehicle
raised her hackles. Jasmine watched as the driver of
the black Suburban exited. Yeah, her day *did*
completely suck. She swore under her breath when
her brother Jared and his security team emerged
from the vehicle.

Muscle filled out Jared's six-foot-six-inch frame,
and his black hair blew in the night wind. He'd
grown it out recently. He looked more relaxed and
happier than she'd ever seen him. "Hey, little girl,
heard you took out a pretty big dude tonight. I see
you didn't come away unscathed."

Jasmine looked at her brother and held up her
hand. "Why are you down here, J? This isn't just a
random BS security job, is it? If it were, there
wouldn't be a need for the head of domestic security
to grace my obviously lowly presence."

"Pouting, Jazzy?"

Jazz walked to the Suburban and opened the
front passenger door. "Yeah, I'm pissed. Why the hell
did you send me down here? Any newbie personal
security officer could've done this job."

She slammed the door and waited for Jared and
his team to get back in the vehicle. One of Jared's

security detail walked past him and whispered, "Never piss off a King."

Jared snorted. "Better advice is never to piss off a King *woman*."

"My window is down. I can hear both of you." Jasmine wasn't going to let them get away with anything.

Jared got behind the wheel and started the vehicle toward where Jasmine assumed Guardian's temporary field offices were located.

"I think I need stitches. Swing by the hospital, would you?" Jazz's arm was throbbing.

"Got a doctor with us, and we need to read you in on the events surrounding tonight."

"I was there, remember?"

"Yeah, the dude you took out tonight was hopped up on something, but we have a real problem, and the raging bull isn't involved. Whoever is after Nelson is still out there."

Jasmine closed her eyes and leaned her head back on the headrest. "You didn't divert me here for a security detail. I am going to be his babysitter, aren't I?"

Jared smirked. "Did you get to meet him tonight?"

At her low groan, he turned and looked at her.

"Jazz, if you don't want the assignment, I could give it to Jade. I'm sure she could handle it."

Her head snapped toward him at the taunt. Jared's laughter shook his shoulders. The jerk was baiting her as usual. "You can kiss my ass, Jared. She's on loan to the DEA, so stop picking on me."

He looked at her and deadpanned, "Jazz, honey, I've been kissing your ass since the day I was born."

The rumble of laughter from the rest of Jared's team brought a small, unwanted lift of her lips. She slapped his arm and snarked, "Let me know next time? I'll pretend to enjoy it." That small upturn of her lips remained despite the pain that radiated from the cut on her arm. She closed her eyes and relaxed into the leather seat until Jared turned into the field office's parking lot.

Jasmine walked into Jared's temporary offices and was once again amazed at the technology that traveled with her brothers. Four of her brothers and two of her sisters worked in various capacities for Guardian. Jared ran the domestic branch of Guardian Security, in charge of all domestic security issues, including Jasmine's specialty, personal protection.

Jared waved her toward the back room. A man in blue scrubs greeted her, unwrapped her arm and cleaned the wound. His obvious Scandinavian accent intrigued her. "Not from around here?"

The medic shrugged his shoulders. A southern accent replaced the Swedish lilt. "Well, ma'am, I guess that depends on where you think I am from."

Jasmine laughed. "All right, I get it, don't ask."

The doctor's light blue eyes locked on his hands as he fixed a syringe. "This is going to hurt."

Jazz shrugged. "Yeah, life hurts. You learn to deal with it."

The doctor chuckled. "Pretty jaded view of life for one so young and so pretty."

She clenched her fist as he injected a numbing compound around the cut. He disposed of the syringe in the sharps container, draped the exposed skin around her wound with a sterile dressing and prepared his needle and suture for use. Turning, he tapped her arm near the wound. "Can you feel me touch you?"

"No, *you* I cannot feel." Jazz laughed, probably harder than she should have. But hell, it was funny.

The Swede chuckled. "That statement would predispose me to believe you could feel someone else."

He peered up at her for a brief moment. His eyes were lighter than the singer's, almost a soft baby blue. Jasmine felt the warmth from his gaze and smiled at the man's calm demeanor and tender treatment. He was probably a couple of inches taller than her. He was fit and strong without being massive. His white hair was cut short on the sides and left longer on top. When he bent over her, his scent was clean, nothing distracting or heavy, but comforting nonetheless.

He drew the first tiny stitch through the muscle under her skin. "It's a shame you can't feel me. I've been told a person might enjoy my touch."

Jasmine studied him like a scientist would a sample under a microscope. "Hmm, is that an offer or observation, doctor?"

The Swede's eyes traveled to the hallway where Jared was talking with several people. "I believe... an observation with the hope of an offer, yes?"

She followed his eyes and shook her head. "Afraid of my brother?"

The Swede cut the suture and shook his head. "Afraid of *him*? No." He looked directly at her and continued, "Of you? Maybe."

She smiled at that. The man's calm, authoritative presence made the statement ridiculous. This man wasn't someone she'd ever classify as weak. His broad shoulders and back rippled as he worked on her arm. Afraid of her. Right. His sense of humor earned him an introduction. "I'm Jasmine."

"Oh, believe me, I know." The doctor smiled at her and winked. "Maliki Blue."

"Nice to meet you, Maliki."

The man smiled and returned to the task at hand. Jasmine watched him in silence as he finished the sutures and bandaged her arm. He handed her a small pill vial. "Take one every six hours for swelling and pain."

She shook her head and put the vial on the counter. "No way. One of my brothers got hooked on that stuff. I'll be fine."

The doctor shook his head and sighed. "If I had a dollar for every time a King had told me the same thing, I'd be rich. It isn't a narcotic. It isn't habit forming, and it's definitely within the King guidelines of 'I'd like to suffer rather than help my body heal itself.'"

A snort of unladylike laughter punched out before she could stop it. "You seem to know my family well. How is it I haven't met you before?"

The man shrugged and washed his hands. "I've been... around."

"Ahh... got it. Well, thanks for the patch job, Maliki." She peeked at him from under her lashes.

"You should call me. My brothers aren't always around." Jasmine winked and slid off the table. The doctor's face flushed a wicked shade of red. Too sweet, a man who blushed.

"To do that, I'd need your number."

Jazz grabbed a pen and looked for a piece of paper without success. She grabbed Maliki's newly washed hand and wrote her digits on the pad of his thumb. "Don't wash that hand again before you put it in your phone. I'd hate to assume you weren't interested."

"I'd never let you assume that." Maliki smiled and winked again.

"Jazz, you done in there?" Jared called down the hallway.

Dang it, with her brothers keeping gorgeous men like Maliki away, she might die an old maid. Jazz gave the doctor one backward glance and held her thumb and pinkie in a phone shape. "Call me," she mouthed and headed down the hallway.

"All better?"

Jared's teasing irritated her. She hauled herself down the short hallway and flopped into a chair in the conference room where his team had gathered. Dammit. She was seriously jet lagged. That feeling of being tired and having the eerie sensation that she stood three inches from falling off a ledge sucked. It was an itchy nervousness coupled with the utter exhaustion she always got when traveling home from overseas. Jazz realized her brother was looking at her. *What did he ask? Oh...* "I'm peachy, thanks."

One of Jared's team approached him and pulled him to the side. He glanced up at the rest of the people in the room. "Give me two minutes. This can't wait." Jared turned back to the person he was working with and continued his conversation.

Jasmine reached up and pulled a handful of hairpins from her hair, allowing her mass of thick, wavy, black hair to fall to her waist. She leaned back in the chair and closed her eyes, listening to the conversation around her. Jared turned back to the people in the room. In his usual clipped, professional manner, he ran through the information they currently had on Nelson.

"If you have finished your nap, Jazz, we can get this briefing over with."

Jasmine didn't open her eyes but fired back, "I've heard every word y'all said. Your team is doing forensics on a note scrawled on the photo found on Chad's tour bus. The road manager found it and was the only one to touch it. The door lock was manipulated, but there is no surveillance that showed anything. The time frame for the plant of the photo is extensive. Nelson, the band and a few roadies, plus his normal security team left the coach at two in the afternoon, worked out at the local CrossFit gym. The facility was one that the musician's handlers rented out, so there was no way for anyone to steal or duplicate security badges. After the workout they went straight to the arena to practice. The band and Nelson stayed backstage and did interviews and fan meetings. The mad bull that charged the stage tonight was after a local hire electrician who was handling the power cables, not Nelson. The two have a previous history and the story jives. He's not our guy."

She opened her eyes and found her brother. "Did I miss anything?"

Jared leaned back in his chair. "Yes, a couple of things. We had our profiler do a workup on a potential subject based on the threat and handwriting. Male, thirty to forty years old. The person is high functioning, and intelligent. The pattern of language, sentence formation, and block writing depict a disciplined author. Based on the content of the note, our profiler believes the subject feels threatened by Nelson."

"Okay, whack job... got it."

"It may be more than that, Jazz. We have received word from the FBI that Nelson has been tied to two ongoing murder investigations. They're getting twitchy because of Nelson's direct connection to the cases. We've been retained to protect him by his people, and the FBI is eyeing him as a suspect in a potential investigation."

"Wait, Nelson's a suspect in two murder cases? And what? You think he put that photo in his own bus?"

"Can't rule it out. The handwriting wasn't his. We've had our specialists make a comparison, but that doesn't make him innocent. Needless to say, we have a shitload of work to do, and while that's happening, it will be your job to keep him close in case he's guilty, and protect his ass in case we do have a whack job."

"So you want me to keep this guy under surveillance in case he's a murderer, and if he's not, protect him from someone who is?" Jasmine held her brother's gaze.

"Pretty much. Cole Davis, the agent in charge of the investigation, has worked with us in the past, and he is reading us in on the information tomorrow morning before we meet with Nelson's people. We brought in a small team who are working with his original security team and holding down the hotel where Nelson and the band are staying tonight."

Jazz dropped her head to her hands and squeezed her eyes shut. Yep, today sucked. No two ways about it. The superstar was going to be a handful. A snuffled huff turned into a tired, maniacal laugh. Oh hell, he was probably more than a handful, based on her up close and personal observation tonight.

"You good to go or do you need to sit this one out?" Jared looked more than a little concerned and motioned toward her arm.

"I'm good. When and where do we start?"

"0900 hours. Come on. I'll take you to the hotel. You look like crap. And what is up with the Orphan Annie clothes?" Jared lifted from his chair, walked to the door and held it open for her.

"You redirected me practically in midair. I only had a couple of minutes to dash into the one and only Walmart I saw on the way from the airport and buy clothes. It was either this or the white pencil skirt and the pink silk shirt I had on. Then on the way out of the store, I got caught in a downpour. Thanks to Georgia's glorious weather, my Prada skirt, shirt and favorite Jimmy Choo shoes are ruined. By the time I made it to the Georgia Dome, I looked like a drenched raccoon. I changed in the bathroom. My makeup had melted off my face. Thanks to the humidity and rain, my hair took on a life of its own, so I pulled it all back and pinned it up. Believe me. Today sucked on too many levels."

"Huh. That would explain the au naturel look."

"Yeah, definitely not my best day. My bags should be on their way here from D.C. by now. I hope."

"I'm sure. Hey, I still think you're cute." Jared pushed open the outside door and walked with her to the Suburban.

"Yeah? You're prejudiced."

"True." He opened the vehicle door and waited for her to get in.

Jazz leaned back in the seat as he shut the door. "Thank you. I think."

Jared started the vehicle and pulled onto the nearly deserted roadway.

"Why are you here? I mean, I get that Nelson is a high-visibility client, but we have field operation managers for a reason." Jasmine rolled her head on the Suburban's leather headrest and took in her brother's profile. The subtle strobe illumination of the streetlights that lined the wide avenue sent flashes of brilliance that were quickly muted.

"There were other reasons to be in the area. I'm

doing some legwork for the Archangels." Jared gave her a sideways look.

"Care to share?"

"Can't." He put on his blinker and merged onto the interstate.

Jasmine let the subject drop. The Archangels were Gabriel and, now, her brother Jason. She had a damn good idea of what work Jared was doing for them. No doubt it involved the looming Russian threat. She hadn't had a full briefing, but since she was part of the King family, she needed to make sure her situational awareness was ramped up. Too much had happened for anyone not to take the situation seriously. After the attempt on Jared and his husband, Christian, and the Russian tie-in to the child abduction ring Christian had uncovered, the Russians were a threat *everyone* took seriously.

She picked at the blood-soaked shirt she was wearing and sighed. This had been a day from hell. Her arm hurt and her ears were ringing from the volume of the music at the concert. She yawned and tried to pop her ears. Yep, she'd probably suffered significant hearing loss standing that close to the massive, throbbing amplifiers and speakers.

Throbbing. The vivid memory of Chad Nelson's chest, shoulders, and well-fitting jeans snapped front and center into her mind's eye. She looked out the window. A warm sensation washed over her. Lord, that man was something. Totally not her type, but he had charisma, and if you liked country music, he obviously had talent. *Enough. You don't like country music.* The entertainer had all the female adoration he needed. Maybe a bit too much adoration.

A glimpse of Maliki's smile came to mind. The doctor worked for Guardian. He knew her life and her brothers and still wanted her number. His warm smile and emotion-filled light blue eyes were exactly what she liked in a man. *Lord above.* Two men who flipped her switches in one night. Well, one man and one client. The thought made her smile. She wondered when Maliki would call or text and how long would the case with Nelson take? Hopefully not long.

Clearing her throat, Jazz turned her attention back to Jared. "Do you think one of your minions would be able to check and see if my bags made it to Georgia yet?"

"I'm sure that was handled, but if not, we'll make sure it happens. We'll get you into your room and let you wash off the day. If the luggage isn't in, we'll have a boutique deliver something appropriate. We've got a meeting with the FBI at nine. If you're still waiting for clothes, I'll take the meeting by myself."

"Thank you."

"Don't mention it. After that, we are meeting with Nelson and his entourage. Regardless of the baggage situation, we both need to meet with them. I'll get you up to speed and then I'm turning it over to you. I'm not running it through the field manager. Nelson is too high profile. You'll report directly to me on this one."

"Going to suck for your personal life if I have to call you in the middle of the night." She laughed at the thought of interrupting her brother's slumber.

"I'm used to it. Our ADD sister in charge of IT doesn't sleep and calls at the weirdest times. If you need anything, I'll be available." Jared signaled as he took the off ramp.

"The girl never really sleeps. I don't know how she does it. She's wired on Red Bull, coffee and sugar 24/7. But dealing with late night notifications is a part of your job I don't envy. Always on call? No thanks."

Jared shrugged. "Occupational hazard. I made sure Christian knew what he was getting involved in." The streetlight illuminated his wide wedding band. Jared's satisfied smile filled her heart. It had been so long since he'd been this at peace with himself. Seeing him happy settled a piece of her soul and meant the world to her.

Jared pulled into the parking garage and escorted her to the lobby of the hotel. He handled getting her key card from the hotel clerk, a good thing seeing how she was blood-drenched from head to foot. She wore Jared's jacket, and it hid the majority of the mess, but she stayed away from the few people talking in the lobby. Lord above, she was done for the day. Wiped the heck out. Jared strode toward the elevator, and she followed him like a puppy. He took her to her room and opened the door. Her bags sat inside, and she sighed in relief. At least she could get out of the blood-soaked bargain store clothes and turn back into herself.

"Go get yourself clean. Order some food and get some sleep. We're meeting with the lead agent at 0900. We'll leave here at 0815." Jared pulled her in for a quick hug and kissed her forehead. "Night, brat."

She chuckled at the endearment. "Night, J."

CHAPTER 3

*J*azz's phone vibrated on the bathroom's marble vanity. She finished applying her mascara before she glanced at the text from an unknown number.

Good Morning. How is my favorite patient?

Joy bubbled up at the message. She smiled and leaned against the counter as she responded.

Be truthful... I'm your only patient, aren't I?

She laughed and added an emoji with its tongue hanging out.

Yes, but u r still my favorite. R u free tonight?

Jazz pulled her bottom lip into her mouth and worried it with her teeth.

Won't know til l8r, but I want 2 b.

She wasn't going to play games with the good doctor. She wanted him to know she was interested. Hopefully, he wasn't averse to her being forward. No, that shouldn't be a problem. The man knew what she did for a living. Jasmine sent the message, entered his name into her contacts and slid into her Dior skirt. The phone vibrated again just after she finished buttoning up her shirt. She dabbed on a touch of perfume and picked up the phone.

Maliki: *Have dinner with me.*

If I can, yes.

Maliki: *Text me when you know.*

I will. :>)

She'd enjoy spending time getting to know the man. His quiet strength had calmed her shattered nerves last night—unlike the client she needed to deal with today. Oh, the singer was sexy as hell, but the man's legendary womanizing preceded him by miles. She'd had her fill of cheating men who could charm snakes out of trees. Her ex-fiancé had taught her that lesson. The hard way.

She finished dressing and grabbed her shoes. A knock at her door echoed through the hotel suite. Jasmine slipped on her heels, hopping on one foot as she hurried across the carpeted expanse to answer the door.

"Well, there is the sister I know and love." Jared's taunt earned him a soft punch in his not-so-soft abs. "What? Besides yesterday, when was the last time I saw you without makeup or not in designer clothes?"

Jasmine cocked her head to the side and had to think about the answer to that question. "That's a two-part question. Designer clothes since I got my first paycheck and could afford them, and makeup... ummm, the day before my thirteenth birthday."

"Right, because when you turned thirteen, Mom let you and Jade wear makeup." Jasmine laughed at the thought. Jade had been wearing makeup at school for at least a year before her mom officially gave them permission to wear it. Of course, Jade was the adventurous one of the two. Twins, but they rarely, if ever, acted the same way. They were opposites and happy to live that way. Jasmine loved her sister fiercely, but the woman drove her batshit crazy. Gonzo. Like, not wanting to stay in the same room for more than an hour with the woman type of crazy.

"If Mom only knew." Jared opened the door and made a grand gesture of allowing her to go first.

"Oh, believe me, she knows. She just picks her battles with that one."

"Don't we all?"

"We do. But I'd give anything to be as free-spirited as she is. She's a wisp of laughter dancing on a sunbeam."

Jared and Jasmine shared a smile. That was how their dad had described Jade. The bittersweet memory halted conversation for a while. Finally, Jared chuckled and quipped, "That little wisp can kick some serious ass."

"We all can."

"Granted, but she enjoys it. Speaking of which, how is your arm?" The elevator door opened for them.

Jasmine shrugged. "I'll live." She'd worn a pale green, long sleeve silk blouse to conceal the bandage on her forearm. The dark charcoal gray pencil skirt and her favorite three-inch black stiletto Louboutins with the beautifully detailed cutaway at the arch of her foot completed her business attire. She knew how to dress, had the money to do it, and loved all things girly. Once again, the opposite of Jade.

"I still want the doctor traveling with us to take a look at it before we part company. Infection is deadly." Jared escorted her through the lobby and out to the waiting SUV.

Jasmine smiled at the thought of seeing Maliki

again. Hopefully at dinner, but she'd take an extra meeting at the direction of her brother. At that thought she turned, snapped her fingers and pointed at Jared. "Oh, right! Speaking of which, thanks for nothing." Jasmine slipped on her Chanel sunglasses and waited for him to get settled into the vehicle.

"Excuse me? What did I do?" Jared pulled away from the hotel and merged into Atlanta's morning traffic.

"The doctor."

"Yeah, I assumed that when you said 'speaking of which,' but what the hell did I do this time?" Jared hit start on the vehicle's GPS and changed lanes.

"You were you. He almost didn't ask for my number. How am I ever going to have a relationship if everyone who works for Guardian is intimidated by my brothers?"

"I doubt I intimidate Maliki Blue. Why do you need to date someone from Guardian?"

Jasmine did a double take at her brother just to make sure he was serious. "Because nobody on the outside is going to put up with the insane schedule we work."

"Wrong." Jared dismissed her comment out of hand.

"Excuse me?"

"Tori, Ember, Faith, Christian and Keelee." Jared held up his hand and lifted a finger at each name he called out.

"Not fair. Tori *was* in the business. Still is, part time," Jasmine reminded him.

"That still leaves Ember, Faith, Christian, and Keelee who are not in the business, married to extremely busy men and able to live happily with people who work for Guardian."

Jasmine waved a dismissive hand in the air. "Good for y'all. It's not like I'm looking to do anything other than date right now anyway."

"You haven't dated in eons."

Her jaw dropped at that comment. "I'm not *that* old, Jared."

"When was the last time you went out with someone?" He turned his head and gave her a sideways glance.

Nope, she wasn't going there. After her Fiancé Fiasco, as she'd labeled some of the most depressing days of her life, she refused to discuss her personal life with her family. They were too far up in her business with what they already knew. Time to redirect the conversation.

"Stop the inquisition. Pull over at the next Starbucks, please." She wanted a coffee. Jazz hit several buttons on the GPS looking for the store.

"Will you leave that alone? I'll get you your nonfat soy thingy. There's a place in the lobby of the office building where we're meeting Cole." Jared punched three buttons, and the GPS resumed its original function.

"You know this guy well?" Jasmine switched on the radio and started looking for something decent.

"Cole? Yeah, he was my liaison agent with the FBI when we took down the Morales cartel. He's one of the good guys. He'll go places. What happened with the doctor?"

"You switched subjects. Why?"

"I'm interested in what Maliki said to you."

"Not much, because my brothers are uber-macho and run the company where he works."

Jasmine turned suddenly and pointed at Jared. "You couldn't recruit Cole Davis, could you?" Jasmine knew Guardian could lure the best away from the lower paying government jobs.

Jared clicked his tongue and then flashed a self-deprecating smile at her. "Nope. He's an original G-man. FBI through and through. But he's one I would trust, so having him give us the rundown on their involvement made it worth my while to stay down here for an extra day or two." Jared turned down the radio that Jasmine had just turned up.

"Hey, I love Adele!" Jasmine turned the music back up. Not much, but enough to say she had.

"You'd better start liking country music. At least until you put this case to bed."

"Not going to happen. Not my taste, and I'm too set in my ways to change. I mean, who needs the whining, crying and dying of country music?" Jasmine looked out the window, recalling last night's concert. There had been a couple of ballads, but the majority of the music the man had sung had been upbeat party songs. A few had a good beat to them, too, but no… because if she liked some of the music, she'd have to admit she liked the man. Wow… where did that come from? Talk about some faulty logic. Whatever, she didn't need to be anywhere near that 'Wouldn't you like to give up control?' country bumpkin. *As if.*

They pulled up outside a tall office building made of white concrete and mirrored glass that could have fit nicely into any city. "J, I thought we were stopping for coffee?" Yes, she whined—unapologetically and with emphasis.

"Like I said, in the lobby, Miss Crabby Pants."

Jared laughed when she stuck out her tongue at

him. She loved that she could play with him. Once they were in proximity of anyone else they were both all business, but in the sheltered minutes that they were alone, they always reverted to the kids who had grown up in a quaint, small town in Mississippi.

Ten minutes later, armed with a venti, triple shot, sugar-free, nonfat cup of heaven-on-earth, they walked into the regional offices of the Federal Bureau of Investigation. When Jared grabbed Cole Davis' hand and shook it, her mental snapshot of who she thought he was reversed in a hurry. For some reason, she expected an older, potbellied, political type. Instead, Cole Davis was tall, good looking and charming. They settled in a small conference room, and Davis shut the door.

"Cole, this is my sister Jasmine. She'll be working personal security and/or guard detail for Nelson, depending on how this plays out."

Jasmine offered her hand, which was immediately engulfed in a firm shake.

"Good to meet you." He turned to Jared. "I didn't know you had any sisters."

"Three, all in the business, and all three of us are damn good at our jobs," Jasmine interjected.

Davis smiled and gestured toward the conference

room table. "I would expect nothing less from any King. Let's sit down." They sat as Cole spoke. "All right, Jared, I'll get right to it. I've been promoted, so I'm pulling up stakes here in Atlanta and heading to D.C. That being said, I'm going to pull in a favor. I want Guardian to take this case. I'll give you everything we have, but the new guy coming in will have more than enough on his plate. He doesn't need this. Hell, any way you slice it, this case is a hemorrhoid on the ass of this agency. If we screw up and arrest the guy and he's not guilty, we've got egg on our face. If we find out he's involved and arrest him, we are charging one of the most beloved country singers in history with murder and we are the bad guys—even though we aren't. If we don't find out who is doing this and fail to stop another murder, we're painted as negligent. The press has been sniffing around these murders, and it won't take long before this media shit storm hits the fan. Take this ugly bitch for me and not only will you clear any tabs you have with me, but I'll owe you one hell of a big one."

Jasmine couldn't help the small smile that tugged at her lips. The man didn't pull a single punch. She respected the hell out of that.

Jared shifted in his seat and played with a pen

that someone had left on the table. He finally spoke, "You never were one to mince words, Davis. I can't help but get the feeling there's something else here. What aren't you telling us?" Jared leaned forward onto his forearms, giving Davis his complete attention.

Cole turned slightly in his chair and thumbed the folder in front of him. He pulled his gaze from Jared and looked directly at Jasmine. "We are assuming Nelson has a... well, hell, for lack of a better word, we think he has a kink. Are you sure you wouldn't rather put someone else on the case?"

Jasmine was immediately intrigued. "A kink? I've read his jacket. He's phenomenally successful, plays hard and parties hard. He has no lasting relationships, but he's reputed to have been with multitudes of women. The man is a branding mecca with the Midas touch. Everything he touches bypasses gold and platinum and turns to rhodium. He employs some of the best talent in the country, and they keep him on top of the charts and out of the news, except when he wants to be seen. What are we missing?"

Davis glanced between her and Jared. The guy started to speak and then stopped. He flipped open the file and pushed a single piece of paper toward her. It was a membership application to... well... maybe Mr. Country Music wasn't all talk after all.

"I take it that club is exclusive?" Jasmine had to admit the thought of Chad Nelson wearing leather and wielding a whip spiked her temperature, but that wasn't her scene. A good looking man in leather, though? Yeah, she could have a field day with that visual.

"Yes. His lawyer gave it to us, and along with traffic camera footage we obtained that put him at the club, this is his alibi when victim number one was murdered."

"So you have no idea what goes on inside this club?"

"No, we can't say for sure, but we have a pretty damn good idea."

"What did Nelson say when you interviewed him?" Jared started jotting down notes.

"That's just it. We reached out to his manager for an interview and a lawyer responded. We've never talked to the man. We don't have enough to arrest him. To bring him in and question him would put the FBI and Nelson in every tabloid on the planet, and since the man lawyered up, we've been biding our time. It wouldn't assist us to tip our hand. We took this information and continued the investigation. He is a person of interest, but we don't have enough to punch the ticket and bring him in."

Jared nodded and glanced at Jasmine. She lifted an eyebrow in question. He shook his head and gave Agent Davis his attention again. "We're not making any changes to personnel. Jasmine will be the Guardian officer handling Nelson's security. I'll lead the investigation, and we'll have our people running down any information we need to grouse out. I know what Jasmine can do, and I have no doubt that Nelson will be safe or, if we find out he's behind these murders, she will cuff and stuff him faster than either of us could. She's that damn good."

Jasmine felt a warm blush hit her cheeks. Rarely did she receive compliments from Jared, but when she did, they meant the world to her. Yeah, she knew she was good at her job, but getting that validation from someone who mattered? It was heady. Davis started pulling papers out of the folder and turned them to face Jared and Jasmine.

"Okay then, here's the scoop. We have two prominent people who have sued Nelson. Both are now dead. Murdered. Victim number one is Natalie Plate. She was a studio executive who filed a forty-million-dollar lawsuit against Nelson, alleging he failed to fulfill the recording contract she had with him over four years ago. The lawsuit is stalled but still relevant. Ms. Plate's assistant found Natalie in her office, bound to a chair, dead. Single tap through the center of her forehead. She was dressed in the same clothes she'd worn the day before, and according to the coroner's report, the time of death was sometime between nine and midnight the previous night. There are no surveillance tapes that are useful. Too many exits and way too much foot traffic in the building to be able to identify anyone who would be there late."

"How is there too much foot traffic that late at night?" Jasmine picked up the police report but waited for Agent Davis' response.

"The offices are on the same block that house three theaters, multiple restaurants, a gym and a nightclub. The city is revitalizing the area, and the mix of zoning is pulling in people, but the studio offices did not have camera surveillance."

Jared pulled pictures of the crime scene toward him and searched the different angles.

"This wasn't an emotional crime," he mused.

"No. We noted that too. The investigation found out she had other lawsuits filed against a few of the entertainment stars she used to manage. So others may have had a motive, but as Nelson stood to lose the most we looked into it. We can't find any personal contact between Nelson and Plate in the last four years. He severed all ties with that recording company. It was a vicious split. Like I said, we contacted his people to set up an initial interview and got thrown to the lawyer. But we were able to verify his whereabouts." Davis tapped the application on the table.

"How did you verify he was actually in the club? I'm assuming this type of establishment doesn't have a sign-in roster or available surveillance." Jasmine pulled another report toward her, consuming the information while listening to the conversation.

"We have excellent video coverage of the exterior of the facility via traffic cameras and one private security system in the building next door that we were able to... acquire. We know he arrived at eight and didn't leave until after two in the morning. All exits are covered, and the video feed is authentic. It wasn't doctored."

"Victim number two?" Jared asked as he scribbled something down on a small notepad he'd pulled out of his pocket.

"A studio musician who is, or rather, was suing Nelson for ten million dollars. Jarvis Colston claimed Nelson stole a song he pitched to Nelson several years ago. Nelson was on stage in front of fifty thousand witnesses during that murder."

"But..." Jasmine egged the agent on.

"But, this is the second case where the victim's death has directly benefited Mr. Nelson."

"So you're assuming a contracted or hired assassin got rid of his legal issues?" Jared leaned back in the chair and rubbed his jaw.

"It's not out of the realm of possibility."

"True, but why would anyone do something so overt? Who would believe a person would do such a thing. Unless that was his goal?" Jasmine looked at the second crime scene photograph. The musician had been shot at point blank range in his car outside what looked to be a roadside bar.

"Exactly." Jared tapped the table with his fingertips and looked from the documents to Davis. Jasmine allowed her mind to wander as her brother contemplated the organization's involvement in the case. She had to admit, if Nelson was behind killing the people who were suing him, this brand of insanity might just work. He was worth hundreds of millions of dollars. Would he resort to hiring an assassin to take out people who were after his money? It was possible. She'd seen people killed for less. So, yeah, Mr. Music had a motive, and he had the means to hire the job out. As for opportunity? Hell, if he put out the contract, it wasn't a stretch to believe the assassin would know when to take down the mark. Nelson could even dictate the times, so he had an alibi.

Jared pulled the photos closer and reached for the folder. "We'll take it. You owe me, and believe me: I'll collect." Jared shook Davis' hand before Jasmine shook the agent's hand too. She couldn't help noting the man looked relieved.

Jasmine gathered the remaining paperwork from the table while the men said their goodbyes and made a promise to meet up in D.C. when Davis was settled. She placed the files in her Dolce & Gabbana tote, grabbed her coffee cup and followed Jared out of the door. No more than ten minutes in the FBI's office and everything she thought she knew about Chad Nelson had been ripped into confetti and thrown in the air. Someone was killing his enemies. Jasmine stood beside Jared waiting for the elevator and finished her coffee. She'd grab another one on the way out.

"J, I'm not going to the meeting with Nelson and his people. I have an idea." Jasmine grabbed his arm and pulled him toward the coffee kiosk instead of toward the SUV. He chuckled and pulled out his wallet when she ordered for both of them.

Jared leaned forward. "How do you want to play it?"

She shook her head and waited until they both had their caffeine fix. "I have an angle, but I need a meeting with him, no reps, no lawyers, no managers, nobody. Just us. Can you arrange that?"

Jared nodded. "Yes, of course. What is the angle?"

"Get me the meeting tomorrow—late morning. I need to check into some things. I'll lay it down for you tonight. If you don't like it, we'll push on with your plan, but I think I have a way to get into his inner circle. Seems to me Nelson is not the only one in that massive business machine of his that might profit from getting rid of these lawsuits."

Jared stopped and gave her an appraising look. "Very astute, and I like the road you're traveling. All right. I'll handle the meeting and make sure I get Nelson alone tomorrow. Call me when you have the logistics figured out, and we'll hash out a way forward."

"Fantastic, but I have a dinner date, so it will be before six or after ten." She allowed herself a self-satisfied smile.

"Maliki?"

"Maybe."

"Huh. Guess I'll have to work on my methods of intimidation."

She put on her sunglasses and pretended she didn't notice his laughter.

CHAPTER 4

C had drained the last of his coffee. His patience vanished along with the last dregs of the caffeine. "Tell me there is a reason I am awake, dressed, and sitting at a conference table at the ass crack of dawn." Nobody spoke, but everyone cast furtive glances at each other. For Pete's sake, the suits obviously had bad news to tell him, but it seemed none of them had the balls to give it to him. *Fantastic.* Man, he needed sleep. Coming down from the grind of the tour and the last concert was never easy. Add a sprinkle of a long-legged, dark-haired angel who had moves that rivaled Jason Statham, and it equaled an up-all-night insomnia fest. His eyes itched. The unexpected *urgent* meeting that couldn't be put off was nothing but a gathering of the legal beagles and recording company suits. He glared at the corporate drones that circled the chrome and glass behemoth someone had the audacity to call a table. How many of these people did he actually know? He honestly couldn't remember a single name. Sure, he'd seen and talked to several of the lawyers, but Robert Hawkins, the man he paid mountains of money to represent him, wasn't in the room. Maybe this press of people was what he paid for. But this silent bullshit was for the birds. What in the hell was the purpose of him being here? Hell, he didn't know, and it was too damn early to try to play mind reader. He dropped his face into his hands and rubbed his unshaven cheeks roughly before he sighed, "All right. I'm out of here." He started to stand.

That got one hell of a response. Every swinging dick in the room started to speak at once. Kirk, Chad's road manager, personal assistant and long-time friend, put his fingers to his lips and shredded the air with an earth-shattering whistle. *Huh, looky there. The suits can be trained.* They shut up and gawked at Kirk like he'd grown three heads.

"Ladies and gentlemen, the man who pays your salaries asked you a question. My bet is you lawyer types have the scoop." Kirk pointed to the man in the middle of the table. "Mr. Lawyer, answer Chad's question, please."

Well shit, he needed to give Kirk a raise. Chad swiveled his head to the pudgy jowled man in the three-piece suit. If the damn thing were white, he'd look like Boss Hog from that old show, *The Dukes of Hazzard.* His band watched a shit-ton of old TV shows on Netflix while they were traveling. He closed his eyes and rubbed them. Maybe he needed to cut back on binge watching 80's sitcoms.

Boss Hog cleared his throat. Chad opened his eyes and swept a disgusted look around the room before he leaned forward and waited for Boss to explain this shit show.

"Well, Chad, we are waiting for several more people to arrive. I understand they have been delayed. I can only give you the most basic details." The condescending tone chapped his ass. Yes, he was raised in Tennessee. Yes, he had an accent and was country to the core, but he was also the man who built his brand. *Enough of this shit.*

"You know, that doesn't work for me. As of last night, I'm done with my tour. I have interviews to prepare for, then I'm disappearing for a while to rest and write music. Either you tell me what the hell has your balls sweaty, or I'm out of here. In case you've forgotten, you work for me, I don't work for you, nor do you dictate that I show up for a meeting that isn't." Chad changed his gaze to the record executives he saw huddling in the corner of the room against the wall. "Nor do you. My contract is being renegotiated as we speak. I have fulfilled all my contractual obligations. You don't have any reason to be here. Spill the shit, or I'm rolling."

"You can't leave." A slender man, all of maybe twenty-five years old, spoke up.

"Oh yeah? Watch me, Bubba." This shit was over.

"I mean you can, but you shouldn't. What your management team isn't telling you is that you are in danger. There is a situation, and it doesn't appear like a simple stalker. There have been serious threats, Mr. Nelson, and you could be in serious trouble. Your management team has hired Guardian Security to oversee your safety. They have been delayed to coordinate with the FBI."

"What's your name, Bubba?"

"Lance Meade."

"What do you do, Lance Meade?"

The kid turned red and gave a small laugh. "I... ahh... I'm an intern. Here for the experience. I'm in law school."

Chad turned his glare to ten other suits at the

table. "None of you have the balls to tell me what's going on? I had to grab a clue from an intern?"

Boss Hog floundered, gaping at him before he turned a warning glare toward the kid with the balls. "Well, we didn't want to worry you."

"You didn't want to worry me? That's bullshit. You wanted to muscle me into whatever agenda you have built that will benefit you. I'm country, sir, not ignorant." Chad stood and put his hands on his hips. "All right, gentlemen, it's time to play hardball. I want all the information you've got. You will brief me before the people from..." Chad looked at the kid again.

"Guardian, sir."

"Right, Guardian, get here. As a matter of fact, Lance, be a good boy and go tell the secretary to make the wonderful people from Guardian comfortable when they get here. I'll send for them when I have the entire story and not one second before."

"But Chad, you don't want to make this guy wait. He's one of the most powerful men in the country, if not world. You could jeopardize their involvement," Boss Hog squealed.

"Then you better talk fast." Chad's head whipped to the door at the sound of the deep voice. He couldn't help the laughter that escaped.

"Dude, did they cast you for the next *Men in Black* movie?" The guy was decked out in all black—as were the four men who flanked him. Not a speck of color. Black shirts, ties, and suits. The badge and shoulder holster that flashed a matte black grip when the man unbuttoned his jacket and sat down sealed the bad-ass persona.

"I'm Jared King, CEO of Domestic Security for Guardian International." Jared gave a wry glance around the table before he continued. "Your handlers have retained Guardian to protect you. We believe there is a credible threat against you, but we need to talk privately. Your minions are unwelcome and unwanted."

Well, that set off another round of geese squawking. Good lord, the man caused a clamor. Chad motioned to Kirk and the man rent the air with another ear-shattering whistle. The man-in-black's smirk turned into a genuine smile when the babbling ceased immediately.

Boss Hog cleared his throat to speak, but Chad held up a hand and silenced him. "Nothing. Not another word until we talk—alone." Chad motioned toward the newly arrived MIB clone.

"Chad, you can't do that. You need legal representation." Boss Hog's squeal made Chad's shoulders raise around his ears. Sharp and flat at the same time and three octaves too high.

"Dude, I haven't done a damn thing wrong, and *there are threats against me*. I don't need a lawyer to complicate anything. Now you and your cast of thousands get out and don't come back in here until I call you." He motioned toward Kirk. "Get ahold of Millicent and get her down here."

"Who is Millicent?" Mr. King, at least Chad thought that was what the guy had said his name was, asked as he leaned forward and accepted a folder from one of the other walking mountains he had with him. He watched the door shut behind Kirk, who was the last person out of the room.

"Millicent Wicker. She's the president of my PR firm. Keeps me out of the news unless I want to be there. She's damn good at her job. If this shit is going to blow up, she needs to be ahead of it." Chad drew a deep breath and released it slowly, bringing his heart rate to a near normal level.

The man across from him nodded his head slowly and motioned toward one of his men. Chad started to ask the man who in the hell would want to hurt him when he was stopped with a raised finger. The motion shut his mouth and pissed him off at the same time. The man motioned toward the speaker

phone in the middle of the table. That simple movement set two of his team into motion. One man
unhooked the speaker phone and took it outside.
Through the glass door that separated the conference room from the holding area, Chad watched as
the phone was deposited rather unceremoniously on
a couch in the hall. Another man unplugged wires
and disconnected the huge television and computer
system at the end of the conference table.

"I'm not a fan of monitored conversations."

Chad shook his head and leveled a confused look
at the man across from him. "This must be a serious
threat."

"While I am concerned about the threat to your
safety, my primary concern will be to ascertain
whether or not you are guilty of murder."

Every nerve in his body clenched and he stopped
breathing, waiting for the man to explain or laugh or
something... *"What?"*

"The FBI thinks you're implicated in not one, but
two, murders."

*"Murder?" The damn FBI thought he'd killed some-
one?* Well, he had... when he was enlisted, but hostile
conflict notwithstanding, he hadn't so much as made
an aggressive move toward anyone in years. He
stared straight at the man across the table who'd

dropped that bombshell. The direct gaze said more than his words did. "You think I killed someone? That's... how... what in the fuck is going on?"

The man smirked at Chad. "Not a murder, Mr. Nelson. Plural—two murders. Both were people who had lawsuits pending against you."

Chad's head whipped around to where the lawyers had been sitting and then back to Mr. King. "What? Who? What lawsuits?" Hell, he was being sued? Probably, it happened all the time. But... how... when... by who? How in the hell could someone think he'd do that? He shook his head and stared at the conference room table. He lifted his gaze and leveled it on King. "Dude, I swear on my daddy's grave, I have never killed a soul that the government didn't order me to kill. I don't know what the fuck you're talking about. Do I need to get a lawyer back in here?"

"You have that option, but right now you are not a suspect, more of a person of interest. My job here is to determine if you did, in fact, murder or hire the murders of Natalie Plate and Jarvis Colston."

"Natalie? Nat is dead?" Chad wrapped his arms around his gut. Fuck, he was going to be sick. Now that he thought about it, he knew Nat was suing him. He also knew she didn't have a leg to stand on.

Well, according to his lawyers she didn't. He'd forgotten all about the lawsuit she had against him.

"Executed. A bullet through her forehead."

Chad closed his eyes and swallowed hard. His gut clenched tight, and he pushed back the rolling sensations that hit him. Thank God he hadn't had anything to eat, or he'd have lost it. The FBI thought he'd killed the woman who'd given him his first recording contract. No… just… no.

"She gave me my break in Nashville. She got greedy. I fulfilled my contract. She didn't have a case. I would never hurt her."

"What about Mr. Colston?"

Chad pulled his eyes back to the man across from him. "Who?"

"Jarvis Colston. He was also suing you. He said you stole a song he pitched to you seven years ago."

"Mr. King, I refuse to listen to other songwriter's songs. My administrative staff returns all sheet music or tape submissions to the artists. All my music is my own. If he is suing me, it is without merit, and every piece of mail I get is logged, opened, photographed, and if it is music, returned with a delivery confirmation of the rejection. I never listen to submissions, and that's a fact. I insisted on that clause when I signed my first contract. I don't collaborate or sing other people's music." Chad dropped his head into his hands and took a deep breath. *Of all the things that could have happened at this meeting... hell... how do you process shit like this?* "What do I do?" Chad lifted his head and waited for an answer.

"Let me do my job. I'll handle the investigation. If you're guilty, I'll prove it. If not, my organization will track down and bring in whoever is out there killing your enemies."

"Enemies? Hell, man, enemies try to kill you. These people only wanted money, which I don't fucking care about because I have more than I could spend in three lifetimes!"

"Exactly. Enemies try to kill you. You have legitimate death threats against you, which my organization is also investigating."

"So you're what? You're guarding me?" Chad was fucking lost. Murder, death threats... hell, when did his world turn into... this?

"One of our best security specialists will be assigned to you until we finish our investigation on the murders and the threats against your life. Until that specialist arrives, you will have a team assigned to protect you from whoever is stalking you."

"Who would do that? Threaten me? Fuck, man, I

just want to write music and sing." *God, please just give me one solid piece of information to wrap my head around.*

"We don't know. We have a profile, but undoubtedly, it is someone with insider knowledge of your schedule." Mr. King looked at his watch and opened the file. "We have a lot to go over, Mr. Nelson. This will be our initial interview. Everything you've said and are going to say will be a matter of record. As I stated before, at this time you are not a suspect. I will not be advising you of your rights unless you implicate yourself."

Chad closed his mouth. Literally. He was lost in a tornado of emotion and information. "I don't need a lawyer. I haven't done anything wrong."

Jared King nodded and grabbed a Mont Blanc out of his jacket. "All right, let's start from the beginning."

CHAPTER 5

Jasmine opened the door to the outer offices that Jared now occupied. Her brother's team was still working at ten thirty at night. Reggie, one of the team members who had been with Jared longest, smiled at her and waved her through to her brother's office. She peeked in to see Jared with his feet propped up on the desk. His view was fixed out the window, and his cell was against his ear. She crept in the door and stood silently, not wanting to interrupt his call. He must have caught her movement out of the corner of his eye. He looked over, did a double take and motioned her in.

"I'm sure whatever you decide will be fine." Jared lowered his eyes as a smile crept across his face.

"Babe, seriously, you have expert assistance. You've reached a consensus. Just pull the trigger and submit the request to purchase the buildings." Jared listened for a moment, shook his head and laughed. "Christian, the money has been allotted. The buildings are structurally sound. There is enough room for expansion, and they are located in the heart of the area you are trying to reach. Pull the damn trigger." Jared paused and glanced at Jasmine before his gaze focused out the window again. "All right. I love you, too. See you soon."

Jared hung up and turned back toward her. "What have you done?"

"What? You don't like it?" Her hair was now streaked with dark red lowlights and lighter red-gold highlights. The length was cut in a new style with bangs. She'd altered her conservative makeup while channeling her twin sister. The results were rather dramatic.

"I... well... you look... different. It is going to take some getting used to the change. My main curiosity is what you think you're going to do with this..." Jared's brow scrunched as he tilted his head in confusion.

"Some of his band members, his road crew, his road manager and countless other people who surrounded him saw me at the Georgia Dome. I have to be able to pass as someone entirely different if we don't want whoever is after him to know he has a personal security officer."

"Well, I think that happened with this miraculous transformation. You were rather road-worn yesterday." Jared ducked sideways in his chair at the playful swing she took at him.

"Seriously? Anyway, I've got a new wardrobe coming in. It should be delivered to my hotel tonight. I've got an insane idea for a cover story. From what your case notes implied, you don't make him for the murders, right?"

Jared rubbed his jaw and thought about his answer. "Meh... it's a double-edged sword." He listed his head from side to side and hissed out a stream of air before he answered. "His responses were spontaneous. The shock was real. If he was lying, he's the best damn liar I've ever met. My gut is telling me this guy didn't know about the murders."

Jasmine sat down in one of the two chairs in front of the desk. "So we are more than likely looking at an insider who wants the lawsuits to go away and wants Nelson dead. Who benefits if he dies? Who stands to inherit? Where do the pieces of his empire land and under whose control?"

"The insider wanting the lawsuits gone is only one option, and we are working on that now. His businesses are vast, and his music empire is second only to Lucifer Cross. I scratched the surface of the structure with his initial interview. We've been granted access to records, stockholder's reports, lines of authority and powers of attorney. The true power behind the organization is too gray right now to be defined. The only thing I know for sure at this moment is that we don't know anything." Jared sat down beside her and yawned. "Sorry, anyway, since you obviously have a plan, how do you propose to run the show tomorrow?"

Jasmine opened her purse and pulled out a piece of paper. She handed it to Jared and watched as he read the details. His face remained impassive until he had reread the point paper.

"I'm not a fan. You've never gone undercover before. While I can applaud the initiative, you're a personal security officer. You aren't an undercover police officer, nor have you had the training that Jade has had to assume this role."

"Granted. Like the point paper stipulates. I go in under this pretense. If for some reason I get made, Nelson and I are immediately in the wind. We'll get out, ensure we don't have a tail and contact you for assistance if needed. But if I'm not made, I have the inside scoop on the dynamics of the people closest to him. I'll be able to neutralize any up-close threat. It is the practical solution to preventing access to the principal without letting the perp know we're watching."

Jared leaned forward in his chair and braced his elbows on his knees. "That's a solid plan until you ask yourself one question."

"And that is?"

"What if the inside threat and the murderer aren't the same person?"

Jasmine draped her arm over the back of her chair. Well, shit, there was that. "Okay, you tell me, what if they aren't the same person?"

"No matter what my gut instincts are telling me, at this time we can't eliminate anyone from this scenario, including our client. Do I think Nelson knew about the murders? No. I believe it was genuine shock that I witnessed this morning, but if he contracted the murders out and didn't know that the assassinations had already taken place, that shock would be honest too."

Jasmine nodded. They had no idea who was responsible, and she was walking into one hell of a convoluted mess.

"Now the question is, knowing where we stand, do you feel comfortable assuming this role? You don't have undercover training, but as you are more or less doing the PSO work you've been trained to do, I'll back you if you think you can handle it."

Jasmine puffed out a lungful of air and considered her options. "I'll regret it if I don't try. The man is irritating and arrogant. If you find evidence to support the theory he hired the murders out, I'll be very happy to slap a set of cuffs on him. If he didn't do it and it is someone else…" she spread her hands out and shrugged, "…I'll still be in a position to do my job and protect him from whatever inside threat he's facing."

Jared popped the paper she had handed him with a flick of his finger. "Okay, now that we have settled that, how was your date?"

Sadness tugged at her at the memory. "It was okay. We had a nice time, but he's been through some things recently." She held up her hand, forestalling the inevitable question. "We didn't discuss specifics, but whatever it was has impacted him. Suffice to say we had a lovely dinner."

Jared leaned back in his chair and rubbed his jaw. She watched as a myriad of emotions jetted across his face. "I've been concerned about him. I'll call

Dixon and Drake. If there is a position open at the training complex, or if they can invent one, I'll offer it to him. He needs time to process the events that have transpired around him, and I'm sure Adam wouldn't mind an extra hand with the rehab facility."

Jasmine lifted out of the chair and moved over to kiss her brother on the forehead. "Thank you. You're a good guy."

"Shhh... don't tell anyone. I have a reputation to uphold."

"Your secret is safe with me, J."

His laughter followed her out of the room.

CHAPTER 6

C had leaned back against the seat of the SUV. He was exhausted. Hell, he'd lapped exhausted about ten times and was still running in the 'I'm so tired' race. After King had grilled him for hours yesterday, he'd sequestered himself in his hotel room and freaked the fuck out. He couldn't eat. His head was fucking killing him and sleep had been impossible. The entourage that he normally traveled with was banished from his vicinity as soon as he hit the hotel. He had to process what the fuck was happening to him, and he couldn't do that with people around. Even Kirk was kept out, compliments of two huge men at his hotel door. Hell, he'd even turned off his cell phone after five text messages from Kirk and Millicent. Now he was being transported to a meeting with his lawyers by the same man who had shattered his perception of reality yesterday.

"I appreciate what you did yesterday. Nobody's been upfront with me in a hell of a long time. Probably too long."

Jared King threw him a glance. "You think?"

That pulled a sad chuckle from him. He watched the city pass by for a moment. "I've put together one hell of a management team. I did it for a reason. They take care of all the shit that circles my head. Without the distractions, I'm free to write and perform my music. They make money off me, and I get to do what I love. Obviously, I've lost control of a huge portion of my life. Or given it up. I'm not sure if it was intentional or not, but it happened."

"It isn't difficult to be consumed by what you do."

"Speaking from experience?" Boss Hog had said the man was one of the most powerful men in the country. Chad was pretty sure the add-on of 'if not the world' was splashed on to scare him into doing what the lawyer wanted.

"I run the domestic side of a huge security corporation. I've been lost a time or two. Made some poor decisions thinking that what I was doing was for the best, so yes, I'm speaking from experience. I'm no novice at screwing things up."

Chad laughed at that. Maybe it wasn't funny, but damn, it was nice to know he wasn't the only one who could fuck things up. He turned his attention to the road. The signs weren't right. "I hate to tell you this, but I think you are lost."

Jared shook his head. "No, I'm not, but this was a necessity as we needed to talk with you again without any of your entourage present. As we discussed yesterday, your life is being threatened, and until we find out who it is, everyone except you is a suspect."

"Dude, everyone I hang with has been with me for years."

Jared nodded. "Our profiler tells us this person may have been harboring this resentment for years, but a recent event has triggered the escalation of his delusion."

"You are telling me one of my friends may be a lunatic?"

Jared nodded. "Yes."

Chad leaned back and shook his head. "And the week started out so well…"

Jared chuckled and pulled into a long row of warehouses. His vehicle slowed and turned into one of the buildings. Another SUV that Chad hadn't noticed while they drove pulled up beside them. The team inside the second vehicle deployed after the garage door was secured.

"All right, Mr. Nelson, we are going through that door. Wait until my team opens the door for you."

"Overboard much?" Chad whispered to himself. If someone was going to kill him, would they follow him to a deserted warehouse, get inside it and try to shoot him when there were enough MIB guns around his vehicle to slaughter a herd of bison? Not likely.

Chad exited the vehicle when the door was opened and walked with Jared into the office. He stopped dead in his tracks. Jared closed the door behind him. Chad couldn't move.

"Hello, Mr. Singer Dude."

He recognized the voice but nothing else. "Um… hi?" he grappled, trying to remember where he'd heard the woman's voice before.

"Had any radio show award winners backstage lately?" The woman purred. *Holy shit!* Reality dawned on him. It was the spitfire who had taken down the bull of a man at the Dome. But what he was seeing was one hell of a stretch from the long-legged filly he'd seen that night. Well, the long legs were there, and Lord above they were sexy, but holy hell... what had happened to the woman he'd met?

She'd changed. Good Lord, how she'd changed. Dark red and gold shimmered in the black hair that hung free around her face. The result was stunningly beautiful. Her hair fell just below her ample breasts. She wore a pair of skin-tight, strategically ripped blue jeans, high heeled boots and a white tank-top that pulled tight across her breasts. Her hair and makeup transformed her from a plain, naturally beautiful woman to a sexually brazen siren who caught, and demanded, a person's attention. The only indication she was the same person was the cut on her forearm. She leaned against the edge of the table and licked her lips. He'd seen sex kittens before, but holy hell, this sexy spitfire had it going on and then some. She wasn't a kitten. Lord, the woman was a full grown, hunting, prowling, sexy-as-fuck feline. His cock started to stand up and take an interest, too.

Chad swallowed, twice, and cleared his throat. He shifted to try to relieve the building pressure behind his jeans. "I wouldn't have recognized you in a million years."

She smiled and flipped her hair behind her shoulder. "That is the idea."

"You work for him?" Chad was putting the pieces together—slowly.

"Score one for the country boy." She slid onto the top of a desk and dangled her legs.

He cast a glance at Jared and then back to the filly with the attitude. "What's going on?"

"You have someone wishing to do you harm. We feel the threat is legitimate—so much so we are inserting an operative into your circle of close friends to keep an eye on you and them," Jared answered, but Chad didn't pull his eyes from the woman.

"The question now is, can you introduce me as a love interest to your inner circle? Nobody can know I am your security detail, not your mom, manager, or candlestick maker. Do you understand?"

Chad looked between her and Jared. "Yeah, I get it." The spitfire could kick ass and take names, but he wasn't too sure he was happy with the idea of her being in harm's way. If someone was coming for him, he sure as hell didn't want her to be the one to stop the bullet.

"Good. We need to build a realistic way that would explain how we met. I'm thinking before your meteoric rise to fame, something that nobody could dispute."

He took off his ball cap and ran his hands through his long black hair. "Yeah, okay. I can say we first met when I was in the military. We have been talking on the phone, and you are coming to see me. Sparks fly after that, right?"

Jared nodded and pulled out a pad of paper and a pen. "Where were you stationed and what years?"

Chad listed his duty assignments and the dates.

"May I have your private cell phone number?" Chad told him, and Jared looked across the table at Jasmine. "You got your field phone?"

Jasmine nodded.

"What last name are you using?"

Jasmine smiled. "Cousins."

Jared nodded. "Mr. Nelson, we are going to manipulate your phone records. Load her cell phone number into your phone and put it in your favorites. We are going to ensure that if anyone looks, they know you two have been talking. A lot of talking. Late at night. Nobody can know that she is a plant."

Chad nodded. "Yeah, I got it. But seriously, my phone records? I'm having a difficult time thinking it's one of my crew."

"Who handles your cell phone bill?" Her voice pulled his attention toward her again.

"I don't know." And he didn't. Bills got paid, it was transparent to him.

"Until we catch whoever is threatening you, we're leaving nothing to chance. If this last cell phone bill shows you two talking and nobody sees it, no harm, no foul. But if someone is validating her cover? It is worth the time and effort. I'm going to step out and work these issues."

Jared's comment blanketed another layer of discomfort over him. His skin itched. He felt cornered. Trapped. The total loss of any perceived normalcy made him feel like he'd tried to straddle a tornado and ride it. The fucker was going to buck him off way before the buzzer sounded. He threw his Atlanta Braves baseball cap onto the desk next to the gorgeous, kick-ass-and-take-no-prisoners woman who was going to be his personal security. He once again ran his hands through his hair. No, he didn't like this. Not at all.

Jared turned to leave but stopped before he exited the office. "Mr. Nelson, that woman is my sister. She is one of the best personal security opera-tives we have. If you tell anyone that she is not who she claims to be, you may jeopardize not only your life but hers as well. If that happens, four of the deadliest brothers in the world will hunt you down and make you wish you hadn't. Do you understand me?"

Fuck, like he needed to be measuring dicks with Mr. MIB right now. He was having enough trouble dealing with the events of the last two days. He really couldn't handle anything else. "Dude, shelve your threats. I did two tours in the sandbox, and I don't scare easy. I'm buying what you are selling. I know how to run with an op, and I won't compromise it. Good enough for you?" He'd hated every minute of every day he'd served, but he'd been a damn good soldier.

Jared nodded and mocked, "Hoo-ah, or whatever. Color me *not* impressed," on his way out the door.

When the echo of the resounding thud of the slammed door ended, he looked at the woman seated on the desk. "I take it he isn't impressed," Chad drawled.

The vision in front of him chuckled, "No, he rarely is. My brothers are pretty tough, Marines and Air Force background, but Jared is a cop through and through."

Chad copied Jared's mocking tone, "Well Semper Fi and Aim High." He turned his attention toward her. "What's your name?"

"Jasmine." The name suited her. The woman

beneath all the makeup and pretense was a beautiful flower. Not that the trappings didn't enhance her beauty, they did, but she didn't need it.

"How long have you been doing this job?"

"Why?" She reached for her purse on the corner of the desk.

"Well, if I'm honest, I'm not sure I like the fact that you would be putting yourself between me and a bullet or a knife or hell... even a fist."

Jasmine froze, then turned her eyes toward him to nail him with a stare that would freeze the balls off of Frosty the Snowman. "Let's just say I've been doing this job long enough to know male chauvinist pigs who don't think a mere woman can protect them can endanger a mission faster than any psychotic assassin. You want to catch this bastard, you do what I tell you, when I tell you, and I'll keep you alive."

"Wow. I take it you've fought this battle before?" Chad had to admire the woman's spunk. She gave him a single slow dip of her head. Her eyes glittered with what he figured was one hell of a lot of anger. "Well, since we are being brutally honest, let me put it out there for you. I was raised to protect women. Sorry about that, but it is true. My instinct is, and always will be, to make sure ladies are treated properly."

"Like you treat the *ladies* backstage?" The taunt fell from her lips and lanced him to the core. He'd been a man whore. He'd built that reputation, but one night many years ago had changed everything.

"Not all of those women are ladies, but I treat them with respect. Regardless, I'm trying to explain why I have a difficult time processing the fact that *you* are here to protect *me*. I don't need a reminder that my past is sordid, I own that, but it *is* in the past."

Jasmine stood and placed her hands on her hips.

If he'd said that he didn't do a once-over and appreciate the view, he'd have been lying.

"Yeah, I can see that."

Busted. Fuck. "I'm willing to try, but I'm not going to allow you to come into my world and emasculate me in front of my people. They'd know in a heartbeat that shit was all wrong. I don't attract or even like bossy, demanding women. I never have, and if I suddenly knuckle under to a new pretty face, well... your cover is shot."

"I can work with that. I will only dictate your actions when you are in jeopardy. If I can, I'll do it in a way no one else will know."

She held his gaze and didn't back down for a second. The woman had nerves of steel, and surprisingly, he was intrigued. Not usually what attracted him to a woman. The exact opposite yanked his chain.

Chad smiled his best stage grin and asked, "When do we start this?"

JASMINE CONSIDERED THE QUESTION. The sarcastic portion of her mind wondered what exactly Chad defined as *this*, but with the benefit of years of training, she cloaked the claws on her attitude. "I'll call you tonight to confirm. I'll get your personal cell phone number from Jared. By tonight our backstory will be airtight. The variable will be your staff. If you don't think it's pushing it, I'll fly to Nashville in a couple of days. That should give you time to get back to Tennessee and plant some seeds. How apt are they to believe you have a love interest?"

Chad leaned back against the wall. "They are paid well enough not to ask questions about my private... encounters. Those that will ask, I can handle."

Encounters? Not relationships or affairs, but encounters. Very telling. Jasmine let the comment pass without comment but cubby-holed that bit of information for later. "Will you be able to meet me at the airport?"

His vivid blue eyes searched her face, and he nodded. "Why?"

"If we use the fans and the scene they will cause, it may legitimize the reality of a relationship."

"Yeah, we can do that, but without sounding too vain, I usually stir up one hell of a fuss when I appear at a public location. Besides, won't a big scene piss off the man in black?"

Chad's reference to her brother pulled forth a small laugh. "No, we can pre-position and control the area. Will the people closest to you question it?"

"Shit, who knows? Most days I have my own time. I write, play, sing or just listen to music. They leave me alone for at least a couple hours a day. It's not like I have a life outside of my music, so I'm usually available when they need me. I keep to myself and rarely go out, so they may question the suddenness of the situation, but they can't disprove it."

"Do those rare outings include your trips to Club Chameleon?"

She watched the expression slide off his face. The shuttered mask he slipped on added to information points she was gathering about the superstar. The man radiated anger.

"How did you find out about the club?"

"The FBI. They have shots of you going into and coming out the night of one of the murders."

"That part of my life isn't open for discussion, and I won't let you or anyone else dissect it. That club has nothing to do with your cover."

"All portions of your life fall under a murder investigation. Why do you think the FBI knows about your membership? They think you hired someone to kill the people who are suing you." Jasmine watched the storm of emotions stomp across the man's expressive eyes. When anger and rage fled, a flood of confusion and anguish pushed itself forward.

"I've killed. On the orders of others while I was in the military." Chad closed his eyes and clenched his hands in a spasmodic effort which seemed to control his emotions. "I will *never* again be responsible for taking another life." Chad drew a deep, shuddering breath. "I don't have anything to do with the murders of those people. If I had my way, I would have settled those cases out of court. I fought to have them taken care of immediately, but the lawyers and my management team convinced me that settling would sway the public to think I was at fault. I wasn't, in either of those cases."

"If you aren't guilty, Jared and his people will prove it. They are the best at what they do. In the meantime, there is a credible threat against you. While the security team you've been assigned can take care of external threats, we believe you are most vulnerable to an internal threat. Hence me."

"No... the more this soaks in, the more uncomfortable I am with the whole thing. I'm capable of taking care of myself. Especially now that I know there is a threat." He shrugged his shoulder and continued, "Heck, I've been trained to take care of myself. While I appreciate the..." He swept his hand up and down, indicating her transformation, "...I think you should call your brother back in here. I've changed my mind. I'm not going to put more people in danger."

"I don't doubt for a second that you can take care of yourself. The fact of the matter is that this threat might not be one you see or one that you can fight by yourself."

"Right. No offense, darlin'. I saw you in action, so I know you can scrap with the best of them, but if someone is coming after me, do you really think you could stop them?"

The man sounded resigned and defeated. She couldn't let that continue. Jasmine slid off the table and walked up to him. She ran her fingertips across his cheek and swept them through his thick hair. Her voice was icy and clear. "Oh, I *can* and *will* stop them. We will convince everyone that we are a couple, and no one will suspect I'm more than your current flavor of the week. However, what you need to remember is that I sleep with a .45 caliber automatic. I am a black belt in three different disciplines, and even though I may act like a woman in love for your crew—I'm not. I'm here to do a job. I'm one of the best at what I do. I have extremely sharp nails, long teeth, and my bite can kill. Unlike you, I have no doubt I may take another life in the performance of my job, and that is something I have come to terms with long ago. I don't need or want your knight on a white horse act, Mr. Nelson. I'm here to do a job and nothing more. I'm not calling my brother. We *are* doing this, and we *will* make it believable."

Jasmine slid her body against his and purred, "We are going to need to be very believable. Do you think you can kiss me like you mean it?" The contact of his body against hers sent erratic tendrils of sensation through her.

The singer gazed at her for several long seconds before he put his arms around her waist and pulled her firmly against him. The tug forced a small huff of air from her lungs. "I guaran-damn-tee it. But I still don't like this, not even a little bit. I don't need you in harm's way." He lowered his head and softly caressed her lips.

The same desire she'd felt for him in his dressing room that first night rocketed through her veins. She pulled away slowly and took a deep breath. The arc of sexual electricity between them crackled, bringing goose bumps to the surface of her skin. This was what she'd wanted with Maliki. *I'm so screwed.*

He smiled wickedly, almost as if he could sense her thoughts. He ran his hands up her back and added, "To make this work, you have to understand that the closest members of my entourage know I prefer my women... compliant."

Jasmine leaned forward again, wrapped her arms around his neck, looked at him through her lashes and purred, "Anything for you, Chad." She lifted an eyebrow and murmured, "Because it's my job, nothing more—and Mr. Singer Dude, you do need me."

His eyebrows rose as his smile widened. "Yeah, but not to step in the path of a bullet."

Jasmine dropped her hands to his chest and pushed him away. Enough tit for tat. They had an insertion to plan. She chuckled at the double entendre. The sexy-as-sin musician gave her a questioning look. No, no way in hell she'd ever explain that thought. Time to turn the conversation toward the business of getting her into his world. "All right, Mr. Superstar, you sell the bill of goods to your inner sanctum the way you need to. Fill me in on what happens tonight when I call you. And would you do me a personal favor?"

Chad's eyebrows rose in question.

"Stay alive until I can get there. All right?"

"Oh, I'm not planning on getting myself killed, especially not when I have a front row seat to this show."

CHAPTER 7

Is that what a person looks like when they're having a stroke? A vein across Chad's manager's forehead bulged obscenely and turned a dark blue color. His face and neck flushed a vivid red and spittle clung to his lips as he shouted, "What the hell do you mean you need to go to the airport? Do you realize how much your security detail is going to bitch? Not to mention your agent, the record company and that guy from Guardian who told you to keep your ass here. We've only been home for three days. They haven't found the person who is threatening you."

Chad shrugged. "I don't care. I need to meet someone at the airport. If we don't advertise it, I can sneak in, meet her flight and leave without anyone knowing."

"Bullshit! You are the most recognized face in the business. You have a certified death threat against you, and you need to keep your ass right here in this house."

Chad laughed and stood up, towering over his manager. "I pay you. Remember?"

The manager choked on his anger. His face turned a horrific shade of red-blue. The little man sputtered and paced as his hands flew around in disjointed exclamation points. "Who is it that you're going to meet? I mean, I can pick them up. This isn't good. You can't do this."

"Terry, I'm picking up a personal friend—a close personal friend." Chad picked up his guitar and strummed a couple of cords. "Her plane lands at three thirty. Either you work the security detail to make sure they are ready, or I *will* go by myself."

"How come this is the first I am hearing of this friend? What is she, a groupie? Or one of your whores that you sneak out to tie up and beat? Seriously, now is not the time for that shit."

The fuck did he say? Chad's head whipped around, nailing his manager with his eyes. "What?" The steel and ice in his voice froze the space between them.

He saw the change in the man the second Terry realized what he'd said. Fear fixed on his face, draining the torrid flush to a sickening pallor.

"I'm sorry. I didn't mean anything by it, Chad. I'm just worried about you, about the threat…"

"Three people know about my visits to the club. You are not one of them. *Who. Told. You?*" Chad stepped closer, and the little man cowered.

"Nobody?"

"Fuck you, Terry! Who told you?"

"Millicent. She wanted me to be aware in case you ever needed someone to come get you."

Millicent Wicker. The one fucking person he thought he could trust with all his secrets. The one who obviously disregarded the non-disclosure agreement. Chad felt his blood boiling and struggled to push down the rage that was building.

"What?" He couldn't form any other words with his teeth clenched and grinding.

"She told me what happens in those places."

"Bullshit! She knows nothing about what happens in that club. People like you and Millicent only read the bastardized guesses of small-minded people. What I do in my private time has *nothing* to do with you, Millicent, or anyone else on this planet."

"Okay, Chad. I get it. I promise I won't talk to anyone about this again."

"Again?"

"Uhhh…"

"What the fuck, man? Who did *you* tell?" Chad moved until he was inches away from the man. His teeth clenched so hard he could feel them breaking. His one remaining illusion of privacy was being shredded, and there was absolutely nothing he could do to mitigate what had happened. And *that* pissed him off.

"Well, when that agent from the FBI called? Davis, I think his name was? He needed to account for your whereabouts. He wouldn't tell me anything other than the date. He was curious about where you were, and that was one of the nights you went to the club. I knew because you took the Audi and the clothes you wear when you go there are… different. I told him he needed to talk to your lawyers, but then I called your lawyer to give him a heads up. I didn't say a word about you going there to the FBI, but it scared the shit out of me! Why did the FBI want to know where you were? Are they tracking the stalker, too?"

Chad strode across the space that separated them. "If you open your mouth about me again, to anyone, I will ruin you. You will not work for another person in this or any other entertainment industry. You will write down exactly what Millicent told you and when. But right now... you need to get out of here, Terry. Get out, *now!*"

Chad saw nothing but the man's backside as he streaked out of the room. Fucking Millicent. How many others had she told? Chad paced and pulled out his phone. He needed to... hell... what did he need to do? This wasn't fucking happening. He couldn't bring attention to the club. The ultra-rich, celebrities and political powerhouses who attended that club didn't need this. *Fuck!* Legally, he couldn't say a damn thing. He needed to ensure nothing else got out. If Millicent was the one releasing his private information... he'd terminate her services... bring a damn lawsuit against her, maybe. *Son of a bitch, why in the hell would she...*

"Dude, the entire compound heard you screaming at Terry. You okay?" Chad swung around at Kirk's question. He shook his head and continued to pace.

"Whoa, Chad, man, talk to me. What the hell has you so worked up?"

His friend's puzzled expression only added to his anger. He'd trusted two people with this secret, and one of them had fucked him royally. Kirk and Millicent had an on-again-off-again, friends-with-benefits thing going on. Kirk knew about the club, too. The third person was the lawyer who'd drawn up the bullet-proof NDA that both Millicent and Kirk had signed. "I need you to call Millicent. Get her down here."

"Hell, she just flew back to New York yesterday after talking the stalker issue to death. Seriously, I'm not as young as I used to be. I need a break. The woman wore me out." Kirk flopped into the deep leather cushions of the couch.

"I don't fucking care. Get her here." He whipped out his needle-sharp response faster than a rattler could strike.

Kirk's eyes did the saucer thing. *Good.* About time somebody got the idea he was pissed. "Dude, seriously, chill. I'll call. What has your panties in a wad?"

Chad stopped pacing and gritted his response through his teeth. "She will be here tomorrow morning, or I will take action. Got it?"

"Fuck, man... yeah, yeah, I got it. I... she... Chad... are you okay?" Kirk pulled out his phone. His hand was shaking as he unlocked it. Chad couldn't help wondering if he was upset his quasi-lover was in trouble or that Chad was madder than a fucking junkyard dog.

Kirk lifted the phone to his ear. Millicent's voice caught and held Chad's attention. Although he couldn't hear the exact words, the tone wasn't that of a lover.

"Milli, you need to come to Nashville. Be here by noon tomorrow." Kirk looked up at Chad and shook his head. "Sweetheart, you're up a creek without a paddle. Get here if you want to have a career." Kirk hung up the phone and threw it onto the coffee table. He leaned forward and looked up at Chad. "What can I do?"

"I'm going to the airport this afternoon. Arrange it with the new security team or make sure Terry has done it."

"Why are you going to the airport?"

Chad looked directly at Kirk and gave a half-hearted smile. He didn't feel like playing the game Guardian had set up, but he needed to sell Jasmine's story. Hell, maybe Guardian could put a lid on this shit for him. That thought caught and held.

"I finally convinced her to come down."

The tall blond froze instantly and glared at Chad. "Who? Millicent?"

"No. Jasmine."

"Wait. What? Who the hell is Jasmine?"

"Someone I met while I was in the military."

"Yeah? That's a long time ago."

"Mmm... she was special, but things were complicated. I got all reflective one night a couple of months ago and looked her up. We've been talking for a while. I finally convinced her to visit now that I'm on a break from touring."

Kirk flopped back on the couch. "No shit?"

Chad looked at him and dipped his head. "No shit."

"Cool, when are we going to pick her up?"

Chad shifted his eyes to the man he considered his best friend. "We?"

Kirk gave him a weird look. "Well, yeah, man. We always go together."

Chad shook his head. "Not this time, dude. I think I would like some alone time with her, if you know what I mean."

Kirk stood up. "Yeah, right. Sorry, didn't think that one through. I'll talk to the security detail. What time?"

"I need to meet her flight at three thirty."

"Okay. I got it." Kirk walked out of the room and closed the door behind him.

A swirl of thoughts swam across Chad's mind. He

was so damn tired. He hadn't slept for shit last night, or for that matter, any night since Jared and Jasmine King had walked into his life. The cold hard facts were undeniable. The FBI thought he was a person of interest. Two people were dead, and from what he was being told, he was the only intersecting point. He wasn't responsible for their deaths, yet somehow he'd been implicated. Add the fact he'd had death threats made against him, and you had a perfect shit storm. Not to mention all of that chaos was happening outside of his carefully constructed sphere of self-imposed shelter.

How in the hell had he become so isolated and protected that he had no knowledge of what was happening around him? People managed his life. Hell, they managed his access to information about his life. If it weren't so pathetic, it would be funny. But looking at it now, what he saw was nothing less than tragic. He'd built the perfect business machine, employed the best people and turned his back to play his music while the machine took on a life of its own.

Chad stopped pacing. In a moment of startling clarity, he knew exactly what he was going to do. He took a deep breath for the first time in almost a week. He *knew* what to do. Chad grabbed the guitar and strummed random chords while he mentally ticked boxes off on the laundry list of items he'd need to accomplish to make it happen. Fuck, as the idea grew and took on roots, the list became long, complicated and ugly. A knock at the door caused him to fall back on the couch in frustration. Rubbing his face with both hands, he bellowed, "What!"

Kirk poked his head around the door, "I am sorry to bother you again, but I got the security details worked out. I will come get you when we are ready to leave."

"*We* are not going, Kirk. I am going. No manager, no entourage, just me and the security detail. Understand?"

"Yeah, sorry, a slip of the tongue, but dammit, Chad, right now isn't a great time to be out and about. Not with that threat against you. Are you sure this is what you want to do?"

"Yeah, let the team from Guardian do their job. By the way, this shit falling down on me has made me take a hard look at where I am. I've had a bit of an epiphany. I think I'm done with it all, Kirk. This life is a fucking three-ring circus, and it isn't what I want. Not anymore. I'm taking my life back. I'm meeting Jasmine, finishing my obligations to the label and I'm punching my time card."

"Say what?"

"You heard me."

"No... just hang on a minute. You're quitting? You can't be serious."

"The big top is coming down, my friend."

"Dude, really, you need to slow your roll and think about this. The bullshit happening now, it's temporary. It will pass. Music is your life."

"I deserve more than this."

"*More than this?*" Kirk held his arms out and spun around in the grand music room of Chad's forty-thousand-square-foot mansion. "Dude, you are the fucking king of country music. Your smallest, most insignificant wish is fulfilled in a heartbeat! What in the hell *more* could you possibly want?"

The pleasure of waking up with the woman he loved. A home, not a freaking motel-slash-show-place, and maybe children someday. A life that didn't include sleeping in strange hotel rooms or on the tour bus at least two hundred fifty days a year. The ability to walk down the street or have dinner at a restaurant without being mobbed. Holidays at home with a Christmas tree that he helped decorate instead of a thirty-foot monstrosity that cost a fortune to have someone stage. Hell, those things barely scratched the surface of the *more* he wanted.

Getting his life back was his starting point, though. The rest would follow.

Chad shrugged and kept his mouth shut. Millicent's betrayal still stung; fresh, raw and painful. It was like he'd told Kirk. He was done, and he was pretty damn good with that decision, too.

Kirk must have understood he wasn't going to get an answer. He let out a huge sigh. "Whatever, dude. Just don't do anything stupid while you're upset."

Chad waited for the door to close and sent Jasmine the pre-arranged text message. *Can't wait to see you, pick you up at 3:30.*

CHAPTER 8

The plane touched down with a jolt. The immediate air brake pushed everyone in the cabin forward with a lurch. Jasmine closed her eyes and said a prayer of thanks. If her brother or one of the Wonder Twins wasn't piloting the aircraft she was flying on, she rarely made it to takeoff without a prayer or two sent upstairs. The brakes stuttered as the pilot slowed rapidly to make the cross ramp off the active taxiway. Jasmine turned on her phone and texted Chad.

JUST LANDED.

. . .

She received an immediate text.

*At baggage claim. **Large crowd.***

Jasmine had no doubt. It wasn't the norm for her to do her job on center stage; she was usually behind the scenes. When the aircraft finally parked, Jasmine stood in her four-inch heels and towered over the man in the row in front of her. His eyes were dead level with her breasts. He flushed wildly and tried to move, but was pinned by the people filling the aisles. Jasmine schooled her expression, trying desperately not to laugh. She was jostled from behind and leaned forward, bringing herself just a bit closer. The man made a mewling noise and tried to move out of her way, but only managed a couple of inches. Jasmine cringed inwardly as she retrieved her handbag from above his head in the overhead luggage compartment, hoping the little guy didn't have a coronary.

Once the door opened, she followed the rapid pace of the passengers flowing off the aircraft and the signs for baggage claim. She could hear the commotion before she got to the escalator. Somebody below her on the baggage claim floor yelled,

"It's Chad Nelson!" Jasmine smiled and wondered how he was going to play it. However it rolled, she would keep up her end.

As the escalator lowered, she saw him in his jeans, mirrored sunglasses and ball cap. His broad, muscled shoulders pulled his black t-shirt tightly against his chest. The man was stunning. He smiled hugely as he walked away from a bank of fans that he'd been signing autographs for and moved to the escalator to wait for her. As she walked off the apparatus, he took her hand and pulled her close. The electric shock she'd felt in the office ran through her body again. Chad smiled and slowly lowered his face, taking possession of her lips. His taste and smell swamped her senses. The fans exploded, cheering and screaming his name. She exploded on the inside. Her nerves jolted with the instantaneous chemistry of the kiss. Jasmine took off his hat and ran her fingers through his hair as the crowd of women went crazy. She hadn't done it for the crowd, but no one needed to know that. Lifting his head, he smiled down at her and loosened his hold. "Hi, baby, you look fantastic." There were a series of blinding flashes. How the paparazzi had gotten to the airport so quickly was beyond her.

She reached up and kissed him on the lips softly. "Hi back, stranger. I could say the same."

"Where are your luggage claim tickets?" Jasmine reached into her purse for them and handed them to him. Chad waved over a man and handed him the tickets. "Would you please make sure these get to the house?" The man nodded and departed immediately.

Chad stopped and grabbed her again. He bent her backward, taking her weight in his arms and holding her off the ground as he kissed her deeply in an old-time movie leading-man swoop. The crowd broke into wild screams and applause again.

With an effort, she relaxed in his strong arms and whispered against his lips, "Aren't you overplaying this?" Flashes of light illuminated his chiseled features and his eyes. They were cobalt blue and rimmed with the longest, darkest lashes she'd ever seen. God, the man was drop-dead sexy. Chad squeezed her tight, straightened, smiled and winked. He put his arm around her and headed toward the line of his security that was keeping the fans at bay. Jasmine looked over at the little man who had almost face planted in her chest. He blushed fiercely when she winked at him. Jasmine waved and laughed as she linked her arm in Chad's.

"Who was that?"

Jasmine leaned into him and channeled her inner Jade. She shimmied her breasts ever so lightly against his arm. "Somebody who has the exact stature to meet the girls up close and personal. I think he may have had an aneurysm."

Chad caught Jasmine by the waist, pulling her forward and past the crowd that was being held back by security. "Damn, right now I'm wishing I was four foot nothing, too."

THE MANSION WAS full of people and Chad introduced Jasmine to everyone. Names blurred, but the faces she tried to catalog. She'd notice a detail or two about each person to peg them into her mind's eye. The mental flashcards helped to keep known people sorted from unknowns. Chad rolled through band members, backup singers, a chef, housekeepers, and security, most of whom she recognized from Guardian. The introductions droned on through his manager and his manager's assistant and maybe an assistant to the assistant's assistant, all while he pulled her through the house and up the grand stairway. She could see no way to protect him from anyone wanting access. The entire situation was unacceptable. Chad led her to his private wing of rooms. She mapped the house and counted steps. He closed the door behind them and grabbed her, pulling her close.

Jasmine stiffened immediately. Chad lowered his head and whispered in her ear. "Terry will undoubtedly be here with some major concern, scheduling conflict, or drama that he has to talk to me about. He hates not being in the loop, and I sent him into a tailspin when I told him about you this morning. Trust me. He'll be here, and he needs to see us together."

"No respect for your personal space or time?"

Chad shook his head as he started dancing with her.

"Umm... excuse me, but aren't we missing music?"

Chad smiled and tapped a finger to his temple. "It is always playing in here—notes, tunes, melodies. Sometimes I can't get them down on paper fast enough."

He led her across the floor and twirled her, pulling her back to him. His eyes closed and he stopped dancing. Jasmine froze, not sure what he was doing. He opened his eyes and beamed a huge smile at her. "That is an awesome riff."

He walked to the couch and picked up the guitar, playing several chords and notes, writing them down in one of several spiral notebooks scattered across the huge granite-topped coffee table.

Okay, note to self, the man is ADD on top of everything else. Jasmine surveyed the windows, noted the adjoining doors, and examined the great room, looking for egress points. The music hall was lined with musical instruments. Guitars were scattered in stands around the seating area. A grand piano was tucked into the far corner. A drum kit behind a Plexiglas shield jutted out from the opposite side of the room. Several electronic keyboards flanked the towering drum set.

The massive expanse of the room gave a softness to the notes coming from Chad's guitar. The acoustics sent a shiver down her spine. Ornate decorations caught her attention and reminded her of a turn of the century ballroom. Huge wall sconces dotted the dark hunter green walls. Three gold and crystal chandeliers dangled from ornate ceiling medallions, all of which were outlined by dark wood, with crown molding joining the walls to the ceiling.

The double doors opened, and a little bald man burst into the room with his head buried in a folder full of papers. He glanced up, gave Jasmine a dismissive look and returned his attention to the folders. "Chad, we need to work the interview schedules for the CMAs you are scheduled to perform. Additionally, you will be presenting the award for the Breakout Artist of the Year category with Francine Young."

Chad put down his guitar and patted the couch next to him. He grabbed her hand as she sat down. He kissed her cheek and covered her hand with his, forcibly pulling her fist apart as he intertwined his fingers with hers. She consciously relaxed her muscles and schooled her features as she watched the little man. The one thing she hated seeing while acting as a personal security officer was the way her primaries were treated by those who were supposed to take care of them. If this man's disregard for Chad's personal time and space was any indication, he had a problem.

"Now, we are scheduled for two after parties, one at Sony, the other at Red Cliff. We have you with Millicent for the red carpet walk and the appearances..."

"Millicent? Wait, as in my PR manager Millicent?" Chad quizzed the man.

Terry nodded tentatively.

"Hell no, I'm not escorting Millicent. Why would I? I've never taken her to any events. Cancel that. I'll be escorting Jasmine to all future engagements."

Terry looked up and switched his gaze from Chad to her and back again. Finally, he ended up staring at her and gaping. The little man's face flushed crimson red. "Listen, no disrespect, Chad, I have had this scheduled with Millicent and Francine's manager since the schedule came out months ago. I told you when you and Kirk were on that damn video call from Phoenix during the dust storm. You can't change it now."

The singer picked up the guitar and started strumming. "I've found that when people preface a sentence with 'no disrespect' that is exactly what they mean, Terry. I *can* change it, and I am. If you said anything about it, I don't remember it. Jasmine is the only woman I will be seen with in public."

The little man's eyes bulged as he sputtered, "Chad, really, I don't see how this… this… person… can…"

Jasmine had to give it to the singer; his reaction was immediate. He stood and spoke with controlled venom. Jasmine took note of that fact. Chad Nelson wasn't a pushover by any stretch of the imagination.

"You are walking a thin line, Terry. Listen to me clearly and hear what I say to you, because I will not repeat it. *Jasmine is mine.* She will be my escort to all functions we are currently obligated to attend. After that, either she or I will decide which ones *we* will attend. I will not hesitate to find a manager who understands. Do I make myself clear?"

"Crystal clear, but do you have any idea how much work will go into changing all this? You've never cared before. Why would I suspect anything had changed? Until this morning, I had no idea *she* existed. Threatening to fire me because I didn't know about your friend and doing my job is bullshit, Chad."

"No, thinking that I'd ever take Millicent to an event is bullshit, Terry. Telling me who I'll escort is bullshit. Running my life without any regard for what I want is bullshit. It stops, and it stops now."

The little man nodded and trembled with whatever emotion he was suppressing. Jasmine reached out a hand and placed it on Terry's shaking arm. "I understand my sudden appearance is making things difficult. I told Chad I should have waited to come down, but... perhaps we should all take a break and relax? Can your scheduling wait until tomorrow? I'm positive *you* could make sure Chad and I are left alone for the rest of the evening so he can relax? We'd appreciate it." Jasmine watched the cogs click in the little man's mind. He weighed the options and knew where he needed to land.

"Of course. I will ensure you are not disturbed for the rest of the evening. We can discuss the schedule tomorrow. Perhaps over lunch?"

Jasmine smiled sweetly at him and nodded. "That would be wonderful. Thank you so much for being so protective of our private time. It means so much to us."

The little man beamed. She could bet he was working the angles in his mind. It was confirmed when a brilliant smile plastered across his face. "Of course, no problem at all. I will see you both for lunch." He nearly skipped out of the room.

Chad lifted her hand and kissed the back of it. "Very well played, Ms. Cousins."

She leaned back into the couch and sighed. "Most people are easily manipulated." He pulled her over, and she lay, albeit stiffly, against his chest for a moment. The delicious warmth of his body and his scent surrounded her. *Aaannnddd* that was enough of that. She pushed away and sat up. "Where's my room?"

Chad stroked the back of her arm with a finger. "We're sharing my room."

Jasmine shifted so she could stare at him. "Excuse me?"

"It is a king sized bed. You can have half of it, and I promise not to ravage you unless you want me to, but if we didn't share my bed, the love story would be kinda weak, don't you think?"

Jasmine got that, but somehow she'd thought... or maybe she hadn't thought. Damn, being in the same bed? She hadn't shared a bed since she found out Evan was cheating on her. But this was work. Chad was a client, not a lover, and she was a professional. She'd figure out a way of not making this any more difficult than it already was—maybe.

"Okay, but there are ground rules."

"Such as?"

Jasmine held up her fingers, "One, sex is not on the table. I am here as protection for you." *There, problem solved.*

The grin on Chad's face slid off, and he cocked his head. "Go on."

She continued, "Two, I will play the doting lover to you and only you. I'm not a wallflower, and I will not be relegated to the corner like some naive sixteen-year-old in a *Dirty Dancing* movie."

He smiled slightly. "And?"

She held up the third finger. "When this is over we part company—permanently and irrevocably. You go back to being the wild ass country star you are, and I slip back into the shadows that I love living in."

He shook his head. "Afraid I can't deal with those conditions, and as they were not part of the original agreement, I don't think you have a leg to stand on."

Whatthehelldidhejustsay? "You can't be serious."

Chad shrugged nonchalantly. "This is on you. Your one condition for this little scheme when we started it was that I could convince people you were my love interest. When you set that condition, sex between us was not taken off the table. I'm not going to do anything to force you to have sex with me, but that doesn't mean I'm not going to try everything I know to make you want me as much as I want you. I don't agree to rule number one, and I intend to make every attempt to break your resolve at the earliest possible opportunity. Rule number two won't be a problem. Watch, listen, do whatever you need to do until we interact as a couple. At that time, I'm the one who takes the lead. Always. Rule number three is also moot. I may be portrayed as a wild ass country star, but I assure you my partying days are long past. I'm a simple country boy, and sweetheart, you are far too beautiful to live in the shadows."

Jasmine stood and looked at the man reclining on the couch. "This little scheme? You mean the one where I protect your ass? The one where I'm here to make sure you don't die? Well, wake up and take notice, Mr. Singer Dude. You don't have much choice in the way this goes down. If I decide I'm out, Guardian swoops in and your world implodes. You will be a captive within these walls until you are exonerated or charged, and your stalker is caught. So, since we have those points settled, would you please show me the bedroom so I can unpack and freshen up?"

Jasmine didn't trust the confident, self-assured look on the musician's face. He smiled that patented stage smile and led her through the cavernous music hall and out the double doors she had noticed before the manager had blasted into the room.

The master bedroom was just as vast as the music hall. The same hunter green adorned the walls, but the masculine touches to the room changed the ambiance from turn of the century opulence to a dark, wood-warmed retreat. The king sized bed was elevated and had steps leading up to the mattress. Shades of green and blue colored the expensive Aubusson carpets, floor-to-ceiling drapes and exquisitely covered furniture that formed a conversation group by the freestanding fireplace. Jasmine took it all in while searching for access points that she'd need to protect. There appeared to be only one other door, which probably led to the en suite. It would seem that access to his inner sanctum was restricted through the music hall's door. She could work with that.

Her luggage was sitting on the plush leather and suede bench at the foot of the bed. She unlocked and opened the small case, lifted the tray-like shelf to expose a false bottom to the makeup case and lifted out her .45 caliber and extra clips. Jasmine loaded the weapon, chambered a round and thumbed the safety. "Which side do you sleep on? I need to be on this side."

Chad shrugged. "Doesn't matter. I sleep in the middle."

Jasmine gave him her best withering look and walked to the side closest to the door, the one that would put her between a threat and Chad when they slept. She positioned the weapon under the pillow. Walking back to the case, she lifted out her concealed weapon, a Glock 43. The light, slim-lined weapon fed into a concealed carry holster that attached to the waistline of her skirt and tucked into the hollow of her back. With the flowing muslin top, no one would notice the weapon unless they touched it, and nobody was getting that close. Two leather harnesses and fine-edged throwing blades came out of the case. She opened a dresser drawer and hid them below his shirts. Her shoulder holster for her .45 would stay in the suitcase until she needed it.

"How did you get them through airport security?"

She shook her head as she pulled out a Taser and loaded the battery. She tossed that on top of her purse. "I didn't. I gave you two baggage claim tickets that were issued by the airline and one that was created by Guardian. This case was prepped for me locally and added to the conveyor belt by Guardian when the luggage was being offloaded in the baggage handling area." Jasmine pulled out her handcuffs and badge and dropped them on the bed before she shut the lid.

Chad's eyes lingered on the cuffs. She couldn't be sure what he was thinking, but with what she knew about his membership at Club Chameleon she could well imagine the thoughts running through his mind. He finally blinked and focused on her before he cleared his throat and motioned to the music room. "When you've freshened up, we'll grab a bite to eat. There are some things I should probably inform you about."

"Things other than sleeping arrangements?"

"Yeah, I've had some shit go down. Your organization needs to be briefed, and I need to take some steps to ensure it never happens again."

"Is everything all right?"

"No, I can honestly say things aren't all sunshine and roses. We can discuss it over dinner, then you can call the man in black if you think it's necessary."

"All right. Give me two minutes." She replaced the false bottom and grabbed her toothbrush and toothpaste out of the other bag. Chad left the room and shut the door quietly behind him. Seeing the country boy suddenly subdued didn't make her happy. The guy looked like the weight of the world was sitting on his shoulders.

Jasmine flipped on the bathroom light switch and took in the elegant grandeur of the appointments bathed in the light from two crystal chandeliers. A natural stone-and-travertine-lined shower ran down the entire side of one wall. Two walk-in closets the size of her kitchen back in Virginia consumed the other side of the room. Two opulent crystal bowls topped a natural stone vanity and were topped off by floating mirrors that seemed to hover in space. A partial wall and a fireplace hid a huge step-down tub that could hold a party of six. "Well, color me impressed, cowboy." Jasmine turned and did another three-sixty. "Color me impressed."

CHAPTER 9

"So… you're just going to walk away from a career you broke your back to build?" The music room remained void of sound for several seconds.

"Yeah." Chad played with the food on his plate. The man hadn't eaten much, and after he'd told her about Millicent's violation of his NDA and his decision to quit, he'd been withdrawn and quiet.

"Is it because a few people found out about the club?" Jasmine took a drink of her water and studied him. Dinner had been sent up from the kitchen and served on a small side table just past the grand piano.

"Yes and no." He downed the rest of his third scotch and sighed. The dark circles under his eyes and the line that formed between them told her the man was exhausted, stressed and probably not thinking straight. He filled his glass with ice and poured the amber liquid over it. Jasmine picked at the remainder of the meal. She sensed Chad wanted, or maybe needed, to talk to someone. In her capacity as a PSO, she'd been a sounding board, a confidante and sometimes took on a parental role. She knew when one of her principals needed to vent, and Chad was a shining example of someone who needed a person with whom he could talk.

He tapped the side of his crystal tumbler and glanced up at her as if he was trying to make a decision whether or not to open up. She wouldn't rush him.

"Look, I go to the club, but most nights I'm not there to look for a scene. Don't get me wrong; I've done them, but for me, it is more about self-discovery than getting off." He gave a rueful laugh and looked down at his glass.

"May I be completely inappropriate and ask what you've discovered?" Jasmine watched as he stood and walked over to the bar that was positioned between a stand full of guitars and the overstuffed sectional. He sat the full tumbler down and stared out into the music room.

He shrugged his shoulder and looked over at her.

She could feel his assessment... whether or not he dared to reveal himself to her. She got that. His world had been torn to shreds, and he didn't know who he could trust.

"I can assure you that nothing you say will be repeated to anyone... unless it somehow involves the murders." Jasmine followed Chad further into the opulently decorated room and tucked herself into the corner of the massive sectional so she could watch him. His eyes held a spot on the wall, but she could tell he was far, far away from this room.

His gaze shifted back to the tumbler on top of the bar before he gave the slightest shake of his head.

"Sometimes talking about things with a stranger helps."

He glanced her way and tightened his jaw. Chad's shoulders dropped, and his back still toward her, he spoke quietly. "At the very beginning of my career, just after I hit the top of the charts, I was up to my elbows in women, money, and fame. I drank hard, did drugs, and partied all night—every night. I was performing in Nashville, the last show of my first headline tour. I guess I'd invited my mom to the show, or at least she told me I had. Anyway, after the show, a couple of the boys and I were relieving some stress." Chad threw a glance her way, took a deep breath and continued, "Looking at it without the drug haze, we had an orgy. My mother walked in on that."

Chad closed his eyes and dropped his head back. "Needless to say, it was a wake-up call. I used the break between tours to detox and get some counseling. I cleaned house. Got rid of the people who were with me for the drugs and the scene. I hired a personal trainer and through him met a guy who had been through some of the same things I had been through. He's famous. Anyway, he invited me to go with him to Chameleon. He's a Dom. The evening was very... enlightening. I'd be lying if I said I had any idea BDSM existed before that night."

Chad moved to the far side of the couch and sat silent for several minutes. Jasmine tried to imagine the guilt, embarrassment, hell, the horror she'd feel if her mother walked in on her while she was intimate with her ex, and his mom had seen so much more. No wonder he'd had a come-to-Jesus moment. Jasmine prompted, "So you took up the lifestyle?"

"No, not really, at least not the way most people assume. I've learned how to use all the implements, to bring pleasure from pain, but as much as the women I do scenes with seem to enjoy the interaction, I'm not a sadist. Although the pain brings them pleasure, the acts leave me feeling empty. But over the years I *have* taken on the tenets of the lifestyle. Safe, Sane and Consensual. I'm a Dominant, and I embrace that. I seek out a specific trait in the women with whom I'm intimate. She allows me to control the encounter. I give her what she needs, and she gives me what I need."

Jasmine hesitated before she asked, "What do you need?"

A sad smile spread before he spoke. "When you boil it down, I guess… a connection. One that is on a pure and honest level. No pretenses, no games. Not someone who is after my money, the fame, or the prestige of being with me."

Jasmine gave his comments careful considera-tion. They struck a chord deep within her. After all, she'd been searching for a connection when she'd dated Evan. She'd accepted his marriage proposal hoping to find the thing that Chad described. She cleared her throat, hoping the action could clear her mind. "I've done this job long enough to know there are types of people who will always look to be part of that fame and fortune." *Like Evan… like his groupies.* Jasmine watched as he leaned back and closed his eyes.

"Yeah. That's why I keep the people I trust close.

And look what that's done for me. I have lost my grip on my reality. Hell, I don't have even a small portion of my life under my control, and let me tell you, sweetheart, it sucks. It took your brother's little one-on-one with me a couple of days ago to figure all that out, but it's true. The smoke and mirrors that my business erected allowed me to think I had a say in things in my life, but I don't."

Jasmine sat in their shared, comfortable silence. She weeded through the man's comments. His trips to the club were him seeking what he instinctively knew he was missing in his life, but had no idea how to get. She knew that feeling. Her ex-fiancé Evan had been her attempt to grab onto that connection. Unfortunately, she'd never been able to give him all of her heart, and the emotional distance had cost her. She glanced over at Chad. He wanted a real relationship. He didn't say it, but the truth was there for anyone to see.

His small snore pulled her out of her head, and she glanced at the end of the couch and sighed. *Poor Mr. Singer Dude.* She lifted off the couch and went into the bedroom. After she pulled down the blankets, she returned to the music room and gently shook Chad awake.

"Hey, come on. You need to sleep, and I have some work to do."

Chad woke with a start, leaned forward and scrubbed his face. "I haven't slept more than a couple of hours since the night at the Georgia Dome."

"I can believe it. Go on, get into bed and get some rest. I'm here now, and I've got your back."

Chad stood and glanced down at her. Their gazes met and held. He seemed to make a decision, because he nodded and headed into the bedroom. Jasmine pulled out her phone and sent a text. She wasn't going to call this late, but Jared needed to know about the manager, and to a lesser degree the others around Chad, who had shown the desire to maneuver his life. Manipulation of the people in Chad's inner circle was a hotspot. She needed to find out if there were flames smoldering under the ashes.

CHAD WOKE IMMEDIATELY. He opened his eyes knowing what he'd see. Jasmine lay half on top of him, her hair in a wild mess over his chest, shoulders and face. He blew a small puff of air out, moving a strand that tickled his nose. His arm tingled with pins and needles. He moved it slightly, shifting her shoulder off of it, and squeezed his eyes shut as the blood ran back into it. How in the hell they'd ended up in the middle of the bed with her splayed over him was a mystery, but if the feel of her body against his was the answer, he'd take that mystery box every damn time. He flexed his fingers and made a fist several times before he drew a deep breath. God, Jasmine smelled and felt amazing against him. His morning wood agreed as it plumped against his thigh.

He smiled at the small snore that repeated at a smooth, rhythmic interval. He had no idea how to decipher the complex woman. Hell, she knew more about him than Kirk did, and that said something. Kirk had been with him since the early days in Nashville.

Two voices lifted in anger outside in the music room. He couldn't hear what was being said, but it pissed him off that someone was in his private area without his permission. Chad started to lift Jasmine off him, but she stopped him. He heard the distinct click of the safety being removed from the .45 she'd placed under the pillow.

Kirk's voice came through the door clearly. "You cannot go in there, Milli."

Millicent's scathing reply was low, hissed and

wasn't clear enough to hear, but it was closer to the door and whatever she said didn't matter.

Jasmine lifted up and lay on top of him, freeing her gun arm in the same motion. "Slide the sheet over my shoulders and kiss me like you mean it."

Her whispered comment sent a flame thrower through his body, and without thinking he obeyed immediately and felt the cold metal of the gun settle against his ribs. Jasmine didn't hesitate to drop her lips to his. He grabbed a handful of her hair and pulled her lips tight against his. He demanded entry and ravaged her mouth. When she fucking moaned into him, his raging hard cock pegged her soft stomach.

The door opened, turning both of their lust-filled gazes toward it. Millicent stood frozen in the doorway. Her eyes popped wide open, and her mouth gaped. Kirk stood right behind her. He grabbed her by the waist. "I told you, but you wouldn't listen."

Kirk's comments seemed to unfreeze Millicent. He was going to fire the woman. Chad wasn't opposed to having the conversation covered in almost six feet of Jasmine, but he didn't think Jasmine would be too happy about it.

Chad pulled Jasmine down to rest on his chest.

She turned into his neck demurely, but the grip on the automatic didn't lessen.

"Get out. Now." Chad growled the comment.

"Look, Chad..." Millicent had balls the size of coconuts.

Chad let out his anger and aggression and yelled, "Now!" At the shout, Jasmine squeaked and burrowed closer to him. His hand possessively wrapped around her back.

Kirk unceremoniously pulled Millicent out of the room and shut the door. A whispered fight took place outside the door.

Jasmine lifted her head and looked at the door. She smiled and winked at him. "Good morning."

He let out a long breath. "Lord, it could be." He moved his hips slightly. If she weren't staring directly at him, he'd have missed the flash of lust that raced across her expression when she realized how hard he was.

He heard the safety on her weapon click as she lifted off of him. Her white silk and lace cami did nothing to hide the hardened peaks of her breasts. Jasmine sat next to him, and damned if she didn't give his body the once over. His cock jerked at the attention.

"You need to find out what that was all about, but

I want to be there, and to do that I need to put on my game face. Kirk may have recognized me without my makeup." Her voice carried to him a shade above a whisper.

Chad put both hands behind his head and took in the beautiful woman beside him. "You don't need makeup. You're beautiful without it."

Jasmine made a face at him and slid off the bed. She walked into the bathroom. The skimpy lace boy shorts matched her camisole, and fuck if it didn't showcase the cheeks of her ass in fine detail. He followed her and leaned against the door frame. He'd tucked the tire rod impersonating his cock between the elastic of his boxers and his lower abs, and he prayed the big guy didn't decide to pop out and say hello.

"I need a couple of minutes. You take the shower. I'll wash up over there." She motioned past the wall into the area that held the tub. She grabbed for her makeup kit and stopped in the closet, where she'd obviously hung up her clothes last night, before she headed toward the tub.

"The shower's big enough for two." Chad nodded toward the one and only thing he'd demanded—other than his music room—when this house was built.

"That shower is big enough for twenty, but that's not the point. They need to believe we showered together. You'll have your privacy, and I'll have mine."

Chad watched her disappear and groaned. He reached into the shower and started the steam and rain-head systems. The pulsing side jets followed. He dropped his boxers and stepped into his little slice of heaven. His cock ached for release. His balls were high and tight. He pushed farther into the shower and looked back toward the entrance. Steam rolled, obscuring the view, and he thanked God for that fact. He soaped his body quickly, but slowed when his hand circled his shaft. He imagined Jasmine a few feet away in his bathtub.

He groaned at the memory of the feel of her body against his. And that kiss. That fucking kiss was heaven on earth. She'd moaned into his mouth. That shit wasn't acting. He'd felt her body respond, seen her obvious arousal through the lace of her skimpy top. His hand jacked up and down his weeping dick. If he expected to make it through the day, he needed to bust it now. He glanced back and assured himself no one could see into the interior of the shower. He braced one arm against the tile walls, the hot water drenching him as he increased the rhythm of his pulls. He twisted his hand over the head of his cock and tightened his grip. That flash of arousal Jasmine had allowed to slip through her mask this morning pushed him over the edge. He gasped silently and shot against the wall of the shower, pushing through his hand several times and sending another white rope onto the floor. He leaned into the wall and drew a deep breath. He wanted Jasmine. Not as a bodyguard, not for a scene, or a one-night stand.

CHAPTER 10

*S*hit, shit, shit... *shit!* The shower turned on, and Jasmine drew the first deep breath she'd taken since Chad had kissed her. She pulled her hair out of her face and stared at the huge tub. Her hand trembled as she turned on the water. No... this was bad. *So fucking bad.*

She needed to get ahold of herself. She shed her clothes, drew her hair into a messy bun at the top of her head, and got in the tub. She wrapped her arms around her legs and pressed her forehead into her knees. The argument outside the door had awakened her. How the hell she was that close to him to begin with baffled her. She wasn't a snuggle-type person. Even when she lived with Evan, they'd both had very definite sides of the bed. Yet she'd woken up lying almost completely on top of that sexy as hell singer. *No, no, no, no! You cannot think of him that way. He's your primary. He's a job. Nothing more.*

Jasmine grabbed the soap and a washcloth and started scrubbing. She washed and dried herself in record time. She pulled on Jade's clothes and inwardly groaned at the sex kitten wrappings. What she wouldn't give for a designer business suit and a pair of Jimmy Choos. Instead, she wore a pale yellow, long sleeve, slouch-shoulder crochet top over a white tank top and soft faded jeans that clung to her in all the right places. Her feet slipped into a pair of beaded sandals. She clipped the Glock to the back of her waistband, pulling both shirts down. She tilted in front of the mirror to make sure it wasn't visible. Good enough. She pulled a brush through her hair and hit up the makeup kit, all while cursing herself.

Of all the stupid things. She had *moaned* when he kissed her. Moaned. Like a wanton, lovesick… whatever… she had no idea… but she'd moaned. She hadn't meant to do that. Lord, she didn't even realize she was making the noise until he tightened his grip on her hair, and *that* had sent a hell of a wake-up to her lady parts. Jasmine looked at herself in the mirror. The shower had stopped a couple of minutes ago. She needed to get a grip, and fast. They were going to go out there and pretend to be a couple. Jazz took a deep breath, applied her makeup carefully and then exhaled slowly after she examined her disguise. She pointed at the reflection in the mirror. "Do. Your. Job." Her voice echoed in the vast bathroom.

"What?" Chad's voice floated toward her.

"Nothing. Are you ready?" Jasmine peeked around the corner. He wore a pair of faded blue jeans with a wide leather belt and huge silver buckle, a baby blue t-shirt and cowboy boots. The soft cotton material of his shirt pulled over his chest and shoulders, contouring his muscled body. His hair was wet and curled slightly at his neck. He nodded and held out his hand to her. She walked across the bathroom and took it. Shock at the perfection of his calloused fingertips against her palm pierced through her.

He took a deep breath. "Remember, I'm leading. I know that's against everything you are, but I know these two. I plan on firing Millicent, and that might not go over too well with Kirk. They've been together off and on for a long time."

They walked out into the bedroom, and he stopped and turned her toward him. "We need to make this convincing. Kirk will suspect immediately if you release your inner kick ass bodyguard."

"I understand. I was able to sell the embarrassed little girl when you shouted at them. I can channel that and play timid." Jasmine watched as he searched her face.

Satisfied, he nodded to the door. "Showtime, baby."

Jasmine lowered her eyes and tucked up close to him. She took a deep breath and pulled his scent into her lungs. *Showtime, indeed.*

The woman who'd stormed into their bedroom sat on the sectional with her laptop open, typing furiously onto the poor keyboard. She looked up and did a double take at Jasmine, and that's when Jasmine saw it. Jealousy dripped off the woman's glare just as sure as Jasmine was holding Chad's hand. The woman lifted her brown head of curls like she smelled something bad and then turned her glare at Chad.

"This is between you and Millicent. I'll be in the office with Terry if you need me." Kirk stood and walked out of the room.

"You called me down here without telling me why. Kirk alleges I fucked up, but he won't tell me how. I have a company to run. You've got an hour before I have to leave for the airport. What is so damn important you had to bring me down here to the middle of the sticks again?"

Chad sat down across from Millicent and pulled Jasmine in next to him as he leaned back into the cushions. His demeanor screamed calm, cool and collected, but Jasmine could feel the tension in his body. He was anything but relaxed. "You violated the NDA we have in place. That is grounds for termination."

The woman's jaw flopped open and closed like a goldfish that had been taken out of the water. Her eyes suddenly narrowed and she clamped her mouth shut. "What? I've never violated that agreement."

"Lying on top of everything?" Chad let out a chuff of air. "I strongly recommend you come off that high horse you're riding right now."

Jasmine watched Millicent. The woman regrouped, and Jasmine knew the second the woman had figured out how she was going to charge up the hill to attack the issue again.

"Chad, anything I may have done was to protect you." Millicent sent covert daggers toward Jasmine with a quick, hard look. "Why don't you have your... friend go amuse herself while we... work things out?" Jasmine fought the laugh that bubbled up in her chest. The woman's overt pout and obvious innuendo were borderline comical. Jasmine had to give her credit, though, she was tenacious.

"My friend?" Chad glanced over at Jasmine. He lifted her chin with his fingers, and she lowered her eyes. "She isn't my friend." Jasmine's eyes flew up to meet his, and she stiffened slightly. The stark truth to that comment hurt more than she wanted to admit. "Jasmine is the woman I want to spend the rest of my life with." Jazz searched his expression and saw something she didn't want to classify. Instead, she lowered her eyes and leaned into him. Once she had her head on his shoulder, she rotated so she could see through her hair and observe without actually appearing to be paying attention.

"What?" Millicent's harsh question cracked out like the lash of a whip.

Chad's shoulder shrugged under her head. "Not that it concerns you. I'm waiting for you to tell me exactly how many times you've violated the NDA, and then I want you to give me one reason why I shouldn't terminate your services and sue you for everything you have."

Chad's fingers ran up and down her arm in a mindless caress. Jasmine shivered under the contact.

Millicent put her laptop down and pushed it away from her.

"The only times I have violated the constraints of the NDA were to ensure that you were safe."

"Times? As in more than once?" Chad removed his arm from around Jasmine and leaned forward, resting his forearms on his knees.

"I told Terry about the club and what happens inside that place. He needed to know so he could cover your ass, and it was a damn good thing he did know. How else would he have been able to divert the questions from the FBI to your lawyers?"

"Wow, here's a thought: he could have asked me. And you have no idea what happens inside Chameleon." Chad's voice was low and angry.

"Oh, but I do. I couldn't let you go there without doing a good deal of research. I have to know how to smooth over anything that the press could come up with. This club is a huge target. You're lucky you haven't been outed publicly, and you can thank me for that fact. Chad, you pay me to keep you out of the press. That's what I was doing." The break in her voice was very well timed. Jasmine watched as the petite woman wiped at a single tear that fell down her cheek.

"Put a cap on the tears. They don't work on me." Chad's voice sliced through the air.

"Could we discuss this alone? I don't want to mention any facts in front of your... guest."

Chad stood, his hands on his hips he glared down at his PR rep. He pointed directly at Jasmine. "*She* is the only person who knows *everything* there is to know about me. Stop stalling for time and tell me who else you've told?"

"Terry, Kirk, of course, and Henry Burns."

"Who?"

"He's a private contractor I have on retainer. He's gotten rid of numerous problems for us in the past."

"Excuse me? Us?"

"The paparazzi stalk you. He follows them. If anyone gets near you, he ensures certain things are prevented or avoided."

Jasmine filed the name away. A contractor. Thug or professional? He'd been tracking Chad's movements. That gave him access, and that made him a suspect.

"How long has this man been following me?"

"Off and on for five years."

Jasmine let another data point click into place. The profiler said it was possible this person had known Chad for years, and a recent event had set him off.

"And you didn't think it was necessary to tell me about him?"

"No. He signed an NDA, and he's never actually stopped anyone outside the club, but if he needed to do so, he would have. I didn't think Terry would jeopardize his position by crossing me. I guess the worm is stupider than he looks."

Chad walked to the windows and looked out. Jasmine followed him. He pulled her close. She reached up on tiptoes and whispered. "Keep your enemies close. Don't fire her yet."

She kissed his neck, and he rubbed her back possessively. He kissed her forehead before he turned back toward the woman. Dear ole Milli had been sending daggers in her direction while Chad's back had been turned. Jasmine would bet her last penny the woman was in love, or at least seriously in lust, with Chad. Jasmine positioned herself behind the singer like a shy little girl. God, how she hated acting like this. She'd grown up with a strong, independent woman as a role model. While she could understand the desire to have a man take care of her, this shy, meek act wasn't her—at all.

Millicent stood and held out her hand to stop

anything Chad was going to say. "Seriously, Chad, if we could just sit down and talk through this, you'll see what I did was in your best interest." Millicent slinked over and got far closer to Chad than was necessary. "Please?"

Seriously? With the pouty lips? Jasmine hid her face and rolled her eyes. She leaned her forehead against Chad's shoulder blade and drew a deep breath. She'd been here just over twelve hours and seen two prime examples of the conniving, manipulative people in his world. So far the only one who appeared to have Chad's back was Kirk.

"I need to think about this, Milli. I don't know if I can trust you anymore."

"You can, Chad! I'm only looking out for you. I swear." Jasmine could smell the woman's perfume from where she stood leaning up against the solid frame of the man she was here to protect. Her primary. *Hers.* Jasmine sighed loudly, and Chad turned his head toward her. He reached behind him and pulled her up against his side.

"Give me a day. I have three radio interviews between this afternoon and tomorrow morning. I'll meet with you after I'm done."

Millicent lifted a perfectly manicured eyebrow and smiled. "All right. I'll meet you here at…?"

Chad shrugged. "I have no idea. Get with Terry to figure out a time." He grabbed Jasmine's hand and started back toward the bedroom.

He paused and looked back over his shoulder. "Oh, Millicent?"

"Yes?"

"Nobody comes into my private rooms without my permission. Don't do it again."

Jasmine pulled away from him as soon as the doors shut. She lifted a finger and pressed it to her lips, then pointed down to the floor. A small sliver of the sun that poured through the east window of the music room could be seen under the door of his bedroom. A shadow broke the sunlight and hovered there, not moving.

Chad's eyebrows shot up, and then a devilish smile spread across his face. He reached for Jasmine and pulled her close. "Let's make some noise, baby." His lips touched her ear when he whispered the words. His warm breath sent a shiver of anticipation down her spine. He grabbed a handful of hair and pulled, forcing her to expose herself to him. She had no way to hide from the full intensity of the kiss and the press of their bodies. Her hands rested on his chest and vibrated under the possessive growl that came from him as he broke off the kiss. He grabbed her ass and lifted her. Jasmine gasped and then laughed as she locked her legs around his waist. "Giddy up, cowboy!"

Chad pushed her back against the door and shook his head. "No, ma'am, I'm not riding you. It's time for you to ride me." They both looked down and watched the shadow move away, leaving the small slice of sunshine on the marble floor.

Chad brought his attention back to Jasmine. His strong body braced against hers sent a thrill through her. She tried to steady her breathing, but the adrenaline of the moment and his body against hers prevented that action. His eyes dipped to her lips. He moved in slowly. Jasmine shook her head from side to side. She couldn't give into this, no matter how much she wanted it, God help her. *Oh, shit.* She wanted this man. She arched her back and groaned. "My gun," she mouthed. That broke the spell. His eyes widened in comprehension. He lifted her off the door, and she dropped her legs.

Reaching behind her back, she slid the concealed holster out of her jeans. As she walked across the bedroom and headed toward the window, her fingertips massaged the spot where the metal and plastic holster had dug into her skin. Careful not to expose herself, she took in the view of the expansive drive that cut a semicircle into the landscaped yard. A dark blue BMW sat at the front door.

Chad moved behind her and gripped her hips as he looked over her shoulder at the vehicle. Millicent flew out of the door a few seconds later. Too bad they were too far away. Too bad the window was a solid piece of plate glass, because the woman was going off on Kirk, and Jasmine would have loved to hear her comments. Watching the woman throw a hissy fit, she felt sorry for Kirk. If this bitch had been hooking up with him over the years, he had to know the truth, because it was immediately obvious to her that Millicent wanted Chad. The woman was probably using Kirk. She sighed. Terry the agent, Millicent the manipulator, and Henry Burns, the unknown in the equation, had all earned themselves a thorough background check and maybe a visit by a damn good investigator.

"I'm going to fire that fucking bitch." The anger in the man's voice echoed her own. He dropped his hands and stepped away when Jasmine glanced over her shoulder.

"You gave me the lead time I need, thank you. I need to make some phone calls."

"Yeah. Okay." Chad ran a hand through his hair as he turned toward the bathroom. "I'm going to change and go out to the gym and work out some aggression, because right now, I want to destroy something."

"Chad?" Jasmine called after him.

"Yeah?" He turned, his frustration evident in the tense muscles and clenched jaw.

"Take a member of the security detail with you, please."

"Why? As mad as I am, if someone came after me, I'd welcome it."

Jasmine blinked back her surprise at the sharp edge of his voice. During all the interactions she'd had with him, he'd never been this agitated.

"Anger won't stop a bullet." A statement of fact.

"Right, that's what I have you for, right? So I'm screwed any way it falls."

"What?"

"They kill me; I lose you. You take a bullet for me; I lose you. You find the guy; I lose you. Anyway you cut it, I lose." He quietly shut himself inside the master bath, leaving Jasmine staring at the door. Her brain lay scattered, ruined by the sincerity of his words. She returned her gaze to the window. This case had turned into so much more than a personal protection gig. Emotions were involved, his... and hers.

CHAPTER 11

*C*had exhaled on the exertion. This was his last exercise of the workout and his third set of clean and jerks at his max weight, and he still could feel the anger and frustration coursing through his veins.

Anger at the betrayal Millicent had dealt him. *For his own good. Like he was a fucking five-year-old.* No, there was no way she'd get away with it. She'd built her client list and her fortune on his back, and when he walked away from her *and* let it be known he didn't trust her, game over. She was done. She just didn't know it yet.

He lowered the weights and straightened. When he'd started his workout, it was just him and one of the MIB detail in the gym. Now, every member of his band and the few staff members that worked out with them regularly had come out too. It seemed wherever he went, his crew followed. There were a couple of people he didn't recognize, but that was nothing new. However, after the last week, he questioned it. Especially since they didn't seem to be working out, just hanging around. He grabbed a water out of the fridge and wandered over to his security shadow. He faced away from the center of the gym and spoke low. "I don't know the two guys over by the air assault bikes." The man nodded and moved toward that area. The guys were probably friends of one of his crew, but right now, he wasn't going to take a chance. He groaned at the thought. He hated second guessing everything. He was so far out of his comfort zone, he needed a passport to check the fuck back in.

Chad used his t-shirt to stem the flow of sweat pouring off his face. He couldn't go back to the house. Not yet. Even though he knew what to do with Millicent, he had no idea what to do about his feelings for Jasmine. He wasn't going to try to deny the fact he desired her, because that would be like trying to deny that a raging bull elephant was in the room. But the thing was, he liked her. She was tough as nails, funny, smart—like, sharper than a whip smart—and even after he'd admitted that his life was in complete shambles, she hadn't judged him. That was solid. No flight in her either; she stood her ground. No pretenses. Hell, he could count the people he knew like that on one hand and still have fingers left over.

Chad jumped on the treadmill and set it at a ten-minute-mile pace. He ran for a minute or two before he glanced out the wide open barn doors that allowed the heat and humidity into the gym. He didn't do AC in his gym. He was here to sweat. Two more members of the MIB crew walked through the doors like they owned the place. He watched the men corral and escort the guys he didn't recognize out of the gym. His bass player mumbled a curse and followed them out. *Great, he was paranoid.*

He punched up the speed and the belt under his feet hummed with the increase in pace. *Yeah, as if you can run away from your problems.* Nope, he wasn't a runner. His momma hadn't raised him that way. He'd made the pickling juice he was currently marinating in, and he'd have to figure out a way to fix it. Or turn into a pickle, and he wasn't overly fond of that option.

First, he needed to deal with the interviews and the appearances at the awards shows, the final commitments he had for his label. He needed to talk to his lawyer. If there was a loophole in his contract to get him out of those things, he was taking it. Then... well, then he was going to clean his house, again. He'd take time off, regroup and figure out what he wanted his future to look like. One thing was for sure, he was going to downsize and get a firm grip on *who* and *what* he allowed into his life. A quick glance around his now packed gym under-scored that idea. He grabbed another bottle of water and wrapped a towel around his neck. Yep, he had a plan. The biggest part of it included a woman who thought it was her duty to walk away from him. He'd be damned if he'd allow her to slip through his fingers. That woman was a keeper.

"WE HAVE A PROBLEM." Jared's words sliced through any thought of a rant about Millicent.

"True, but how did you know?"

"I don't think we are talking about the same thing. We have another murder that involves Nelson, a high-end event promoter by the name of Denny

Gates, based in Nashville. The man was suing Chad and his label for a concert they pulled out of due to concerns about venue safety. He was found this morning. Bound and shot. One bullet between the eyes. We are rushing ballistics, but it looks like our perp is at it again."

"Well, shit."

"Eloquent."

"Yeah. Well, I can account for the primary's whereabouts. He was with me."

"Figured. He currently has seven more lawsuits pending against him. We had a team en route to this guy for surveillance when we got word he'd been killed. As a precaution, we are contacting the other people who have cases pending against Chad. Local law enforcement agencies are being contacted for protection efforts."

"This will leak. Someone will say something, and the press will find out. Chad's name will be connected with the investigation."

"Yep, needless to say, this case will soon be an epic shit storm. I figure we have a day, maybe two, before we lose the upper hand and the suspect knows we've identified him for all three murders. If it is a contractor, he'll either lay low or get back with his employer for directions. If it's a floating free radical? God only knows what will happen next."

"I'll cover things here."

"All right, now why did you call?"

"Three people I need your team to check out. Millicent Wicker, she's Chad's PR specialist, and he just found out she's violated the NDA agreement they had in place. He was going to fire her outright, but I was able to convince him to bait her along. She'll be back here tomorrow. I'll need a workup on her. If we need to keep her close, I'll ask Chad to keep her on."

"We were already looking into her because of her business dealings with Nelson. I'll elevate the level on her background. Who's next?"

"Terry Morgan, Chad's manager. Slimy, manipulative, and a control freak. He also has a temper. He's on my scope as a perfect fit for our stalker."

"All right, he's bumped up, too. Who's the third?"

"Ah, he's the one that is the huge question mark. Millicent Wicker hired a contractor to follow Chad and, to use her words, '*make things go away.*' She's had this guy shadowing Chad for years. His name is Henry Burns. I don't know where he's based, but he's been in the same locations as Chad, so maybe you detective-type people can track him down."

"And the plot just gets more convoluted." Jared sighed. "Anyone recognize you yet?"

"Haven't been in the public eye much. Working on selling the relationship angle."

"Really?"

She rolled her eyes at the smart-ass drawl. "Yes, really. I just got here late yesterday afternoon. We had dinner. I did some work, and he slept. Probably for the first time since you sprung this shit on him. You've got to admit, he's been handed a lot in the last week. He's struggling to deal with it."

"You know he hasn't been eliminated as a suspect, right? The man could have contracted the hits."

"No, I don't think he could have, J. I really can't see that happening."

"Be careful, Jazz. Getting too close to the primary while undercover is a huge mistake. It will cloud your judgment. He *hasn't* been cleared. He's a person of interest in three homicides. Separate yourself from this man, or I'll separate you from the case."

"I'm more than capable of seeing every side to this case, Jared. I'm telling you my gut reaction. He isn't involved."

"As long as you keep your head on your shoulders. Don't drop your guard. You are there to protect him—and take him down if necessary."

"You don't need to remind me how to do my job. Since when do you question my abilities?"

"Since I saw the way he looked at you at the warehouse."

"And how did he look at me?"

"Like you were a steak dinner, and he was starving. I've seen that look before. I've been the man who had that look on his face. He wants you. Don't underestimate him. He may well use you if he sees you're interested."

"I'm not and he won't."

"Bullshit, and you don't know that. Look, I have to go. I'll call you as soon as I have any information."

"All right, take care."

"Be smart and safe, little girl."

Jasmine hung up the phone with Jared's words echoing in her ear. *Bullshit, and you don't know that.* Her brother wasn't right this time. She did care. She cared about the man who gave and gave and gave. From what she could see the man didn't take. All anyone had to do was look around this place. He supported a cast of at least forty people.

The music room doors opened, and her primary

entered. She noticed one of the Guardian security team shut the door behind him. Chad looked thoroughly spent. He was a wash of sweat, his gray t-shirt soaked, and a darkened sweat line was also visible on his shorts. The material clung to the man, leaving nothing to the imagination.

"Did you enjoy your workout?"

Chad chuckled and shook his head. "I was able to work through a few things."

"We need to talk."

"Bad?"

"It isn't good."

"Just tell me."

"There has been another murder." She saw the color drain from his face. He closed his eyes and shook his head before he sank down and sat on the floor.

"Who?"

"A man named Denny Gates. He was suing you and your label for an event you backed out of due to safety concerns."

"Shit, I remember that cancellation. The venue was shit. Whoever booked us into it was high on something. The theater was decrepit. The venue couldn't guarantee crowd control, and it was only fire rated for something like two thousand people.

The promoter sold way more tickets than that. We had a clause that allowed us to cancel for security and safety reasons. We did." He looked up at the ceiling as if searching for something. "I didn't know he'd sued us. We considered suing him at one time. We refunded all the ticket costs because he couldn't cover it, and I didn't want my fans to be out money because of his greed. When did he die?"

"Sometime last night."

"I have an alibi." A ghost of a smile slid over his face.

"Unfortunately, that's not going to help when the story breaks. Guardian is interviewing the rest of the people who have suits pending against you, your label and your business endeavors."

Chad nodded and pushed himself off the floor. He motioned toward the bedroom. "Going to shower, say a prayer for that guy, and try to get my head around this."

Jasmine watched as he went to the bathroom. He pulled off his t-shirt on the way to the bathroom and then was gone from her sight.

An hour later, Jasmine sat on the bed and pretended to read a book about the Grand Ole Opry that she'd found in the music room. The shower had turned off about twenty minutes ago, but Chad still hadn't come out of the en suite. She'd closed the bedroom doors while she waited for him. The man's world had been knocked into an abyss, and she had no idea when or if Guardian was going to be able to pull him from the spiral.

He finally emerged once again, clothed in his jeans and a fresh t-shirt. He padded over to the bed and flopped onto the pile of pillows. "You know what sucks?"

"Besides all of this shit that is going on in your life?"

"Yeah, besides that."

"No, what sucks?" Jasmine reclined onto the pillows and rolled onto her side.

He lifted his arms and tucked his hands behind his head. "Of all the people in my life, a person I barely know knows the most about me. That and the fact that you've already judged me based on my past."

"I did. But I re-evaluated after being around you. I can see some of the background I received tainted my opinion of you. Every good PSO adapts to the current situation and learns to make adjustments."

"Think you'll ever let me kiss you without a witness?" Chad rolled onto his side and reached out to stroke her hand with his index finger.

"I…" A knock at the bedroom door prevented her answer. *Thank God.* She'd dodged a bullet with that one.

Kirk's voice boomed through the door, "Chad? Yo, dude, time to hit the phones. Terry says you have a telephone interview in twenty minutes."

Chad rolled off the bed and walked out into the music room. Jasmine heard the men talking about the interview. She sauntered into the huge room and sat down at the baby grand piano, being as unobtrusive as possible. Kirk stopped speaking and looked at her. "I have to ask. Have we met before? I mean before yesterday when Chad did the whole whirlwind intro through the house?"

Jasmine shook her head and smiled. "You don't look familiar. I haven't left Wisconsin since I got out of the Army. Have you ever been to Madison?"

"Only for a concert about four years ago." Kirk studied her with an intensity she didn't care for. Of all the people at the Georgia Dome last week, he had been around her the most, both while she was standing in the wings of the stage and in Chad's well-lit dressing room.

"I'm getting the weirdest sense of déjà vu. I rarely forget a face. But anyway, here." He handed an envelope to her. Jasmine looked to Chad in question. His brow creased in confusion.

"What's this?"

Kirk shrugged. "Beats me, I found it inside the music room doors lying on the floor when I came in a couple of minutes ago. It's got your name on it." He sucked in some air and winced comically. "I also stepped on it, so I'm hoping there was nothing breakable in it."

Jasmine took the envelope by the very edge and placed it on the piano. She'd open it once she had gloves on.

"See you in the office in fifteen?" Kirk asked.

Chad nodded. "I'll be there."

Jasmine watched the man leave. As soon as the door closed, she motioned toward the envelope. "Don't touch it." She sprinted into the bedroom and threw open her makeup case. She tipped it over and rifled through the dumped contents. Finding a small baggie with a pair of evidence gloves in it, she hurried back to the music room. The envelope had been tacked down at the point of the envelope flap only. Jasmine carefully examined the outside. Her name was inscribed in harsh block lettering. It was also misspelled.

Chad stood behind her and placed a hand on her

hip as he leaned over to see. The touch sent a shiver through her that she promptly ignored. His low chuckle let her know Chad noticed the response. *Great.* She drew a deep breath and carefully opened the envelope and retrieved the paper. There was no powder or foreign object left in the envelope, so she opened the single sheet of paper.

It was a photograph of her and Chad printed on plain bond paper. It had been taken that night at the Georgia Dome when Chad had escorted her back to his dressing room. The block letters at the bottom read *Dead x 2.*

"Fuck me." Chad's whisper echoed her sentiment.

"Okay, we go to plan B." Jasmine grabbed her phone and punched a text out before she slammed it down on the side table. "Go, pack a bag. Enough for a week or more. We are out of here."

"Whoa, there. I have obligations I have to meet. I can't go anywhere."

"You can and you will. There was always a possibility that someone would recognize me. Well, they obviously did. Now, get your ass in gear and let me do my job." The door to the music room opened, and three men from Guardian's security detail filled the doorway. "We've been compromised. I need a Suburban. Sweep it to make sure there are no tracking devices." She held up the note "This needs to be processed. Someone stand guard outside and escort us out of the house when we're ready." A chorus of 'yes, ma'ams' echoed as she raced into the bedroom. Chad followed her in and stood as if shell-shocked. "Chad."

He turned to her and blinked. "Chad, you are in danger. We have to go. Whoever has threatened your life has now threatened mine as well. If you won't leave to protect yourself, leave for my sake. I'll have my brothers take care of your damn obligations. Go, get what you need."

She spared him a glance. He was pissed. At her? At the situation? Who the hell knew? She grabbed the phone and put it on speaker while she packed.

"What's up, Jazz?" Jared's voice floated across the expanse of the room.

"Chad's road manager found an envelope with my name on it slid under the door of Chad's music room. It was a picture of us together at the Georgia Dome. He's grabbing a week's worth of clothes, and so am I. I have our team collecting the evidence for you. The vehicle is being swept, and we will be out of here in under five minutes."

"We'll shut down the compound. No one in or out. We have a roster of all people allowed on the grounds since we set up four days ago. At least we will have a finite pool of people to sift through. Where are you going to go?"

Jasmine glanced at the clock. "We aren't going to make it too far today before we need to pull over and stop. I'm taking him north."

"I can send a jet."

"I'm not waiting around here to give this asshole any opportunity. He's included me in this last threat. Who knows what this guy has planned. A sniper shot, knifing, maybe poisoning our food? Hell, we are out of here. At least on the road, I know how to gauge and react to a threat." Jasmine heard Jared's fingers hitting the keys of his computer as she packed.

"All right, it's just about twelve thirty. Going the speed limit, you can make it from Nashville to Kansas City in about eight hours. From there it will take you ten to twelve hours to get to the ranch. That's doable. I'll make arrangements for lodging and call you with the details."

"Great. Will you let Dixon and Drake know?"

"That will be the highlight of my day. Be smart and be safe." Jared disconnected, and she zipped her bag shut. She slipped off the long sleeve shirt and armed up: the .45 caliber in her shoulder holster, her knives sheathed and strapped on, and her trusty Glock 43 at her back. She made no attempt to conceal any of it. Her badge hung on the front left side of her jeans, the cuffs clipped on her back right hip. She was going out of this room with a show of force, and fuck that son of a bitch who was after *her* man. That thought stopped her. She listened to the sound of Chad packing nearby. She'd never had a problem remaining detached and objective when handling a client. What was it about this man? Why did she feel this way? Possessive... invested. Fuck, she didn't have time to examine her messed-up moral compass. First and foremost he was a client, no matter what her emotions were telling her. Chad's safety was paramount, and she'd be damned if someone would hurt him on her watch.

Chad walked out with a medium sized duffle and strode into the music room. He picked up a guitar and placed it into a hardened plastic case. He snapped it shut and looked around the room before he stared across at her. "Let's do this."

Jasmine nodded to the guard by the door, picked up her bag in her left hand and drew her .45 with the right. They hit the hallway and headed for the stair-case. Kirk stepped out of one of the rooms to the right. Jasmine leveled her gun at him.

"Whoa! Hey, what the fuck is going on?"

She hadn't seen the envelope on the floor, and she didn't know whether or not the man had planted it, so she held the gun level as she and Chad passed. Right now, there was only one person she knew for a fact wasn't the stalker, and that was Chad.

"Chad? Seriously, what the fuck?" Kirk called after them. Jasmine took point and trusted her Guardian counterparts to have their six.

"I'll call you later," Chad called over his shoulder.

Not if I have my way. Jasmine kept an eye on her man while scanning the bottom landing. As they headed toward the door, Kirk's yelling brought people out of the woodwork. Jasmine kept them going. Her goal was to get her man out and safe. The front door stood open, and one of the security detail stood in front of the opened Suburban door. He took her bag and assisted Chad with his before he escorted Chad to the passenger side and secured him inside. The keys were in the ignition, and she wasted no time in getting them the hell off the property.

Twenty minutes into the drive, and after she'd played out a hundred different scenarios in her mind, she realized Chad hadn't said a word. His head was leaning against the passenger side window with his eyes closed.

"You okay?" There was no way the man was sleeping.

"Nope. Not even close."

"Everything will work out. It will be all right."

"Yeah? When?" He opened his eyes, turning in his seat to face her. "Someone I trusted to be in my house wants us both dead. How is that going to be all right? Someone is killing people, and the authorities believe I'm connected to their deaths. How is that going to work out? Please, explain that to me!" Anger rolled off the man. She couldn't blame him, but she did need to settle him down.

"I'm not the enemy here," Jasmine reminded him.

He turned away and looked out the window. The road hummed under the tires. Chad cleared his throat. "Take the next exit and head south."

"Why?"

"My mom lives about thirty minutes from here."

"I don't think that's a good idea."

"Is someone following us?"

"No, I don't think so. I haven't seen a tail."

"Then I'd like to stop. I haven't seen her since the tour started last year. When this shit hits the news, I want her to know what is going on."

Jasmine couldn't deny she'd want her mom to know too. Nobody knew where they were going. A couple of hours' delay would get them in to Kansas City about ten… "All right, but only a short visit. We need to get to Kansas City tonight."

"Thanks."

"No problem."

CHAPTER 12

$\mathcal{C}$ had spoke only to direct her through the quaint suburb to a quiet residential area. They pulled up in front of a small, white, siding-clad house with midnight blue shutters that sat at the end of a cul-de-sac. It certainly wasn't what she'd expected given the massive empire Chad had built. He slipped out of the vehicle while she slipped on a jacket that concealed her weapons. He waited for her at the front of the SUV before he walked forward and knocked on the door.

Jasmine studied Chad. The exhaustion of the last week painted his face with broad brush strokes. He studiously avoided her gaze. But she could see the pronounced dark circles under his eyes and the deep furrows lining his brow.

She laid her hand on his bicep and tugged slightly. "Hey." He tilted his eyes toward her, and she smiled at him. "It's been a long time since anyone has introduced me to their mom." A little levity couldn't hurt, right?

The corner of his lips tugged up the slightest fraction. "A guy would be lucky to introduce you to his mom."

Okay, so not the response she was looking for…

The front door flew open. "Teddy? Oh my goodness!"

Jasmine backed away as a woman launched herself at Chad.

ENVELOPED IN HIS mom's arms, he pulled her in for a hug. She smelled like home. Her hugs had always pulled him right back to his youth and the security he'd known growing up.

"Why didn't you tell me you were coming out? I would have baked you something!" His mom pushed away to chastise him, her smile belying any anger at the surprise visit. She glanced over at Jasmine and did a double take. He'd never brought a woman home. Well, minus Wendy Sherman who he'd dated in high school. "Introduce me to your friend, Teddy."

"Sure. Mom, this is Jasmine King. Jasmine, this is my momma, Marie Nelson."

"It's a pleasure to meet you." Jasmine smiled and extended her hand.

"Oh, no honey, the woman my baby brings home to meet his momma gets a hug."

He choked back a laugh as his mom pulled Jasmine down into a hug. Surprisingly, Jasmine didn't seem to have an issue with the contact. He'd thought she'd go all stiff and bodyguard on him.

His mom pulled away, and her eyes bounced from Jasmine to Chad. "Well, don't just stand there, you two, come inside!"

Chad followed the women inside. It was like going through a time warp. Except for the new roof and renovated kitchen, the house hadn't changed. The same dark brown leather couches, framed pictures of horses in green meadows, hell, even the wallpaper on the walls was the same.

"You have a lovely home, Mrs. Nelson." Jasmine moved over to the wall of shame—his school pictures, pictures of him on the football team, his basic training picture from the Army and several pictures of him accepting Entertainer of the Year awards at the CMAs. Hell, looked like she needed to start a new wall or take down some of the older pictures. Not that she would.

"Thank you. We've lived here since Teddy was two. Can I get y'all some lemonade or iced tea? I have some soda too if that would be better."

"Thanks, Mom. Can we go into the kitchen? I need to let you know about some stuff that's been happening." Chad flinched at the worried look she gave him and hurried to reassure her. "I'm fine, but you need to know about a few things before it blows up over all over the news."

His mom nodded, her gray-streaked black hair bobbing with the movement. "Well, all right. Let me get some glasses. Jasmine, honey, grab whatever you and Teddy want out of the refrigerator, would you?"

Jasmine turned her head. A genuine smile spread across her face. "Teddy?"

"Oh, heavens, yes! He's a junior. When his dad was alive, we took to calling that little dickens Teddy as his middle name is Theodore. He's been Teddy to me and the folks around here ever since."

The glasses went onto the table along with the old ceramic cookie jar. Jasmine poured them all lemonade and Chad straddled the chair, sitting down after the ladies.

"So, what's got you all worked up? I can tell you haven't been sleeping. You don't get those circles under your eyes until you've almost hit a wall, so spill it." His mom was a straight shooter, and he loved her for it.

"Jasmine is my bodyguard."

His mother nodded and opened the cookie jar. "Kinda figured that out when I hugged two guns just a minute ago." She handed Chad a cookie and offered one to Jasmine, who declined.

"Mom, there have been some threats made against me. The people Jasmine work with believe it is coming from the people closest to me."

His mom leaned back in her chair and crossed her arms. "You know I've never approved of those people who sponge off you." She turned in her chair to face Jasmine head on. "Why do you think one of those leeches is after my boy?"

"Several reasons, ma'am. Suffice to say we need to get *Teddy* here to a safe place where the only access to him is through us. I work for Guardian Security. That will give us time to process the evidence, look into the people close to him and find out who will gain if this person were to succeed in harming him."

His mom held Jasmine's stare for a full thirty

seconds. He'd been on the receiving end of that look, and it was pure truth serum. He couldn't ever hide the truth from his mom. Not once.

Finally, she nodded and turned back to him. "What else? You said the news. Why would they run a story about this? I mean, that doesn't make sense."

Chad lowered his eyes and crumbled the cookie onto a paper napkin. How the hell did he tell his mom the FBI thought he was connected to three different murders?

"Mrs. Nelson…"

"Marie."

Jasmine nodded and continued, "Marie. There have been three murders that the FBI and my company, Guardian Security, have been investigating. The only thing connecting these three cases is Chad. He is not under arrest. We have no reason to suspect him, but you and I both know the press will spin this any way they can to boost ratings or sell papers."

Marie leaned forward and reached across the table. She pulled the crumbled mess of cookie crumbs to her and wrapped them in the napkin before she lifted away from the table and threw the mess into the trash compactor.

"Teddy, did you have *anything* to do with this?" She looked out the window, not facing them.

He shook his head although she couldn't see it. "Momma, I swear on Daddy's grave, I had nothing to do with it."

He saw his mom's shoulders relax, and her head nod up and down once. "Okay, well then we can weather this storm, too."

He was up, out of his chair and hugging his mom before he had any real knowledge of moving. "I'm sorry, Mom."

"Hush, this isn't of your making." She drew a deep breath and cupped his face in her hands. He could see the unshed tears, and the hurt from knowing that he'd once again caused his mom pain made him feel like the worst kind of scum. "I'll pack a bag and head to Zelda's. She's been after me to visit. They won't have a clue where to find me, but you better take care of yourself. You hear me?" She gave him her *'I'm going to tan your hide if you don't behave'* look.

"Yes, ma'am." Chad hugged her again and glanced over at Jasmine. He did a double take. The woman had unshed tears in her eyes, too. She blinked and looked away quickly, but he'd seen them.

His mom stepped away and put her hands on her

hips, already in action mode. "Now, we need to eat what's in the refrigerator, so I don't come back to a mess. I'll tend to that when I get done packing a bag and calling Zelda. You can do me a favor while I'm here. The post office keeps delivering that mail from the VA centers. Could you please move all of it into the spare room? I can hardly park in the garage anymore."

"What? I thought there were only a few letters?" Chad stepped to the door that led to the garage off the kitchen. He opened the door and flipped on the light. There were stacks and stacks of boxes and flats of letters. Several packages and bundles of letters tipped precariously off of one box near the roll-up door.

"When you started going to the centers, there were only a couple, but they keep coming in. I take it by the postmarks you've been keeping up the tradition of going to the hospitals and homes when you are on tour?"

He nodded and stepped down into the garage. He could barely make it around his mom's old Ford Bronco to the stacks of mail.

"I don't need all of it moved, just enough that I can get around the SUV with my groceries."

"Why didn't you tell me it had stacked up like this? I would have had someone come get it."

"Ahh… kinda makes me feel like I'm doing something for you by keeping it here. It wasn't a problem until they got a new postmaster. He won't store it for you. Obviously, he's not a country fan."

Jasmine laughed at his mom's comment as she followed him into the garage. "I'm going to go pack. You figure out how to stack that higher or make a plan to have someone get it after I get back from Zelda's.

Jasmine carefully picked up a letter and looked at the address.

"Why a post office box here?"

"I go to the hospitals alone, just me and my guitar. It's under the radar. Kirk usually covers for me. I sing and talk with the men and women that are recovering. The VA staff asked for an address so they could send thank you notes. I had a PO box from when I lived here… before that first hit and all the noise, so I gave them that. Mom told me a few letters showed up, so I just kept giving that address." He lifted the package on top of the stack and set it so it wasn't threatening to fall. His mom must have shoved it up as far as she could reach.

"We need to go through these. The rest of your fan mail is processed by your PR firm, right?"

"Yeah, Millicent set up the fan sites, so she has all the mail. Would you look at all this?"

"I'm calling a team to come get these. It won't take long to get them here. Would your mom be willing to stay until they come?"

"Yeah. Zelda is her cousin's wife. They're both widows, and she lives only a couple hours from here. That's where she hid out when I went through rehab and restructured my life the first time. No one bothered her."

"All right. Do your best not to touch any of the envelopes. Use the cardboard, and we'll move these over here and on top of this small stack."

They made quick work of moving the fan mail to make a wider pathway around the old but meticulously maintained vehicle.

"May I ask you a question?" Jasmine led him back into the kitchen.

"Shoot." He didn't have anything to hide. The woman knew everything about him anyway.

"The house and the Bronco?" She wiped her hands on a paper towel and leaned against the sink. His arm brushed hers when he soaped up his hands.

He was acutely aware of how close they were and the fact that she could move but hadn't.

"She refuses to take any money from me. I replaced the roof, and she allowed me to redo the kitchen, but..."

"She doesn't like the people who live off you, does she?"

Chad turned off the water and took the paper towel she offered. He spun and leaned on the counter right next to her. Their arms touched from shoulder to elbow.

"No. She raised me to stand on my own two feet because that was the way she was raised. No matter what I say, the argument is always the same. 'This house is paid for. It's mine, and I love where I live. Why do I need a brand new house?'" He shook his head. "I bought her a house, right on the river in Nashville. Beautiful brick house. She flat out refused to move. Thanked me for the thought and told me next time to buy her a bouquet of flowers." He chuckled and nudged Jasmine. "Said she'd tan my hide if I spent any more money on her. If she needed anything, she'd ask."

"I like your mom." Jasmine leaned into him. It wasn't an overt thing, but the contact between them grew. "We really should go soon."

"You never did tell me where we were going."

"Kansas City, tonight. South Dakota, tomorrow."

Chad looked down into her beautiful green eyes. Even with all the 'girlfriend' makeup, the woman cranked every gear he owned. He felt her attraction and started to lean down to kiss her when his mom walked in. Jasmine pulled away and moved to the table.

"Well, dang it, my timing sucked, didn't it?"

Chad laughed at his mom's comment. He couldn't help it or hold it in. His mom was an observant woman.

"Mom, can you stick around for a couple of hours? Jasmine is having her people come pick up the fan mail. They need to process it."

"Process it? What for?" His mom cast a worried look at the garage.

"With the threat against Chad and the recent murders, we can't leave any stone unturned." Jasmine took a drink of her lemonade after she spoke, but it didn't hide the red tinge of blush that colored her cheeks.

"Oh… all right. You two are leaving soon?" His mom thrust her hands on her hips when they both nodded. "Well, I'm not letting you leave without taking something to eat. I hate throwing out food.

Come on, pull out that fried chicken, and there is some potato salad. Teddy, go into the sunroom and grab the picnic basket. Wherever you're heading, you'll need to eat." His mom turned to Jasmine and smiled. "So, Jasmine, tell me about your people."

Chad spun on his heel, hiding the smile that spread across his face, and headed to the sunroom. His mom was a force of nature when she was inquisitive, and right now Jasmine was her biggest question mark. He thought of the sexy woman fending off his mom's questions and decided to take his time finding that basket. Maybe he was just a bit sadistic.

CHAPTER 13

Jasmine opened the hotel room door. Jared had reserved only one room, with one king sized bed. The hotel was sold out because Kansas City's professional football and baseball teams both had home games; otherwise, she would have gotten them transferred to a twin room. Chad had been quiet on the drive. It wasn't a moody silence, more reflective than anything. She'd listened to music the entire way. Her kind of music, not his. He never said a word, just stared out the side window.

In the room, he placed both of their bags on the faux leather bench at the end the bed and shrugged, cracking his neck in the process. "I'm going to go shower." He turned and grabbed his bag and shut the door to the bathroom two steps later.

Jasmine took off her jacket and her weapons. She put the guns on the nightstand beside her credentials, cuffs, and knives. With all the hardware off, she stretched and groaned with the pull. She reached for her cell phone and double checked the door was dead bolted and the privacy bar was engaged.

The shower came on as she dialed. "You're late," Jared's voice rumbled in her ear.

"You know why. Did the team pick up the fan mail?"

"Yeah, I had to pull assets off other events, but we are starting to go through it."

"What the hell is with this room?" She flopped onto the bed and gazed unseeingly at the popcorn ceiling.

"What's the problem? One room, two beds. Deal with it, Jazz."

"One room, *one* bed, Jared."

"I reserved two queens."

"I got one king."

"Okay… so make a pillow wall and tell that son of a bitch if he touches you, he's dog meat."

Jasmine giggled at that. "What if I want him to

touch me?" She waited for several long minutes before Jared answered.

"Jasmine, do not compromise your objectivity."

She could imagine the face he was making. By the sound of his voice, his teeth were clenched, and he was trying desperately not to go off. She wondered if his face was as red as the day Jade had taken his motorcycle and crashed it when they were growing up.

"He's not involved in these murders. You know it, and so do I."

"Even if I make that claim, he's still in danger, and you need to keep your head out of the clouds and keep your eyes open. You can't do that if you are involved with this man."

"So you're telling me you can't take care of Christian?" Jasmine had no idea if she was going to act on her feelings. Hell, she had no idea if Chad was going to make a move, but she'd be damned if she'd let her brother treat her like a fourteen-year-old girl on her first date.

"That's different."

"And that's bullshit! It isn't any different. Tell you what, Jared, why don't you pull your head out of your ass and ask yourself if you'd say that to any other operative, or if it's just me you're treating like a child."

"I'd sure as hell tell anyone in the field on a case the same thing. Get over yourself, Jazz. I don't give a fuck if you want to sleep with the man, but I do care if you compromise Guardian's ability to take care of our primary by becoming emotionally involved."

Jasmine closed her eyes and counted to twenty. He was right. She was projecting. She sighed and sat up. The shower turned off. "All right. I owe you an apology for that one. I'm fine. He's fine. We'll be at the ranch tomorrow, late."

"Let me know when you hit the road."

"Good night, J."

"Night, Jazz. Be safe and smart."

Jasmine disconnected the call and grabbed a few things out of her bag. Chad exited the bathroom in a fog bank of steam. He headed for his side of the bed without a word, and she headed for the bathroom. She paused and said over her shoulder, "Don't open the door for any reason."

Jasmine made quick work of removing her makeup. It seemed like eons ago she had put it on while trying to convince herself she wasn't interested, that the job came first. It was ironic that while she was taking off the same makeup, she was trying to find a reason not to sleep with the man if he made an overture. The job be damned. She took a quick shower and looked at the thin, black lace and silk nightgown she'd brought in with her. The matching lace thong lay on top. She also had an oversized t-shirt and cotton boy shorts. Shit… overt or not? She pulled her bottom lip into her mouth and worried it with her teeth. Jasmine glanced at her reflection and sighed. You want him. Wear the lace. She picked up the silky material and slipped it on. The thong she rolled up in the t-shirt. *No pretense.*

Jasmine turned off the light and noticed the lights in the bedroom were out too. She closed her eyes tightly for ten seconds and then reopened them. She could see well enough to drop her clothes on the top of her bag and make it to her side of the bed. She slipped under the covers and turned to face Chad.

He was lying on his side facing away from her. She could tell by the way he was breathing he wasn't asleep. *No pretense.* Jasmine reached out and traced a finger down the divot of his spine. His muscles shifted under her touch.

"Don't play games, Jasmine." His voice was thick with desire. She could almost feel the heat of his need from her side of the bed.

"I don't play games. I never have."

He turned over and faced her. "I gave up one-night stands years ago."

"You do scenes." She reached up and traced his jawline with her finger. The stubble sensitized her fingertip.

"I have. I don't want a one-night stand with you. I don't want a scene with you." He reached over and pushed her hair away from her shoulder, exposing her neck. His hand cupped the column of her throat, and his thumb caressed her jaw, but he didn't move past that contact.

"What do you want from me?" She swallowed hard. His eyes held hers, and a tempest of emotion showed in his expression.

"I want more."

"I don't know if I'm strong enough to give you more."

"You're the strongest woman I've ever met."

"You barely know me."

"And yet you know me better than anyone on the planet."

"I want to try."

"I need more than a try."

"What do you need?"

"You. All of you."

"I've never been able to give that to anyone."

"I've never wanted it from anyone else."

CHAD PULLED her across the sheets. He needed to feel the soft contours of her body against him. He captured her lips and wrapped his arms around her, anchoring her on top of him as he rolled to his back. Her long legs fell between his, and the feel of her soft body against his straining cock pulled a growl from deep inside him. He needed more. Just like he'd told her. He needed all of her.

He held her still by wrapping his hand through her silky hair. He plundered her mouth, stealing the silken riches buried within. His free hand mapped her back and perfect ass. All warmth and softness and yet so strong and vital. The woman shattered any idea of what he had once thought he'd wanted. Her. He wanted her with a need so strong he was lost in it.

He'd spent all afternoon trying to understand how his focus had narrowed to this woman when he'd sought the exact opposite for years. There was no single reason, but a mashup of minute details. The vulnerability he sensed more than saw. It was the glimpses of the woman and not the professional that enticed him. Her willingness to literally put herself in front of a bullet for him. Not since the military had he felt that level of connection with another human. Her presence stabilized a world that had cartwheeled into chaos. He sighed into the kiss. She was his safe harbor.

Jasmine's tongue danced with his. A soft mewl from her lips when he pulled her away sent a thrill through him. He rolled her underneath him and pushed off his boxers, freeing his cock. The enraged bastard slapped his abs in protest when the elastic of his waistband caught on his hard on. He kicked the sheets out of the way and positioned himself between her mile-long legs. The grip of one hand still firm in her hair, he rocked forward slightly and descended for another kiss. Her arms slid around his neck, and she melted under him. He lifted away from her lips to find the pounding pulse point in her neck.

"Yeah, just like that, babe. Let me in," he whispered as his hands pulled the thin straps of her night gown down her arms. He traced her delicate collarbone and tasted the fresh, sweet flesh of her shoulders. His breath against her heated skin pulled a shiver from her that crawled straight through his skin and nestled deep inside him. His free hand worked to drop the lace of her gown, exposing her beautiful, full breasts. His tongue followed his fingertips in a deliberate Braille reading of her incomprehensible beauty. Circling, swirling, sucking, he memorized the body under him. Her hand weaved through his hair and held him against her breast when he finally took her nipple into his mouth. When he added pressure to the small nips he'd been teasing her with, she gasped, lifted her hips under him and ground against his hard-as-a-fucking-diamond cock.

She released a small moan when he lowered all his weight and trapped her under him. If she bucked up against him like that again, he wouldn't be able to... *fuck*... He'd lose it, and he needed to make this the best thing she'd ever experienced, because, for him, it already was.

He lifted and found her mouth again as his hands lifted her gown, bunching the material at her waist. He was too fucking hard and desperate to try to figure out how to get her out of the lace and silk. His hand trailed her hip... no panties. Surprised, he lifted from the kiss and looked down. He groaned and lifted her leg up to his hip, opening her sex to him.

"You wanted this. You wanted me." He rotated his hips. His cock wept against her thigh.

"I did."

Her panted admission launched his desire to a level he'd never experienced. He had to claim her, own her… taste her. He lifted and lowered himself until he worked between her legs, lifting them over his shoulders. She trembled beneath his touch. He kissed the inside of each thigh and licked a trail to her sex. Everything about her was perfect. Her taste, her scent, the way her body quaked with need under his touch. He opened her sex and with slow, deliberate intent, drove her insane. Perfection. Her hands gripped his hair, his shoulders, and then the bed. Her small pants turned into staccato pleas. He worshiped her with long strokes of his tongue and fingers, punctuated with short hard suction. He stopped just short of bringing her relief. Her body clenched and shook under his sensual torture. Her pleas ceased making sense. The insistence of her body's needs hurtled her toward the edge that he wouldn't be able to pull her back from unless he hurt her, and he'd be damned if he'd do that without a very long talk beforehand. He wrapped his arms around her legs and pulled her down, attacking her with a ferocity that guaranteed her orgasm. Her body arched, even though he pinned her against him.

A strangled gasp of air punctuated the exact moment her body fell over the edge. Chad moved his fingers inside her and continued his assault. She arched again, and her body released the sweet honey he'd been seeking. God, the taste of her desire transcended anything he'd known. She shuddered violently under him before he lifted. Her arms grabbed him and, with a strength that surprised him, she pulled him down on top of her. Their mouths fused as he wrapped his hands in her long tresses again.

He pulled away enough to speak. "I don't have protection. I'm clean." He trailed kisses down her throat. God, the thought of not finishing inside her was almost too much to think about.

"I'm on birth control, and I haven't… I'm good."

He lifted back to capture her lust-filled gaze. "Baby, you are better than good. You're perfect."

Chad lifted her leg and pushed the head of his painful erection against her core. He held her gaze as he pushed forward. The heat and softness as he entered her slowly melted his brain. He became an instinctual animal. This woman was his. *His*. He'd be damned if he'd let another man ever experience the heavenly sensation of her body. Chad dropped his head to her shoulder the moment he ground himself to the hilt inside her. Jasmine's body contracted around him, and he groaned.

"Come on, cowboy. Show me how well you can ride."

He lifted his head and laughed at the huge smile on her face.

"Yeah?" She wanted it hard and fast?

"Yeah. Rock my world. Again."

With that praise, he would have moved a mountain for her. He lifted to his knees and pulled her up, so she was straddling his lap, her knees on the bed and perfect for him to thrust like a jackhammer. He leaned in and kissed her and pulled her hands from his chest to his shoulders. "Hang on, baby."

Chad withdrew and slammed home. Her eyes widened as he started a punishing pace urged on by a need so deep he didn't know where it came from. Her eyes closed, her mouth opened as she gasped each time he pounded into her. He watched a flush spread over her chest, neck and face. She leaned forward and wrapped her arms around his neck. He launched off the bed and pinned her under him. Stopping now wasn't an option. He lifted her leg, found traction with his knees and followed his body's need. Her shouted prayer to God, arched body, and convulsing sheath pulled him into the abyss. He ground in as deep as he could and lost his mind. An orgasm ripped through him, and black and red spots exploded behind his closed eyelids. His heart slammed against his chest, and he gasped for air. He felt Jasmine's shallow pants below him and, with the last ounce of strength he had in his body, shifted his weight off her to allow her to breathe.

He pulled her close to his side and stroked her hair as he tried desperately to fill his lungs with enough oxygen to function on even a basic level.

"Wow." Her whisper pulled a chuckle from him.

"Yeah. That was..." How did he describe earth shattering, reality-bending sex?

"Fucking amazing."

"Better than that." He wiped his sweat-drenched face with his free hand. "Holy fuck, that was..."

"Fucking amazing," Jasmine repeated, and flopped away from him onto her back with her arm stretched out over the mattress.

"Yeah." He lay on his back and took a deep breath.

"Just FYI... I'm going to want to do that again."

Chad laughed and so did she. He looked over at her. Her expression mirrored the happiness he felt.

"Going to have to give me a minute."

"Take two. I'm generous like that."

Chad rolled over and kissed her. Her arms slipped around his neck. He pulled away and wiggled his eyebrows at her. "Never mind, I'm ready now." She squealed as he pounced.

CHAPTER 14

a cell phone's trill woke her. She blinked, trying to orient herself for a moment. Chad pulled her closer and wrapped his leg around her. She relaxed into him before the trill sounded again. She grabbed the phone. His phone. The screen flashed one word, Mom. She elbowed him gently.

"Who's it?" His sleepy voice rumbled through her.

She held it up for him. "Your mom."

He grabbed the phone and groaned. He answered it, not moving from his position wrapped around her.

"Mom? What's wrong?

Chad rolled onto his back. Jasmine sat up in bed.

She could hear his mom's voice clearly in the silent hotel room.

"I've been thinking. Something happened yesterday after you left, and it didn't settle well with me. I'm sorry if I woke you up, but I couldn't sleep. Maybe I'm an old woman, but I think the press snookered me."

"What do you mean, Mom?" Chad rubbed the sleep from his eyes as he spoke.

"Well, right after Jasmine's people left with all the fan mail, I was closing up the house. The doorbell rang, so like a fool I answered it. Two men dressed in suits and driving a black SUV like Jasmine's asked if you were at the house. They said they had something very important they needed to give Jasmine. I told them that you left for Kansas City about two hours before. They thanked me and left. But Teddy, wouldn't they have known that? I mean, shouldn't they have that information?"

Chad stared at her, and she nodded. *Shit.* Did Chad's stalker hire someone? And why would they say they needed to give Jasmine something? *Fuck.* She needed to check with Jared before she jumped to conclusions. She glanced at the clock. Five a.m. Wonderful. She could sleep for another five or six hours. Chad had worn her out. Her body was delightfully reminding her of that fact.

"Mom, I'm sure everything is fine. Jasmine's people probably got their wires crossed. It happens in a big organization like that. If it were the press, they wouldn't have left. They would have asked you all sorts of questions. Are you at Zelda's?"

"Yes. I left about a half hour after those two showed up. Are you sure those guys didn't play me? I mean, something was just off."

"It's fine, Mom, I promise."

Jasmine grabbed her phone. It was six on the East Coast. She tapped out a text to Jared.

DID u send 2nd team to Nelson's mom's house yesterday?

HER PHONE RANG ALMOST IMMEDIATELY. She motioned toward the bathroom and Chad nodded as he continued to reassure his mom she'd done nothing wrong. She slipped from the sheets naked and was rewarded with a low groan. She winked over her shoulder and answered the phone as she shut the bathroom door.

"No, why?"

"Chad's mom just called. She said two men in an SUV showed up after the team left with the fan mail, and according to her, they said they had something important to give me."

"Fuck, no. Who would show up at Nelson's mother's looking for you?" Jared growled the words into the phone.

"I'm thinking the stalker. He threatened both of us."

"That doesn't compute. A stalker by definition is on a personal crusade to reach their obsession. They don't hire out the contract."

"Unless the stalker and the murderer are the same person. He could be using the resources he has to eliminate his targets."

"Fuck, Jazz. I need to get into the office and get you a security team."

"J, I don't think that's necessary. The name you registered us under at the hotel is an alias, and you pre-paid it, so there is no credit card information of mine to hack. The likelihood of a stalker, or even a halfway decent contractor, finding us is one in a couple million. We are heading north as soon as we get ready. By the time you get a team here, we'll be at the ranch having a drink with the Wonder Twins."

Her brother was silent for several moments before he sighed. "I don't like it, Jazz. Two and two doesn't equal seventeen, and that's what this is adding up to be. I need to talk to Nic and probably Jason. Take your time getting ready, but don't leave that hotel room until I get back with you. I'll give you a call when we make a decision."

"You got it. Staying tucked away until you call. Bye, J."

"Love you, Jazz. Be safe. Stay sharp."

Jasmine placed the phone on the vanity. She could still hear Chad's low rumbling voice as he spoke to his mom. Turning on the water, she waited for the temperature to warm, grabbed a fresh washcloth and stepped under the spray. The hot water felt remarkable against her muscles. Her hand swept over her breasts and she winced as it skimmed over a couple of rather large love bites. She looked down her body and shook her head with a smile. There were little bruises from Chad all over her breasts, one on her abs, another on her hip and one at the V of her leg. The door to the bathroom opened, and the shower curtain pulled back.

Jasmine took in the beautiful male form in front of her. A light brush of dark hair flowed from his pecs to a line that dropped down his rock-hard, sculpted abs to the wonderfully proud stiff-as-a-board cock that he held in his hand. Jasmine stepped into him and kissed his shoulder. He was five or six inches taller than her, and with the broad expanse of his shoulders, she felt feminine and petite. She slowly sank to her knees, dropping the washcloth to cushion the hard ceramic of the tub.

His hand slid through the wet mass of her hair at the back of her neck and pulled, forcing her to look up. Dark hunger burned in his eyes, and Jasmine shivered at the power behind his stare.

"Kneeling for me?" His voice carried an edge. She took in the length and size of his cock and lowered her eyes. She nodded her head. The position she assumed should have made her crazy with disgust. She was a strong woman. She didn't have to do this, but God, she wanted to…

Chad tugged her hair lightly, urging her to look up. She didn't want to deal with the emotion, not yet. Instead, she pulled away from his grip and nuzzled the soft skin of his cock. She softly kissed the base before she licked up the bulging vein running under his shaft. Her tongue circled the head before she took him into her mouth. His girth made it difficult to take much of his length.

Hands on her head held her lightly. Chad's hips slowly pulled away and thrust back. Her hands found purchase on his marble-hard thighs. She could feel the tension in his body and heard the breath catch in his throat as he thrust forward. Jasmine allowed him to set the pace and swirled her tongue every time he pulled away. He didn't speed up, even though Jasmine could tell he was close. The slightly bitter tang of pre-cum lingered on her taste buds. He did guide himself further into her mouth. Jasmine expected his slow retreat again, but he stilled. Jasmine lifted her eyes.

"Beautiful." He caressed her cheek and ran a finger over her stretched lips. "Absolutely beautiful."

Jasmine swallowed. The reflective move pulled a tight curse from her lover. He withdrew slowly. She lifted slightly to get a better angle, and when he thrust forward, she moved too, bringing his cock-head to the back of her mouth. She felt him breach her throat and stilled, praying for her gag reflex to relax.

Chad's thighs trembled under her touch. She lifted, took a deep breath and lowered herself, again swallowing almost all of his shaft. Her actions seemed to release his need to go slow. His thrusts no longer held a deliberate tempo. He wove his hands through her hair and held on as she set the pace.

"Close." She acknowledged his warning with a moan around his cock.

His hands tightened, and he stopped her movement. A guttural groan accompanied the strong, hot jets of cum that filled her mouth.

Jasmine swallowed his release and lapped at his cock until he pulled away.

He lowered himself into the tub and kissed her while he stretched out, wedging her between his legs. He pulled away and studied her face. The deep inspection was disconcerting enough to make her feel self-conscious. She blinked and mentally pulled up her professional mask, which had completely disappeared.

"Don't do that." He gently twisted her shoulders until she spun around. He pulled her back, so she was reclining between his legs, her back against his chest. The water from the falling shower hit the middle of the tub. The sensation was pleasant and unfamiliar.

"Don't do what?"

"Hide. You're confused, and that's okay, but don't hide."

That mind reading thing Chad just did bordered on freaky. "How…"

His hands roamed over her breasts, circling her taut nipples. The electrifying sensations jolted her nerves, and instinctively she pushed into his caress.

"You keep a part of yourself hidden." Chad's hands continued to explore, caress and tantalize. He paused long enough to lift her arms and place them behind his neck. "Keep them there."

Jasmine hesitated at the command in his voice. Fingertips of one hand teased her nipples with alternating light touches and piercing pinches. His right hand snaked down her torso and settled on her sex. She bucked into his hand and linked her fingers behind his neck. His fingers opened and slid through her, rubbing the side of her clit with enough pressure to make her legs clench in pleasure. She pushed back into him as his fingers performed a sensual dance across her most intimate places. He was relentless and yet gentle. His touch alternated from almost pain to soothing and feather-light. Her mind and body disconnected. She floated in a sea of blissful sensation.

"That's it, baby. Let go; I've got you." His words rumbled around her in that sexy deep bass voice that had wrapped itself around her heart. His touch pushed her to the edge and pulled her back, over and over again. Finally, he kissed her temple and said, "You can't hide from me. I see you. I see all of you. You're amazing and beautiful. I want you, Jasmine. I want *all* of you."

Her body exploded. The intense rhythm of his fingers carried her over the edge. Her cry echoed in the confines of the bathroom as she convulsed through her orgasm. Heat and pressure held her in its grip. Chad's hand continued its assault. She gasped and moaned in exhausted pleasure when she came again. Her body went limp, the sensations too much and too many to process.

Jasmine felt Chad's leg move and then realized the water that rained down on them warmed. His arms circled her, and he hummed a beautiful tune in her ear. He kissed her neck and shoulder, punctuating the musical serenade. God, she'd died and gone to heaven. She felt as if she could float away on the notes of his music.

"Is that one of your songs?" She couldn't recall the tune from the concert.

"Not yet." He leaned back and hummed the tune again. This time, the notes he hummed flowed into a beautiful arc. He chuckled softly and kissed her shoulder.

"What's so funny?" Jasmine tipped her head back. Her eyes locked on his stubbled jaw. She stretched to kiss him there.

"Funny? Nothing, really. We're on the run from someone who wants to kill us, and there is a maniac out there somewhere killing off people connected to me for reasons nobody understands. And yet… here I am with a new song layering itself perfectly in my mind while I'm holding the most amazing woman I've ever met."

"It's been a hell of a week." She drew her fingertips up his forearm in a mindless caress, his *most amazing woman* comment still pinging through her brain like a bullet ricocheting off a series of metal barriers.

Sensations and feelings floating way too close to the surface of her mind conflicted with her need to keep her emotions in check. She needed to be careful. She could fall for this insanely talented music icon. Hell, they had exactly zero chance of a relationship. She wasn't the person he'd searched for in those clubs. Sooner or later he'd get tired of her. She wasn't into BDSM, and the thought of it wasn't remotely interesting to her. Yet, this man had sought out that lifestyle. Was he still looking for a partner who would be his submissive? That wasn't her. She was a personal security specialist, and a damn good one at that. She turned off the water with her toe and lifted out of the tub. Her phone vibrated on the vanity. Reality was calling, her primary needed her protection, and that reminder pushed away the remnants of a dream that would never happen.

CHAPTER 15

"You're cleared to leave, but you need to exercise extreme caution, Jazz. Nothing about this case makes sense. There are so many questions and not enough fucking answers." Jared growled the comment. His tinny voice echoed from her phone's speaker. She handed a towel to Chad and wrapped herself in one.

"We'll head out shortly."

"I want you to check in every hour on the hour until you check in with the twins. I can't believe I'm saying this, but give the damn musician a gun. We all agree he is no longer a suspect in the murders. This shit is convoluted and fractured, but there isn't a connection strong enough to tie him to the murders as anything other than a pawn. I've checked into his background. We've got his permits covered. Do me a favor and make sure he remembers which way to point the damn thing."

Jasmine slapped her hand over Chad's mouth, preventing any retort. She shook her head at him in warning. "I'll do that. We're going to grab our stuff and hit the road. I'll call you when we clear the city."

"Be careful, Jazz. Nothing about this is adding up. You've got the primary's life in your hands. Keep your head in the game."

"I got this. I'll call soon."

Jasmine removed her hand and leaned over to the vanity to disconnect the phone.

"Jazz?"

She shrugged and headed out to get dressed. "A nickname my dad used to call me growing up."

Chad dropped the towel and turned toward his duffle bag. Jasmine took the time to memorize the line of his back... and that ass. Good Lord, he was gorgeous. "Used to? Did you ban him from calling you that?"

Jasmine blinked and jerked toward her suitcase. She pulled out another Jade-influenced ensemble and cleared her throat before she answered his question. "No, my dad was murdered." She straightened, holding the clothes against her.

"Shit. I'm sorry." Chad spun her around, and his vivid blue eyes searched her face.

She gave a small smile. "It was a long time ago. He was a wonderful man and a great dad."

Chad pulled her into a hug that she moved away from quickly. She drew a sharp breath and refocused. "We need to get a move on."

They finished getting ready and quickly packed. Chad donned the old Atlanta Braves hat he'd worn yesterday and a pair of aviators. The stubble on his jaw highlighted the overt sexiness the man exuded. Jasmine glanced at her watch. It was almost eight. The hotel would be bustling with people. She glanced at Chad again. They'd snuck in last night without anyone seeing him, but this morning? Hell, it would be a trick to get out of the hotel without someone recognizing him. He glanced at her and smiled. "I don't blend in. I'll handle any attention that comes my way."

"Was my concern that obvious?" She checked her .45 and slipped it into her shoulder holster, making sure her credentials and cuffs were secured to her jeans and out of view. The lightweight jacket that she threw on covered her weapons.

"I can read you like a book, Ms. King." Chad

shouldered his duffle and grabbed her bag. They'd left his guitar in the SUV.

Jasmine moved toward the door and spoke over her shoulder as she gazed down the hallway. The only human presence was a maid who struggled to get a vacuum off the huge cart she'd parked about four doors down. Jasmine nodded, and Chad followed her into the hall. The elevator took forever to arrive, and to Jasmine's dismay, it had a couple of people in it. Chad allowed her to go first and turned his back to the people in the car.

"Excuse me? Has anyone ever told you that you look like Chad Nelson?"

Jasmine glanced sideways at the middle-aged woman who was staring at Chad's profile.

Chad chuckled and nodded. "I get that a lot."

"Oh my God! You are Chad! You can't disguise that voice!"

The man beside her grabbed her arm. "Kay Francis, seriously, show some respect. He obviously doesn't want to be recognized."

Chad turned and smiled at them both. "I'd appreciate it if you didn't make a fuss. We just wanted a few days alone together." He nodded toward Jasmine.

"Oh! Now I recognize you! You were the one he met at the airport! It was all over Chad's fan site."

Jasmine lifted an eyebrow and gave what she hoped to be a polite smile.

"Can I get a picture? Please?"

Chad looked at Jasmine. She shook her head. This was exactly what she had hoped to avoid.

"If you promise not to post it to social media until at least noon. I don't want to have to fight my way out of the parking garage."

The woman nearly fell over herself reassuring Chad that she wouldn't. Jasmine even took the damn picture so the lady's husband could get in it. The doors opened, and the couple spilled out into the lobby. Jasmine hit the button to close the doors before anyone else could enter the car. They headed for the parking garage in silence.

In the garage, quite a few people milled around vehicles. The early morning fans were wearing jerseys for Kansas City's professional football team. Several people did double takes as they walked by. There were whispers and phones being pulled out. Jasmine cussed under her breath. They loaded up and pulled out of the garage.

"Well, that went well." His ball cap landed on the dash, and his hand raked through his hair.

"No… no it didn't, but we are on the road now." She maneuvered the vehicle through the Sunday morning traffic. The GPS came online and started her route north. She wanted a coffee, but she'd be damned if she was going to stop anywhere near Kansas City.

"Yeah, and how long do you think it will take for someone to splash the picture of this vehicle on their social media account? Dammit!"

Anyone with half a brain and minor computer hacking skills could tap into traffic cameras to pinpoint their location. "Not long. You were recognized. We don't know if the vehicle has been compromised. Right now the best thing we can do is get miles between us and where we were. Guardian will monitor social media. They can delete posts, blur the plate numbers and do their best to make sure we aren't identified. In the meantime, we stick to the plan. Jared is watching our back. If he thinks we need to detour, he'll let us know." Her voice crackled with pent up anger and frustration.

"The man in black said you should give me a gun," Chad reminded her.

"In the back. Open the metal bin with this. Take your pick." Jasmine handed him a key. She kept tabs on him in the rearview mirror while trying to navigate game day traffic and look for possible tails. Shit, talk about a fucking mess.

"You have two M4s in here?"

"Standard issue for a tactical vehicle. Only a few of us are authorized to drive them, and only if we have been through training. The vehicle is hardened, so it maneuvers like a bogged-down tank, but it's safe, has an arsenal and a duress button. If anyone ever has an issue, we flip up this cover and hit that button. It will bring every cop and Guardian operative in a three-state radius."

She heard a clip slide out of a weapon and glanced back. He'd chosen a .45 and a shoulder holster.

"Dig through your bag and put on a button-down over your t-shirt. Guardian issues only concealed-carry permits. We aren't the Texas Rangers, even though I paraded out of your house like one yesterday."

He laughed and secured the arsenal. After a few moments to grab a shirt and another brief but intense struggle to get six-foot-plus of muscled man over a cramped SUV console, he flopped back and released a huge sigh.

"I'm hungry. Are we there yet?"

Jasmine snorted and laughed at the impish look

on his face. She signaled to take the exit onto the interstate and shook her head. "I liked it better when you were brooding and silent."

"Yesterday was stressful."

"And today hasn't been?" Jasmine scanned the vehicles behind her. The lack of traffic this early in the morning helped. She weaved in and out of slower cars. There didn't seem to be anyone following, or if they were, they were damn subtle.

"One photo with a fan and several people who thought they might have recognized me? Nah, even though it is frustrating as hell not being able to go anywhere without being recognized, I guess it wasn't too bad. I probably owe my hat an apology." He reached for the tattered cap and put it on. Chad pointed to the right as they sped by the FedEx terminal. "Wow, look, the airport is right there. We could get a flight out."

"No thank you, cowboy. I've seen the shit that happens when you go to airports. We are going north *under* the radar."

"That wasn't my fault. I seem to recall you wanted a fuss."

"True, but that was then."

The ride settled into comfortable conversation. The traffic was thin enough to give her the ability to change lanes to pass while not being boxed in between slower vehicles. When they drove through Council Bluffs, Jasmine did a double take at a series of four huge modern art sculptures displayed prominently on an interstate overpass.

Chad chuckled. "Damn, that stuff looks like a transformer caught in mid-morph."

Jasmine cast him a dubious look. "Transformers? Really?"

"Hey, what's not to like about cars, robots, hot girls and things blowing up?"

Jasmine nodded. "Granted, but they come in a pale second to any of the *Die Hard* movies."

Chad shook his head. "Old school, woman. There are so many movies that are leaps and bounds above *Die Hard*."

Jasmine laughed while keeping one eye on the rearview mirror. "Please, convince me."

And he did. They talked for hours about movies, television, music likes and dislikes, both his and hers. Nothing but superficial conversation, but the back and forth banter lightened the mood and ate up the hours.

He opened the glove box and searched through it before he pulled out a pad of paper and pen. His hand flew over the paper. Jasmine glanced down at the quickly drawn musical grids. His hand jotted down notes and symbols in rapid succession, his concentration one hundred percent focused on the work he was doing. The minutes dragged by silently, punctuated by his fingers moving in a coordinated air guitar dance. His humming gave sound to fragmented words and a haunting melody.

Jasmine kept an eye out. I-29 North was a smooth drive. She passed semis and passenger vehicles. She alternated her speeds, tucked in between a couple of big rigs and drove, waiting to see if anyone would attempt to come alongside. The vehicles around her all seemed to be unremarkable. She checked in with Jared twice while Chad was lost in his world of music. Social media in Kansas City hadn't exactly blown up with Chad's appearance, but it was mentioned enough that it was trending on two of the major sites.

Chad finally put away the paper and rolled his shoulders, cracking his neck. He looked up and searched the area. "Where are we?"

"Ummm... the middle of nowhere." Jasmine motioned to the GPS that indicated the road ahead was vacant of any turn-offs.

"Okay, I guess I should ask, where the hell are we going?" Chad reached into the back seat and opened his guitar case. He placed his papers into the case and shut it again.

"One of Guardian's training complexes. Until Jared comes up with a lead or a plan, we're going to hole up at the securest location this side of the Mississippi."

"In the middle of the South Dakota plains?"

The rolling hills of golden field corn waiting for harvest spread out in seemingly endless lines on either side of the interstate. She understood his question.

"In the middle of a ranch near the Black Hills of South Dakota."

"No shit?"

"No shit."

Chad turned to face her in his seat. "So, I know you've done your homework on me, and with what I've told you about my life, I could say you know me better than anyone, but I don't know anything about you. Other than the fact you have brothers, and one of them stepped out of a role in the latest MIB movie. Tell me about Jasmine."

She glanced over at him and searched the rearview mirror again, not at all sure she wanted to let him into her world any more than she already had. When this assignment ended, it was going to hurt to walk away. Hell, she was going to hurt. Did she want to expose more of herself to him?

He reached over and grabbed her right hand. "You're doing it again. You can't run away from me. I've seen who you are. Now, I want to know what made you this way. Tell me about yourself."

"Not much to tell. I have a twin sister, Jade, who is beyond crazy but the best friend I've ever had. She works for Guardian, as does my other sister, Jewell."

"Does everyone in your family work for Guardian?"

"I have five brothers, four of whom work for Guardian in one capacity or another."

"But Jared's the big shot? He runs the company?"

Jasmine lifted her hand and waved it back and forth. "Meh... he runs the Domestic Operations section, which is important. I have other brothers who perform other functions. The one who is the overall boss would probably strongly disagree with your assumption. But Jared is the face of the company, so he gets tagged with that role a lot."

"Your mom and dad had a thing for J names?" Chad pulled off his baseball hat and ran his fingers through his hair. That simple movement made his chest muscles and biceps bulge. It shouldn't have been that sexy or distracting, but dammit... it was.

"A tradition on our dad's side. My baby brother has four boys, Talon, Tanner, Trace, and Tristin."

"Is your mom still alive?"

"Yep. As a matter of fact, she's remarried and lives on the ranch where the training complex is located. Frank, the man who owns the ranch, is my stepfather and my sister-in-law's dad. My mom and Frank met after my brother Jacob and Frank's daughter Victoria were married."

Chad blinked at her, his expression blank for a full minute. "Huh."

"Huh, what?"

"They say family lines are tangled down south. That right there... that's impressive."

"I agree."

"So is this Frank part of Guardian?"

"No, he just sold the land in the middle of his ranch to the company. It's a great facility. There's a hospital, a physical rehab center, training complex, indoor and outdoor gun ranges, a runway and a helipad. I think the last time I heard, the facility had over twenty full-time Guardian staff members working and living on or near the ranch. The little town of Hollister has had an influx of people over the last three years, that's for sure."

"I see." Chad stared at her. In a very disconcerting, direct, I-can-see-right-through-you, fashion.

"What?"

"I'm waiting."

His look never wavered, even when her eyes continued to scan the road behind them because that dark blue SUV had been hanging back there for a while now. She hit the button taking the vehicle off cruise and lowered the speed she was traveling. Might be nothing, but she wasn't willing to risk it.

"Still waiting."

Chad's words pulled her from her consideration of the vehicle behind her.

"For what?"

"For you to tell me something about you."

"I just told you a lot about me." Jasmine noticed the SUV gaining on them and relaxed a little as she brought the vehicle back up to speed.

"No, you just told me about your brothers, your sisters, your mom and stepdad and the town of Hollister. You most definitely did not tell me one thing about you."

Jasmine glanced at him. For a self-proclaimed country bumpkin, the man was sharp. No wonder he'd been able to build a music empire.

"What do you want to know?"

"If you had two wishes what would they be?"

"The first one would be that my dad…" She glanced back at the SUV. It had backed off again. Something wasn't right. Jasmine accelerated and lifted a hand as Chad started to talk again. There was no one in front of them or behind them except that one vehicle. She hit the accelerator, forcing the beast she was driving to lurch forward. The SUV behind her held pace.

"Shit. Here, push and hold #3. That will bring up Jared. Tell him we are on I-29—fifty miles south of Sioux Falls. We have a late-model black or dark blue Chevy giving chase."

Jasmine opened the compartment door next to the steering wheel, flipped up a protective plastic cover and pressed a small black button. The duress would alert every highway patrol, sheriff and municipality cop in a fifty-mile radius. The problem was, they were in the middle of nowhere. The SUV behind them was gaining speed.

Chad looked back while talking to Jared. "Shit, they've got a gun!"

Jasmine jerked the wheel to the left, slicing into the passing lane and obstructing the view of the shooter. "Bulletproof glass, run-flat tires and armored plating. You're safe." Jasmine waited until the SUV had slid in behind her before she broke right and stomped on the breaks. Chad's arms flew to the dash in an instinctive brace even though his seat belt kept him in place as the chase vehicle flew past on the left.

Smoke billowed from under the shuddering vehicle as it skidded to a violent stop. Jasmine gunned the armored SUV and headed straight toward the stopped vehicle. She needed more speed to catch and T-bone the lighter vehicle. A series of bullets hit the windshield. Shit got deadly quick.

"Brace!" Jasmine yelled just as the lighter SUV punched its gas in reverse. The vehicles raced toward each other on a collision course. The smaller SUV had the angle it needed, and the impact sent their vehicle sideways. Jasmine hit the brakes and threw the vehicle into reverse just as the lighter vehicle once again smashed into the back corner panel of their armored vehicle. The impact pushed them to the shoulder of the road. Her tires caught on the edge of the asphalt. The driver of the other vehicle kept the gas floored, pushing them toward the edge of the shoulder. The truck tilted, held on the edge of the ditch and then tumbled down the embankment.

* * *

THE IMPACT SLAMMED Chad's back against the door-jamb and jolted him toward Jasmine. He saw her head strike the door frame as both of their airbags exploded. The windshield shattered into a thousand spider cracks. The vehicle rolled once more, and he was hanging upside down. He released his seatbelt and scrambled over to lower Jasmine. Blood covered her face from a ragged gash torn along her hairline. Her pulse was strong, but she was out. The dust from the airbag explosion hung heavy in the compressed cabin of the SUV. Chad carefully released her restraints and eased her down to the roof. He reached for the keys and pulled them out of the ignition. Scrambling to the back, he fumbled with the lock.

He heard the sound of car doors slamming. The lid to the built-in gun case opened, spilling the contents of the box onto the roof of the vehicle. Chad grabbed an M4, two clips of ammo and "locked and loaded". He'd performed the action so many times during his tours of duty that even after all these years the act was smooth and steady.

Chad heard someone shout. He got down on his stomach and waited, looking toward the direction he'd heard the voices. The side windows had exploded during the roll down the embankment, and the side window airbags hung, shrouding the openings as they deflated. Chad shimmied through a thousand pebbles of safety glass. He settled in his prone position and snugged the automatic rifle to his cheek.

"Take out their feet. Need intel." Jasmine's whispered words were a sweet relief.

He watched as two set of legs came into view. Both wore suits. Both sets of shoes halted momentarily. Chad could see one man bend down, a gun pointed directly at the cab. Only the debris of the wreckage prevented the man from seeing them clearly. He watched as the man motioned his partner in the other direction, which would flank Chad and leave Jasmine exposed. These men knew what they were doing. They were going to try to kill both of them. They started to split up. Chad flipped the safety off, breaking the uncanny silence. The men reacted, but not before Chad shattered their ankles and shins with a steady percussion of automatic fire. Both targets went down screaming. Chad knew that didn't mean they didn't have the wherewithal to keep their weapons or fire them. Chad motioned to Jasmine. He crept from the vehicle on the opposite side. His head and shoulder screamed obscenities at him, but the adrenaline of the crash and the very present danger kept him moving. He peeked around the base of the SUV, lifted the rifle and trained it on the man closest. Chad approached the man farthest from the vehicle, his attention split between the two men. He kicked the man's weapon away. As he watched both men, Jasmine crawled from the wreckage and stood. She staggered to the man closest to the vehicle. Blood oozed from her head wound, but her rock steady aim with her .45 froze the man instantaneously.

"Drop the gun, motherfucker."

Chad had to give it to his woman. She had a way with words. She kicked the weapon away as soon as the guy dropped it. He watched as she cuffed him in record time. His agonized shrieks of pain at being twisted with shattered tibias didn't bother him one bit. The guy under him swore. Or at least Chad assumed it was a cuss word. It wasn't English, and it wasn't Spanish. Chad could speak both.

"What did you say?" Chad put the muzzle of his rifle against the man's temple.

"Fuck you." The man spat the words toward Chad.

"Nah, rather not. Not my idea of a good time."

Jasmine walked over and leaned against the rolled vehicle.

"Jasmine, watch him. I saw some flex-cuffs, and I need to get that bleeding stopped."

She nodded and pointed her weapon. Her breathing was ragged, but her aim was straight and true. Chad made quick work of securing the man, grabbed a first aid kit and headed straight toward her.

Jasmine waved him away. "I need answers." She walked over to the one who had cursed at Chad. He watched as she lifted her toe and set it against the fracture in the man's leg. "Learned this little trick from my brother. We can do this the easy way, or the hard way. Who do you work for?"

The man said nothing. Jasmine pressed weight down onto his leg, and he jerked forward, convulsing in pain. Chad turned his attention to the other man. He needed to stop the blood flow, or the bastard would bleed out. He stripped his shirt and wrapped the man's wounds. It wasn't perfect, but it might help.

Another blood-curdling shriek came from the man Jasmine was questioning. The man he worked on whispered, "Not after you. Her."

Chad snapped his fingers at Jasmine and waved her over. "Why are you after her?"

The man shook his head. "Sending a message."

"A message to who?"

"Guardian."

"What's the message?"

The man shuddered and gripped Chad's hand in pain. "Not safe. Nobody's safe. Zlo knows. Stay out of his business." His Slavic accent was pronounced.

"Who is Slow?" Chad asked.

The man shook his head. "He knows everything."

The sound of a car passing and slamming on its brakes drew his attention toward the roadway. The piercing shrill of a responding police vehicle registered, too. He'd been so focused on what the man was saying that he hadn't heard the vehicle's approach. Jasmine pulled her badge from her belt and held it up. Her face, now painted in a macabre mask of blood, stopped the responding officer for a split second. She motioned toward the two men cuffed and lying in pools of their own blood. "Under arrest. Attempted murder. Guardian's jurisdiction. They need to be Mirandized."

The state trooper acknowledged her and directed a few good Samaritans who had stopped to help. Chad crawled to where Jasmine leaned against the

SUV. He sat down next to her and helped her as she slid down the vehicle and sat at his side. He hurt in places he didn't know he could hurt. Tiny cuts from the safety glass littered his stomach and chest. He grabbed the tail of his tattered t-shirt and ripped a portion of material free. He shook it to make sure there was no glass before he folded it and gently placed it on her forehead.

"A little late for that, isn't it?" Jasmine's voice shook. She was probably coming off the adrenaline rush, too.

"Makes me feel better." Chad tucked her closer to him. "You do not live a boring life."

"Not usually this exciting." Jasmine waved off an ambulance attendant and pointed toward the man who'd talked. "Take care of him first."

The medic nodded and changed course.

"Care to explain all that?" Chad waved toward the men.

"Not sure if I can."

"You don't know, or you can't say?"

"A little of both."

"Not going to settle for that."

"Noted."

"Your SUV is fucked up."

"I don't think that will matter soon."

"Why?"

"Unless I miss my guess, you'll be meeting some of my friends soon."

"Friends?"

"Yep. Kick ass, bad motherfuckers. They're the ain't-going-to-have-to-worry-about-this-shit-any-longer type friends."

"Do you kiss your momma with that mouth?"

"Do you?" Jasmine laughed.

It was better than music to his ears.

Her cell phone vibrated inside the vehicle. She rolled her head. They both just looked at the damn thing.

"I should answer that."

"He's probably worried," Chad agreed.

"That would mean we'd have to move."

A stretcher and two attendants carried one of the two men he'd shot to the ambulance. At least five cops ran around and directed traffic. Another set of paramedics approached them. "Ma'am. Can I take a look at that wound?"

Jasmine nodded slightly.

The medic crouched down and did his best to examine the wound while she was tucked against Chad's side. "You're going to need stitches. There's still glass in there. We need to get it cleaned up. Are you injured anywhere else?"

Jasmine shook her head slowly.

A second man showed up and identified himself as a doctor. He motioned for the paramedic to move. "Ma'am, can I get you to look at my finger? I want to make sure we aren't looking at anything more serious than a gash on your forehead."

"I'm sore from the accident. I don't have double vision. I've had concussions before."

He chuckled at the testy tone in her voice.

"Jasmine, be nice to the man. He's only trying to help."

"Shut up, Teddy. I don't want to play nice right now."

Chad chuckled at her use of his mom's nickname for him. She was still protecting him even though nobody had given him a second glance. She sat forward and allowed the man's tests.

A cop handed Chad a gray sweatshirt emblazoned with a badge on the chest. He pulled it over his cuts. They weren't life threatening. A nice long hot shower was all he needed. He stood and groaned at the effort. "Thanks, officer. Appreciate it."

The man reached down and grabbed Chad's cap too. "Might want to put this on, Mr. Nelson. The lookie-loos are slowing down. Once you get up to the road, they'll see you. We need you and Ms. King to come with us if the paramedics release you. We need statements."

"Thank you. That's considerate of you."

"Hell, I'm not above asking for an autograph, but I can wait until we get back to the station." Huge dimples split the trooper's face when he smiled.

"Officer, you get us out of here without anyone figuring out who I am, and I'll do you one better. I'll come back one day and sing for you and your department. Oh!" Chad swiveled around, looking for his guitar case. It was jammed in the back of the SUV.

"I need that case."

The officer retrieved it and Jasmine's cell phone with a lot less effort than it would have taken Chad. He was sore and fucking exhausted, but he wasn't leaving without the song he'd written for Jasmine.

CHAPTER 16

C had rested his head against the wall in the lobby of the police station. The pleather chair took platinum for being uncomfortable. Fuck, he was tired. Jasmine leaned against him. His mind raced around in circles like he was Jimmie Johnson's number 48 car at Lowe's Motor Speedway; way too fast for anyone to catch up with. Seriously, it was Jasmine's head on his shoulder and her warmth at his side that kept him from going off the deep end. He thought about his realization last night. She was indeed his safe haven, his port in this insane storm that had become his life. He lowered his cheek to her hair, resting with her. She wasn't asleep, but she wasn't far from it.

They'd given their statements and surrendered

the weapons they'd used… well, he'd used. Jasmine hadn't fired a round, and that was making the authorities crazy. The police officers had attempted to interview, or rather, *interrogate* him, but Chad had stopped being cooperative about five seconds into the interview. The way the two cops looked at him and the direction their questions were taking… no, there was no way he was saying a fucking word. He just shut his mouth and asked for a lawyer. He hadn't needed to lawyer up, because all questions came to a screaming halt when their superior walked into the interview room and gave the assholes across the table a cease and desist order. Some bigwig at Guardian had put his foot up someone's ass. Hard.

His concealed carry permit had been transmitted, along with the documentation on his newly minted and *current* weapons qualification for the M4. That was a flat-out lie, but one he'd never dispute. The supervisor slapped it down in front of the officers and left.

Jasmine had walked in as the assholes departed. She nodded to the door, and they left. Had this happened to him last week, he'd be freaking, but something about the calm reassurance of the woman next to him settled his nerves. She melted against him and drew a deep breath. Someone offered to give them a ride somewhere, but Jasmine waved it off with a mumble about "some friends coming" and then collapsed next to him.

The sleepy little town they'd been transported to was like every other small town in middle America. Trucks and SUVs outnumbered cars. The old fashioned main street had very little traffic. A grocery store across the way boasted a total of five cars in the parking lot. Chad assumed at least three of them were employee owned. He watched a tractor roll down the street and smiled. Country didn't change much from one state to the next.

A sound he knew from the past directed his attention away from the tractor. *I must be suffering flashbacks. There's no way...* yet the thrum became a steady *whop, whop, whop*. Chad leaned forward and gazed out the plate glass window. A helicopter came into view and circled the buildings. It landed in a nearly vacant parking lot across the street from the police station and adjacent to the little grocery store. It was a Black Hawk—albeit minus the outboard .50 caliber machine guns he'd been used to seeing. The second the craft was on the ground, two huge men wearing black battle dress uniforms and a third, one of the pilots, who wore a black flight suit, disembarked and headed across the lot. Chad had a feeling these were the friends Jasmine had mentioned.

The two cops that had been so vigorous in their questioning exited the bullpen area and gawked at the bird. Jasmine lifted off the chairs. Black and blue bruising and dried blood couldn't detract from her determined grace and beauty. He grabbed their bags and his guitar case.

"Our ride has arrived. If you need anything further, you know where to find us."

"They can't land there!" The cops pointed at the helicopter.

Chad motioned toward the trio approaching them. "Hey, no problem. Maybe you should go tell them that."

The cop looked out the window and dropped his arm.

Chad sneered at the guy. "Yeah, I didn't think so." Damn, it felt good to have the upper hand… finally… When in the hell had his life jumped off the rails?

Jasmine pulled him by the elbow toward the door. Holy hell, talk about seeing in duplicate. The man leading the procession looked like a harder, larger version of Jasmine's MIB brother. This one had just the faintest hint of gray at his temples. The man's face was impossible to read. His eyes, though... those eyes were deadly, and so were the guns and the fucking knife strapped to his belt. A tall, broad blond man with an eye patch strode beside him. The pilot was cut from the same cloth. Strawberry blond hair and a demeanor that told Chad he'd kill someone as easily as he could fly that bird he'd just landed.

The bigger version of the MIB grabbed Jasmine and buried her in a hug. The blond with the eye patch extended his hand. "Doctor Adam Cassidy." He motioned to the pilot. "This is Dixon, and that guy is Jasmine's brother." He took the guitar case and bags from Chad.

"Chad." Chad shook the man's hand, and the one Dixon offered him. The big guy wasn't inclined to be friendly, and that was more than okay with Chad.

"Have you two been medically cleared?"

"We've been seen. I'm good. She's pretty banged up."

Jasmine pulled away from her brother. "I'm fine."

The doctor glared at her and then nodded once. "We've got to get going. Come on." The doctor motioned to the elaborately painted UH-60. Chad groaned inwardly. He hated helicopters. He'd thought he'd never have to ride on one of those damn things again. Jasmine grabbed his hand as soon as her brother released her. The second they were inside the helicopter, the overpowering rush of sound quieted. The interior of the machine had been soundproofed. There were heavily padded seats, and Jasmine sat next to him on the bench that stretched across the back of the cabin. This was a highly modified helicopter. He glanced out the windows and took in the external gas tanks. The bird lifted off and veered radically to the right. Damn, the familiar lurch of his stomach pulled at his gut. He hated helicopters.

"Tell me exactly what happened." Jasmine's brother leaned forward. He pinned Jasmine and Chad with a cold stare.

"We were en route to the ranch. I spotted them tailing us on the interstate. Did the usual moves to see if they were following. They had me convinced they were nothing more than another vehicle on the road. I realized my mistake when we ended up nothing but us as far as the eye could see. They tried to take us out with gunfire. The bulletproof glass held. I executed evasive maneuvers. The driver somehow managed to pull a modified pick on me and the right rear tire bit the drop off to the shoulder of the road. Just as I was correcting the bastard hit me again. We rolled down the embankment. The responding highway patrolman said he thought we rolled two and a half times. Something hard met my head. I went black. I came to out of my seatbelt and behind Chad. He had an M4 and was in a defensive position. He took out both men. He also got one man to talk."

Jasmine's brother turned his glare to Chad. The big bastard stared at him for a solid minute. Chad held his gaze. Damned if he was going to tuck tail and run from a little intimidation. Okay, one hell of a lot of intimidation.

The corner of the man's mouth rose ever so slightly. He extended a hand. "Joseph King."

Chad took his hand and nodded. "Chad Nelson."

The man laughed. "No shit."

Chad chuckled at that. Okay, so her brother had a sense of humor. "The man said he was after Jasmine. He said she was to be a message. A warning. He said Slow was sending that message."

"Zlo." Her brother repeated the name using the same accent as the man who had warned them.

"Yeah." Jasmine leaned back into Chad and pulled his arm around her.

The doctor smiled and looked out the window of the chopper. Her brother didn't. He stared long and hard. Chad lifted an eyebrow in question, and the man grunted before he leaned back. Chad knew the words meant something to them, but he didn't know what. He was sure Jasmine and her brother knew, too. Come hell or high water, he was going to figure it out. He glanced out the window at the horizon. What a fucking day.

He closed his eyes and pulled Jasmine closer. She was the only connection to any semblance of normal he had left. His life had spun so far out of control it had crashed and burned. Murderers, stalkers, car chases, people trying to kill them to send messages. Yeah, it had been one hell of a week.

CHAPTER 17

*J*asmine moved, waking him from a light sleep. He glanced around the cabin and then out the window of the helicopter. The landscape had changed dramatically. The warm orange glow of the setting sun cast rays of light through the backdrop of massive pines, deep rolling hills and never-ending pastures. Chad leaned forward and looked at the magnificent shadows of a mountain range, the dark forms silhouetted in a picturesque diorama.

Jasmine tapped his arm. She pointed out the other side of the cabin at a massive log-cabin-style ranch house. Shit, it was a freaking mansion. Two gigantic barns, four huge grain silos and numerous outbuildings settled in front of a large rolling hill. The helicopter banked, going around the hill. Chad blinked and leaned forward. Behind the ranch, cleverly camouflaged by nature, sat a huge complex of buildings. A road led off to the left and three... no four... houses had been tucked into the rolling hill landscape. The helicopter circled wide and approached from the other direction. He noticed a bank of windmills and rows upon rows of solar panels in an open field in a small valley to his right. As the bird moved, an airstrip and helipad came into view. The pilots sat the bird down expertly in the middle of the helipad.

Joseph opened the door and walked away. No 'bye, see ya' laters' or, for that matter, any acknowledgment that the rest of the people on the bird existed.

The doctor chuckled. "I'm going to insist on you two getting a once-over."

Chad held out his hand and helped Jasmine out of the helicopter. "I'm sore, but I'm good. So, thanks but no thanks on the exam, but she was unconscious for a couple of minutes."

Jasmine frowned up at him. "I'm fine."

"So you say." He motioned toward the doctor. "You need to be checked by a real doctor. Well, the guy at the scene was good, but he only gave her a quick check."

Chad did a double take as the two pilots walked up to him. They were identical twins, and holy shit, did he mean identical. The doctor made the introductions again. "This is Dixon and that one is Drake. Besides being able to fly anything you can launch into the sky, blow up things and drive you insane within three minutes of meeting you, these two run this training complex."

The doctor motioned to the hospital. "Guys, Chad here protected this one after the vehicle accident knocked her out. He took out both assailants and managed to make one talk. Would you take him over to the main ranch house and get him hooked up with a room? I'll send Jasmine over as soon as I'm sure she's good to go."

One of the two nodded, and both of them smiled at the same time. How the fuck did they do that?

"Good to meet you. Dixon has all your albums. Plays them all the time. He's a huge fanboy."

"Seriously, Drake? You're telling him *I'm* the one with the fanboy crush?" Dixon jabbed his thumb toward his twin. "Truth be told, this guy not only owns all your songs but sings them in the shower."

"I do not! But if I did, I'd be awesome. I'm that good."

"Good? You sound like a she-cat in heat."

"I think I'm insulted. No, I know I'm insulted. That karaoke bar last year—where were we? Doc, hey wait a minute, where were we?"

The doctor shook his head and walked away, grabbing Jasmine by the arm.

"Doesn't matter, and I think it was Singapore?"

"Nah, we went to the disco in Singapore."

"True. Maybe it was Seoul?"

"Could be… Hey, Chad, you coming? House, shower, food…" The guy pointed. "…this direction." The men looked at him like he had two heads, but it wasn't *him* that was off his rocker.

"Do you think he got hit on the head too?"

"Nah, he's just afraid of your fanboy bullshit."

Chad swung his head back and forth between the two men and the building into which Jasmine and the doctor had disappeared. Lord have mercy, he wasn't in Nashville any longer, Toto. He turned on his heel and started after the twins. He was life's crash test dummy this week.

JASMINE LABORED up the ranch house porch stairs, one painful step at a time. Her stepfather, Frank, sat in the swing. He smiled at her and scooted over to make room. She wandered over and sank into the swing.

"Hear you been busy." A tired smile crossed her face at the sound of Frank's gruff comment.

"It's been a day, that's for sure." She tucked her feet onto the swing and Frank pushed off. The steady creak of the chains as they moved was soothing. "Momma know? About the accident today?"

Frank grunted. The affirmation was loud and clear.

"She okay?"

"She don't like it, but…" He shrugged.

Jasmine filled her lungs and sighed. The smell of something wonderful cooking filled her senses. She was home. This ranch was home, now. Frank had made it that way for all of the Guardian family.

"That singer. He something to you?" Frank pushed them in the swing with the toe of his boot.

"Why do you ask?" She glanced over at him. The question surprised her.

"Joseph thinks he is."

"Frank? Are you and Joseph… gossiping?"

"Like a bunch of teenage girls." Amanda walked

out on the porch. Before she could take two steps, Jasmine launched out of the swing and hugged her mom.

"Honestly, the entire conversation had about ten words and four or five grunts, but I swear those two have your future decided."

Jasmine laughed at the comment. She could see that conversation happening. "Have you met Chad?"

Her mom sat down next to Frank, and Jasmine sat on the edge of one of the Adirondack chairs nearby.

"I have. He seems like a wonderful young man. Dixon and Drake took him up and gave him a room. I'm assuming he's cleaning up and getting some rest. Are you all right?"

Jasmine nodded. "He took care of me when I was out of it. He's a good man, Mom. Different than his public image. I met his mom yesterday. I think you'd like her. She's a straight shooter."

"I'm sure I would, honey. Is there a *reason* I would meet his mom?" The teasing lilt in her mom's voice made her blush.

"No, not really. As soon as Jared figures out what the heck is going on in Chad's life and fixes it, well... no... not really."

Frank grunted and Amanda smiled at him. "I agree."

"Lord, momma, do you understand him?" Jasmine laughed at the look of indignation Frank gave her.

"Honey, he says more without words than most people say with them." Amanda patted her husband's thigh and leaned in to kiss him.

Her heart clenched. She was so happy her mom had found someone. Those two were so good for each other.

Frank pushed the swing again and smiled.

"Jazz, why don't you go clean up and then bring your man down for dinner. I'll have it on the table in about twenty minutes.

* * *

FRANK WATCHED his stepdaughter go into the house. Amanda dropped her head on his shoulder. "She's falling in love."

"He's not going to be an easy one to love." A superstar with the world at his fingertips. If this turned out to be something... well, he needed to have a talk with that boy. He wasn't above going toe-to-toe with any man that was getting close with his girls.

"Easy love? Is there such a thing?"

"Yep. Us."

Amanda chuckled. "Took one hell of a rocky road to get us here, though."

Frank hummed his agreement. They'd both lost their first loves and raised their families alone. But now... now was good. Now, he knew soul-deep contentment. He loved his new extended family and had found a peace he'd never known could exist.

"Worth it to end up with you."

"I love you, too."

Frank leaned down and kissed her. He'd found the type of love he wanted for all of his family. If Jasmine had a chance at this kind of love, she'd be lucky.

JASMINE KNOCKED SOFTLY on the door between her room and Chad's and waited. The Wonder Twins had put Chad in the room next to hers, which was Jade's room. The interconnecting door was locked from Jasmine's side. She'd unlocked it before she knocked.

Chad opened the door wearing a pair of well-worn jeans and nothing else. His hair was wet, and emblazoned on his chest was a huge tapestry of connecting dots. Red pinpricks and small scratches covered his chest and sculpted abs.

"Oh, lord! Why didn't you say something?" Jasmine reached out and stroked her hand lightly over his pecs. The springy hair tickled her hand.

He grabbed her hand and lifted it to his lips. "I'm fine." He lowered his head and caught her lips in a whisper-soft kiss. "You need to shower. You still have blood in your hair."

Jasmine reached for her hair and stepped back, immediately self-conscious. "Oh, right… I'll go…" She turned, but was caught in his arms almost immediately.

"Let me take care of you." He kissed her temple and took her hand, leading her into his room and the en suite. He flicked the lever on the massive shower system and turned to her.

"Um… dinner…." She knew her mom would come looking.

"How long do we have?"

"Twenty minutes."

"Perfect." Chad tugged off her jacket and slipped her shoulder holster off. His lips distracted her as his hands removed her gear and clothes quickly. He dropped his jeans and backed her into the shower.

"Water temperature okay?" Chad's question took a couple of seconds to register.

It could have been arctic cold, and she wouldn't have cared, not with him holding her the way he was. "Perfect."

"Lean your head back." Jasmine did and winced as the jets of water hit the rather large bump on her head. Chad opened the shampoo and carefully worked it through her hair, being extra careful around the knot on her head and cut on her hairline. He washed her hair a second time and then soaped up a cloth and washed her body. The caresses were careful and gentle, but not sexual. He turned off the shower, escorted her out and dried her with a large bath sheet. Jasmine moaned when he dropped his head and kissed her.

"Five minutes left. We need to get dressed. But just so you know, after dinner I'm going to make love to you. All. Night. Long." Chad turned her toward her door and swatted her on the ass. "Go. Clothes."

Jasmine glanced over her shoulder at him and smirked. She dropped the bath sheet and slowly walked out of the room. Chad's growled curse put a happy smile on her face.

She combed out her hair and put it up in a high ponytail, loosening it, so her hair didn't pull on her sore scalp. She walked to the closet and sighed. Her own clothes. Finally. She pulled on a pair of Prada yoga pants, a soft sports bra, and an oversized Michael Kors t-shirt before she slipped her feet into a pair of soft, hand-stitched, Italian leather ballerina slippers.

Chad was on her bed when she walked out of her bathroom. His arms behind his head, legs crossed, relaxed and oozing sex. He glanced at her and smiled. "I like that look on you. No makeup and relaxed. You're beautiful."

Jasmine headed for the door. "And you're a hot mess. Come on, Mr. Singer Dude. The parental units get fussy if they have to keep dinner waiting." She paused at the door for him.

Chad rolled off the bed, stood and stretched. His shirt lifted, revealing his dark happy trail. Jasmine licked her lips. The man was so freaking sexy.

"Keep looking at me like that, and we won't make it down for dinner."

Jasmine popped her eyes back up to his. Busted. She lowered her eyelids and smiled demurely. "I have no idea what you're talking about, Mr. Nelson." She stepped out the door when he started prowling toward her. "But maybe you could refresh my memory after dinner?"

Chad grabbed her chin in his and dropped a kiss on her lips. "I can guarantee it."

Jasmine grabbed his hand and walked him down to the dining room. She watched as Chad's gaze bounced over the ranch house and took in the high ceilings, exposed, polished pine logs, the great room fireplace that was so large you could park a truck in it—all of it was breathtaking. She could remember the first time she'd been here. Her stepfather didn't flaunt the fact he had money, but this house? Yeah, it was spectacular.

"I feel like my ten-million-dollar home in Nashville was designed by Liberace compared to this." Chad studied the massive antler chandelier that spanned the voluminous entryway. "That's got to be a herd of elk right there."

"It is amazing, isn't it? I'll give you a tour of the ranch tomorrow." She pulled his hand and led him into the dining room, where she stopped and gaped at the people surrounding the table.

She'd expected her mom and Frank, but Dixon, Drake, Joseph, Ember, Jared, Christian, Jason, Faith,

Reece, Adam, Keelee and their young daughter Elizabeth all sat at the table.

Jasmine's face burned with embarrassment. She tried to drop Chad's hand, but he held it tight. He smiled and waved with his free hand. "Hi, I'm Chad Nelson. She's obviously embarrassed, so I'm guessing she had no idea y'all were going to be here for dinner. Where do you want me to sit for the inquisition? Here?" He motioned toward the two open chairs and pulled Jasmine with him.

Jasmine wanted to melt through the beautifully polished wood floor. The smirk Chad had on his face did little to ease her discomfort with the situation. She saw the performer take over. Chad was all gloss and polish. He masked his discomfort with the veneer that he'd perfected during his career. The thought of him having to hide, here, where he was supposed to be safe, angered her.

Chad sat down and looked at Frank. "So, are we doing introductions?"

Jasmine sighed and shook her head while looking around the table. The depth of anger that filled her was the only thing that kept her mouth shut. If they'd done this to Jason when he was dating Faith or, God forbid, given Ember the third degree when

Joseph brought her to the ranch, her brothers would have gone ballistic.

Her mom cleared her throat. "I'm sorry, Chad. I can assure you my sons will not be holding an inquisition." She glared down the table at Jason and Jared.

Dixon chuckled and looked at Drake. "Better than a soap opera."

"Wassa soap opera, Uncle Dicks?" Reece asked. The entire table chuckled and seemed to exhale a collective breath.

"It is a bunch of grown-ups on television acting like the world is falling apart around them," Drake answered the boy.

"Are you going to pass the chicken, Grandpa? I'm hungry." Reece sat up on his knees and reached for his bread.

"Hold your horses." Frank cleared his throat, and Reece dropped the biscuit. Frank bowed his head, and the entire family followed suit. Jasmine glanced at Chad, who winked at her and held tight to her hand.

"Thank you for the bounty of this table, the hands that cooked it and the loved ones in our midst. Thank you, Father, for your continued blessings and the safety of our family."

A whispered *amen* around the table broke the floodgates wide open. People talked over one another as food made its way around the table. Jason caught Jasmine's attention and motioned toward Chad. She narrowed her eyes and glared back at her brother. He smiled, and she saw the devil dancing in his eyes. *Great.*

"So, Chad… heck of a day, huh?" Jason stared directly at Jasmine when he asked.

Chad finished the bite of mashed potatoes. He nodded his head and wiped his mouth with his napkin. Leaning back, he put his arm on the back of Jasmine's chair. "You could say that."

"I believe I did."

"You must be another brother."

"I'm Jason. This is my wife, Faith, and our son, Reece." Reece waved from the end of the table where he was sitting on his knees between the twin towers of Dixon and Drake. Jasmine smiled at him and waved back; so did Chad.

"You do the Guardian thing, too?" Chad asked as he buttered a biscuit.

"Yep. You could say that."

Christian snorted into his iced tea. Chad looked at him and cocked his head. "I'm Christian." He nodded toward Jared and continued, "He's my husband." Every person at the table except Elizabeth and Reece watched Chad's reaction.

"Damn. That's… I can't see how… I'm so sorry."

Jasmine blinked at Chad's sighed response. If Chad couldn't accept her brother and his husband…

"You deserve some sort of award for long suffering. Living with the Man In Black there has to be a barrel of laughs. He is about the grouchiest man I've ever met… aside from that one." Chad nodded toward Joseph. "Does he ever smile?"

Christian's face blushed a vivid red, and he nodded but didn't answer.

Chad laughed and held up his hand. "Don't say a word. TMI already."

Jason laughed and nodded toward Joseph and Ember. "I've heard you've met Joseph. This is his wife, Dr. Ember King."

Adam cleared his throat and motioned to his right. "This is my wife, Keelee, and our daughter, Elizabeth. Keelee is Frank's daughter.

Chad acknowledged each of the introductions, and thankfully, the conversation moved toward the training complex's day-to-day operations.

"Are you a c'lebrity?" Reece's voice carried over the low hum of dinner conversation.

Chad winked at the boy. "Yep."

"What's a c'lebrity?"

Chad looked up at the ceiling. "Well, nowadays, it means someone that is famous for something."

"What are you famous for?" His question came out garbled.

"Reece, do not talk with your mouth full."

The little boy swallowed. "Sorry, Momma." He looked back at Chad in expectation.

"I can sing. Some people like it."

Ember laughed and Reece glanced at her. "Honey, Mr. Nelson is probably one of the best singers in the world."

Reece's eyes rounded as he looked back a Chad. "Can you sing for us?"

Every head, including Frank's, swung toward Chad. He smiled and nodded. "Yes sir, I can."

Jasmine put her hand on Chad's thigh. "But not tonight, Reece. We've had a really big day."

"But when?"

"Tomorrow after dinner, maybe? We can go out on that big porch, and I'll sing lots of songs for you. Okay?"

"Deal."

When dessert was done, Jason looked at Jasmine. "We need to talk. Privately. Frank, may we use your study?"

The man nodded once. Jasmine stood at the same time as Joseph, Jared, and Chad.

Jared lifted an eyebrow and gave Chad a pointed stare. Chad shrugged. "This involves the situation that happened today. The one I was up to my eyeballs in. It also involves her. Since she's my personal security officer, anything that affects her affects me. So let's not whip them out and measure 'em right here, shall we?"

"Whip what out, daddy?"

Drake grabbed Reece and lifted the kid to his shoulders. "Never mind, little dude. We have horses and puppies to pet!"

"Yay!"

Dixon laughed and finished his coffee in one gulp. "I'm going to hate to miss this, but I think I better rescue Reece from Drake."

Jason rubbed the back of his neck and motioned toward the den. "Come on, let's get this over with. It has been a long day for everyone."

Jasmine followed her brothers as they trekked to the den, and Chad shut the door behind them.

Jason sat down on a loveseat. He waited until everyone else was seated. "From the information that you obtained, we believe the people who went after you today were..." Jason looked at Chad and paused for a moment before he continued, "...with the group that had previously targeted key Guardian personnel."

Jasmine nodded. The same group that had gone after Jason, Gabriel, and Jared. The Russians. She'd known that as soon as she'd heard the Slavic accent.

"We've upped protective measures. Jacob and Tori refuse to leave D.C. They are both buried in overseas operations. We've put Charlie team on them in addition to their regular security team. Jewell has a specialist with her twenty-four-seven. Lima team is here with Faith and me and will continue to shadow us. Jared and Christian have Omega team with them. Jade is undercover, so the likelihood of the Russians finding her is next to nil. Once she surfaces, we'll assign her a team. You are going to stay on this ranch with him," Jason pointed his finger at Chad, "until we find out who is taking out the people who are suing him. This is the safest place on the planet."

"Don't forget the stalker," Jared added.

"Right." Jason conceded.

"Where are we with that?" Chad leaned forward.

Jared shrugged and released a long sigh. "We have a lead. It's thin, but I've got investigators on it." He looked at Jason and explained, "The contracted 'fixer' that Ms. Wicker employed. Jewell's people found a credit card we can presumably link to the man based on numerous hits of time and locality close to where Chad was. We're tracking him. Don't know if it will pan out, but…"

Jason nodded. "All right. In the meantime, we keep him here and alive. Jazz, he's your primary. You're glued to his side."

Joseph chuckled, that evil laugh of his drawing every eye toward him. "I don't think that will be a hardship for either of them."

"Dude, five or six words all day and then you drop that?" Jason shook his head and laughed. "Next thing you know we'll be braiding hair together."

Joseph growled, "Fuck off."

"Ah… see, there's the brother we all know and love. Chad, to protect you, I'm going to ask you to stay here at the ranch. Nobody can know where you are. Do you have any obligations that I need to take care of other than the interviews Jasmine told us about yesterday?"

"I have no problem staying here as long as you can guarantee my mom is safe."

Jason closed his eyes and shook his head before he spoke. "I should have said something earlier. We have two men on her. She'll never know they are there unless there is a problem."

"Thank you. I'll need to contact my legal team, have access to email and telephone. I've decided to step down from recording and touring." He glanced over at Jasmine and winked. "I'm firing my PR firm. I need to get ahold of my life before I move forward."

"We can arrange that. We have untraceable phones here that we can provide you. I understand that your life has been turned upside down, but I would caution you against making any dramatic changes until things have settled down. May I suggest you just indicate you are taking a hiatus? If, when we have this situation dealt with, you still feel the need to follow through with your desire to walk away, then do it. Making an extreme gesture at this point may push our perpetrators into the woodwork and make it impossible to smoke them out."

Chad nodded. "I can live with that."

"Good, now you will have to excuse us. We do need to discuss other business not related to this situation." Jason leaned back in the chair.

"Well, you don't need to tell me twice." Jasmine smiled at Chad as he stood and headed to the door.

As soon as the door shut behind Chad, Jasmine launched out of the chair. "You assholes! How dare you? Joseph, when you brought Ember to the ranch, what would you have done if someone had treated her the way you guys treated Chad tonight?"

"That's different…" Jason started to speak.

"Bullshit! You can't push a double standard on me. You!" She glared at Jason. "If anyone had questioned the way you felt for Faith when you were dating her, you'd have ripped out their throat. As a matter of fact, I seem to recall you and Jared having a huge conflict over that exact issue. And *you*!" She turned on Jared and pointed a finger at him. "*You* have absolutely zero right to come here and question my involvement with Chad. You are the *last* person to give advice on relationships!" She was so pissed her hands shook.

"Jazz… sorry." Joseph's quiet comment from the far end of the room calmed her rampage.

Jason cleared his throat and leaned forward. "You're right. We're assholes."

"Damn straight you are." Jasmine threw herself down in the chair and winced as the muted aches of the day protested when she hit the cushion.

"When are we going to stop playing defense and start going after these bastards?" Joseph poured three tumblers of Frank's scotch. He reached into the refrigerator and grabbed a can of soda for Jason.

Jared stood and walked over to the bar. He grabbed two tumblers before he came over to her and leaned in, kissing her forehead. "I'm sorry, too. I love you, and I let that color my reactions."

Jasmine accepted the scotch. "Thank you."

Jason popped the top on his soda. He took a sip and waited for everyone to sit down again. "Our asset has just taken up residency in his chalet in Switzerland. His background is rock solid. The operation and inquiries have started. It won't happen overnight, but I expect the mouse to start smelling the cheese that our asset has set out."

"That's all well and good, but the Russians have us firmly in their sights. We need to put them on their heels. Thinking from a strategic standpoint, if we go after them in the States, it will draw their attention to us and will allow the asset to work himself into their circle with less chance of discovery."

Jasmine cocked her head. Joseph rarely spoke, but when he did, he didn't mince words.

Jason set the soda can down and stared at Joseph. "Gabriel is due back in the States in two weeks. Until then, we wait. Once we have him back inside the borders, we can start making strategic strikes. We have identified suspected players, but we need to work out a strategy so the Russians don't figure out *how* we've identified their players."

Jasmine took a sip of her scotch before she spoke. "Start with the two that attacked me today. Use them. If we could get more information out of the one who spoke with Chad, we can start an offensive move."

"I agree. They are under armed guard now. As soon as they are medically stable, they will be in our custody. We get information from them and use them as the ignition point." Jared took a long sip of his drink and motioned to Joseph. "What would you do?"

A wicked sneer spread across Joseph's face. "Add smoke to the ignition point. Kill them."

"The two from today?" Jared said.

Joseph nodded his head. "Make the Russians believe they died today from injuries they sustained during the accident. If the Russians think their people are gone when we start striking at targets, they'll be confused. Confusion is our advantage."

"They'll need confirmation," Jason added.

"They'll need dead bodies. The accident could cause such grave injuries that a person couldn't be recognized. Official reports, dental x-rays... we've been down this road before."

"Plus it will give us time to work information out of the tough one." Jared nodded. "Yeah, I like it. We can hold them in a secure location while we run the operation with our asset overseas. Our evidence will provide the DOJ all the ammunition they need to give us permission. We can tie in domestic terrorism and present the DOJ with a neat package. Just sitting here waiting for the next shoe to drop is driving all of us insane."

Jason stood and walked over to the window, looking out into the darkness. "I agree with most of that plan. We'll use the two we took into custody today. I'm not going to play with the Russians. I'm going to let them know we are using those two ass wipes. As a matter of fact, we will advertise the fact we have them. Anyone else we catch will be pressed for information in the same way. We have all our players in place." He glanced over his shoulder. "It's time to fight back."

CHAPTER 18

*J*asmine let herself into her room. The moonlight from the windows filled the room with a blue hue. Chad's deep breaths indicated he slept soundly. She tiptoed through the room and quickly got ready for bed. Her brothers had spent over two hours discussing options and possible tactics for the upcoming operation against the Russians. About twenty minutes into the discussion all of the siblings on the ranch had walked to the communications building and pulled Jacob into a conference call. Gabriel was added about fifteen minutes later. A key player in the situation, Jewell was conferenced in once a plan was developed. Her ideas for a separate and mirrored IT system that loaded erroneous information to

Guardian clone servers and redirected the Russians' uber-hacker to follow false leads was incomprehensibly complicated. Jasmine gave up trying to understand the concept after about five seconds. Of the people on the conference call, Jason, Gabriel and Jewell seemed to be the only ones that had a clue what was being discussed and decided. Thank God she didn't have to deal with that side of the business much. She'd settle for the humdrum life of a PSO. *Humdrum... as if.*

Jasmine's head ached. She pulled the covers back and slipped into the body-warmed bedding. Chad rolled over and pulled her close.

"Took forever." He breathed the words into her hair.

"Sorry. Business." She luxuriated in his embrace. Her body melted against his warmth, and she sighed audibly.

"Long day." His words rumbled against her ear.

"It was."

"Hard to believe it was just last night that I made love to you for the first time."

Jasmine caught her breath at his choice of words. She released it, because, hey, he wasn't serious. They'd gotten physical. The sex was spectacular. The events today had driven her emotions all over the place and they'd probably messed with his too. She could fall for the man if she gave herself half a chance, but he would only be at the ranch until his case was solved. After that, he'd go back to his life, and she'd go on with hers. She had a job to do, and he… well, he could do whatever he wanted now that he was retiring.

"You're thinking too hard." Chad rolled her onto her back and peered down at her. His hand softly brushed her hair away from her face.

"Yeah, I am." She couldn't deny it.

"Talk to me." His fingers danced through her hair.

"No pretense?" She peeked up at him through her lashes.

"Never. Tell me what has you worried."

"Us."

"Mmmm… us. Broad topic." He leaned down and kissed her lips softly. Jasmine trembled at his touch. He smiled against her lips and kissed her again.

"What is going on with us?" She reached up and traced his jaw with her fingertips. The scruff of his beard pushed against her sensitive skin and left a cascade of sensations that floated down her arm and skittered across her body.

"I believe it's called dating."

Jasmine's initial chuckle turned into a fit of therapeutic laughter. *Dating?* Of all the words to describe what had been happening to them. Chad's smile above her fed her amusement. "Ummm... hate to tell you this, but our dates, for the most part, suck."

He dropped to his back and clutched his chest. "I'm wounded! You've lanced my heart! How could you not fall at my feet in adoration?"

Jasmine lifted off the bed and straddled him. She mimicked taking the knife from his heart. "Never fear, I'll never let anyone hurt you." She held up her imaginary dagger in triumph.

"I know." Chad's hands settled on her hips. He ran his hands down her thighs and back up again. "And I'll never let anyone hurt you. I'm not one of your Guardians..."

"I've recently discovered I don't need a Guardian." Jasmine leaned forward, dropping onto her hands, draping them in her fall of hair.

"Can you settle for a simple country boy?" He reached behind her neck and pulled her down to his lips. The whisper soft touch of his skin shook her to her core.

"I could, but you aren't a simple country boy."

Chad sat up, and she moved her legs around his waist. They sat eye to eye.

"In reality, I am. I know you had your doubts about me, about who I was…"

Jasmine put her fingers over his lips. "I don't care who you were."

Chad placed his hand over hers and pulled her fingers away from his lips. "I do. I know what I've been. I've made mistakes. I've been lost and looking for something for so long that drifting through life became my normal. I don't want that life anymore. I want what I think can grow between us."

Jasmine searched his eyes by the light of the moon.

He cupped her neck with his hand and put their foreheads together lightly. "I want all of you, Jasmine. Let me prove to you I'm worthy of that."

Jasmine closed her eyes. Her mind raced with the thoughts, the hopes, and the dreams and collided with the past, her ex-fiancé and her life. How could her life and his mesh?

"Baby, stop trying to make sense of everything tonight. Just promise me you'll give me the chance to show you I'm worthy of giving me your heart."

She opened her eyes again and searched his. The word slipped out, a soft whispered prayer. "Yes."

THAT ONE WORD CHANGED EVERYTHING, changed nothing and yet meant the world. He leaned in and brushed a soft kiss on her lips as he lifted the wisp of silk over her head. He needed her softness against him. He pulled her in. She arched into him and shifted slightly on his cock. The insane sensations of that little movement lit him up like a roman candle on the Fourth of July. He grabbed her ass with both hands and pushed up into her, grinding his length against her core. She was already hot and wet for him. He could feel her against his cock.

"Chad, please. I need you." Her words splashed gasoline on his desire. Fuck, he needed to be buried in her. Now.

He held her as he lifted his cock under her sex. She dropped her head back, her long hair covering his arms at her back. She groaned as he lifted his hips and slid into her. Soft, hot, tight... fuck... so gloriously tight. He pulled her closer so he could taste her. He found purchase on her shoulder and started to piston his hips. Her breath punched out when he slammed into her. Her hands gripped his shoulders, and she adjusted her legs, which had been clenched around his waist. She lifted, using her legs as leverage, and dropped down.

"Fuck... yes... again." Chad panted as he grabbed

her hips. He thrust up as she dropped down. The sexual-fucking-electricity arced between them, building bigger with each synchronized movement of their hips. He felt her nails digging into his back and relished the knowledge that he was making her lose control. She needed to trust him to take care of her, because he would gladly spend his life doing it.

Her body lost rhythm. The muscles in her legs tightened. She stopped moving, and he took over. He needed her to shatter, to come apart so he could put her back together. Put her together in the image of them, not in the lonely world she'd built for herself.

Chad lifted and held her as he took her down to the mattress. He moved her leg over his hip and thrust his hips, searching for the bliss they both wanted. With a strength few women possessed, Jasmine pulled him down and bit his shoulder, stifling a scream that coincided with her body's release. He held her head against him and raced to his finish. Her small pleas for more pulled him back. He ground his teeth together, frantically trying to give her another release. He felt her stiffen under him and lost his ability to think. Hell, he lost his ability to breathe when the orgasm ripped from him. He continued to rock through his release. Her arms slid from his back and flopped out to her side, limp.

His arms were under her back, his head dropped to her shoulder, and he tried to breathe. Air in... air out... in... out... Holy fuck, the woman was going to kill him. He'd never... so fucking good...

He listed to the right, and she lifted her left arm, allowing him to fall. The sweat that pooled between their bodies started to cool immediately. He flopped onto his back, still trying to remember why breathing was a necessity.

Jasmine's hand flopped against his stomach. "So last night wasn't a fluke?"

"Guess not..."

"Damn..."

"Yeah..."

"Chad?"

"Hmm..." Chad pulled her over and up onto his shoulder.

"Don't wake me up if this is a dream."

He kissed her forehead carefully. "We're wide awake."

"Good... that's really good." She nestled into his side. He drew slow circles on the arm that lay on his chest. Her breathing leveled and slowed before she drifted to sleep. He didn't understand life. He'd reached the pinnacle of his profession. He'd amassed an empire and isolated himself from everyone and everything. Then his world had shattered from the inside, sending everything he thought certain about his life into ruin. Yet, in the dust and rubble, he'd found her—the one who fit him perfectly. She made him whole by piecing together the fragmented puzzle he could never solve. The woman filled canyons of need with a single look; became sanity and reason when no one else had even managed to become… necessary. He stifled a yawn and looked out the window at the nearly full moon. He had a shot at a life he'd never thought he'd find. A random rift of notes lingered momentarily in his mind. He hummed the tune and closed his eyes to the echo of the start of a beautiful new melody.

CHAPTER 19

*C*had headed downstairs with his guitar. He'd spent more than a hot minute tuning his baby. He'd promised Jasmine's nephew he'd sing after dinner, and he'd deliver on that promise. In fact, he was looking forward to it. Until the last week, he could count the days he'd not played in the last ten years on one hand. Music was his life. He realized the statement was overdone and trite, but hell… it was what it was. His mom had paid for piano, classical guitar and violin lessons for him when he was growing up. They traveled two hours round trip every Saturday so he could learn from the best in the area. He'd had no idea of the sacrifices his mom had made to ensure he was able to learn. He did now. His mom was his hero. She'd given him the gift of music, picked him up when he was at his lowest, and supported him through rehab and recreating his life.

Chad strode across the football-field-sized foyer and headed for the front porch. He'd told Reece he'd meet him on the swing. The screen door hadn't slammed shut before he stopped dead in his tracks. At least thirty people sat on blankets and folding chairs on the lawn in front of the porch.

Frank appeared at his elbow. "Seems word may have spread you'd be singing."

"It would appear so." Chad lifted a hand and waved. He recognized the family he'd been introduced to, but there were many others. He saw two men in wheelchairs, one wearing an orthopedic boot, and another in a full-arm cast. Jasmine had given him a tour today, but they hadn't gone into the hospital. Now he regretted that oversight.

Jasmine sat on the steps of the porch with Reece. He moved to sit beside them and looked out at the small crowd. "Hey. Reece here asked me to sing for him. If y'all don't mind…" A rumble of laughter stopped his intro. He let it die off before he continued. "As I was saying, if y'all don't mind, I'll sing a song or twenty. But first I need to limber up my fingers. If any of this warmup gets put on YouTube, my reputation will be crushed, so behave, y'all." The laughter skittered across the night air again.

He turned to Jasmine and winked before he leaned over his guitar and began to play.

JASMINE WATCHED as he leaned into the guitar. He smiled at Reece and whispered something she couldn't hear. His fingers flew over the strings, waking the instrument up while caressing the frets with the expertise of a symphony soloist.

The song he played evoked strong, haunting, heart-wrenching emotions. Jasmine leaned back against the railing, mesmerized at how he poured himself into the music. The song he played was classical, not a country song or a cover song for another artist. The movements of the music were completed impeccably, and his interpretation of the composer's muse was eloquent and flowing. She'd just spent six months with an opera singer and understood the labor and creative inspiration behind an artist's ability to make the music more than notes on a page. As the last note ended, he opened his eyes and looked straight at Jasmine.

"What was that piece?" someone asked from the lawn.

Chad positioned his hand on the neck of the guitar. "That piece was *Preludio y Toccatina* by Sérgio Assad."

"Will you play another?" Jasmine's mom asked. They both glanced toward the swing where she and Frank sat.

Jasmine laughed at Chad's response: "Just try to stop me."

He turned to her and in a soft whisper spoken for only her to hear. "This one is for you. It's just like you, haunting, strong and desirable." He turned back to the guitar, and the melody flooded the enraptured audience. He spoke over the guitar. "This is *Asturias,* composed by Isaac Albéniz."

He leaned over the guitar, and his fingers flew over the strings. Jasmine glanced at the ranch hands and Guardian people that had gathered. His performance entranced them. The notes were indeed haunting. If she closed her eyes, she would believe he was playing a duet. The illusion of the long-sustained notes punctuated with the counter melody of the music floated around them. The last note held and floated into nothing. There was absolute silence.

Reece put his hand on Chad's knee. "You play good. But you said you could sing."

Chad laughed with everyone else. "Okay, y'all want me to sing?" he asked as he started strumming. "We'll start with some old cover songs, but fair warning, I will be singing several of my own. Shameless self-promotion, I know. Speaking of 'Shameless'... let's start with Garth's song."

Jasmine sat in wonder at the man's talent. People started throwing out songs for him to play and sing, and without hesitation, he belted out song after song. Chad lifted his guitar and pulled Reece between his legs, bringing the guitar down so the little boy could stand between him and the instrument. Reece's eyes tracked Chad's fingers, and he stood mesmerized. The little boy laughed and ran to his mom when the song was done. "Momma, I want to play the guitar!"

"Sorry to put an end to tonight's fun, but I think I have one song left in me. I have heard, from a reliable source, that my ballad, 'Mississippi Magnolia', has special meaning to a couple here tonight." He coughed into his hand, saying Jared and Christian's names. Christian's head whipped up for a quick look at Chad and then over his shoulder at his husband. Jared smiled and shrugged. Christian leaned back and whispered. Jared nodded and cupped Christian's cheek tenderly before they kissed. Jasmine smiled so hard her face hurt. Now things made sense. Her brother had pulled Chad aside today when they were strolling around the complex, and now she understood why.

Instead of playing the guitar, he propped it against the railing. He put his arm around Jasmine's shoulders and pulled her close. She looked up into his eyes as he took a deep breath and began to sing the song a cappella. His voice wrapped around her, caressing her with its deep, smooth timber. The words were a seduction, and the melody intoxicating. When the last note fell, he leaned down and kissed her. She was defenseless. His beautiful music stripped her of any way to combat her feelings for him.

The kiss lasted only a moment before people wandered up to thank and talk with Chad. Jasmine melted into the background and watched him. After witnessing that performance, seeing his happiness, the way he treated everyone with compassion, respect and friendly familiarity, all pounded home the fact he was damn special. Special to so many people, she had no right...

"Don't throw this chance away."

She jumped and turned at Joseph's voice behind her. "Shit, you scared me. Don't throw what chance away?"

He leaned against the house and nodded toward Chad. "Him."

"I..."

"You're trying to convince yourself to push him away. Don't."

"But..."

"But nothing. You are strong enough to be the person to walk beside him."

Jasmine gave a huff. "He'd rather have someone walk behind him."

"Bullshit."

"No, you don't understand, he's... he prefers..."

"Submissive women?"

"Yeah."

"Does Ember strike you as submissive?"

"Ember? Hell, no!" Jasmine had seen that woman go toe to toe with everyone, including Joseph. The woman had a feisty temper and wasn't afraid to let it loose.

"Talk to her."

A loud burst of laughter caused Jasmine to turn back and look at Chad. He caught her eye and smiled before someone else pulled his attention away.

"Why?" She glanced over her shoulder at her brother. He'd vanished. She spun in a complete three-sixty. The man was a ghost. His words piqued her curiosity, though. She glanced around the gathering. Ember was talking with Faith, Keelee, and her mom. It had been a while since she and Ember had visited. What was the harm of talking?

CHAPTER 20

"*H*e told you to ask me *what?*" Ember stood with her hands on her hips and repeatedly blinked, as if she couldn't quite comprehend the question.

Jasmine quickly glanced around the kitchen, thankful that her mom wasn't within earshot. She'd tried to bring up the subject with Ember several times, but each time she'd chickened out. The last three weeks with Chad at the ranch had been amazing, but she still worried she wasn't giving him what he wanted. She had no idea how to be a submissive person. But the sex between them was phenomenal —beyond that, if possible. Still, Jasmine fought a mental battle every time she saw Chad with one of the women who worked on the Guardian side of the ranch. It wasn't jealousy, but rather an insecurity that maybe she wasn't enough. So, today when she'd found Ember making a cup of tea in the kitchen, she'd asked… although right now she was second guessing that. Big time.

"Look, Chad has… he goes to clubs. I don't know how to be submissive," she hissed. God, she was going to die of embarrassment.

Ember leaned against the counter and lifted her teacup to her lips, blowing on the fragrant brew before she took a sip.

"Neither did I."

"How did you figure it out?" The question was low and barely whispered.

"Do you love him?"

"I… probably."

Ember lifted a single eyebrow and waited.

Jasmine rolled her eyes. "Yeah, I think I do, but I haven't told him because I don't want him to settle for me if I can't be what he needs. I don't want to look back in five years and know I was the reason my relationship failed. Again."

"Evan cheated on you."

"Yeah, because I couldn't give him what he wanted."

Ember snorted. "No, he cheated on you because

he couldn't keep his dick in his pants. Anything else is bullshit. If he loved you, he wouldn't have strayed."

Jasmine sighed and rubbed her forehead. "I'm not sure I believe that."

Ember put her cup down and turned to face Jasmine. "Look, the simple fact is this. I love Joey. I'm assuming he and Chad have similar expectations. I give everything to my husband because I trust him to take care of me. When we make love, it might not be what others consider normal, but that man takes care of me. Lord, girl, does he take care of me."

"Oh, my God… TMI, Ember!" Jasmine put her hands over her ears.

Ember laughed and picked up her tea again. "Do you trust him?"

"Yeah."

"Enough to let go and let him be your safety net?"

"I don't know what you mean."

"I know in every fiber of my being Joey will never push me too far. He'll never take the experience past what I can handle. He is my safety, my shelter. If I didn't trust him implicitly, I wouldn't be able to do the things we do."

"But you're not submissive."

"To anyone else? Hell, no." Ember made a one-fingered gesture to no one in particular as she drank her tea. "But when it comes to that man. I'd kneel at his feet for the rest of my life."

Jasmine nodded and watched Ember look through the cabinets. She pulled down a sleeve of saltine crackers and popped one into her mouth, then offered the open packet to Jasmine. She pulled one out and started nibbling on a corner.

"I don't know what to do." All the self-doubt and fears raced to the forefront of her mind. He'd done scenes with women who knew what they were doing.

"He knows what to do. You need to let him lead." Ember took another sip and popped another saltine into her mouth. Her red hair tumbled over her shoulder. She flipped the mass of curls back and washed down her cracker with her tea.

Jasmine looked from the cracker in her hand to the sleeve Ember was currently destroying. The tea was a peppermint herbal mix that her mom kept around for upset stomachs. Jasmine lifted one eyebrow in question.

Ember's face and chest flushed a vibrant red, and she nodded. "Nobody knows. Not even Joey. I'm going to tell him tonight."

"Oh my God!" Jasmine squealed.

"Shhhh!!!" Ember glanced toward the kitchen door.

Jasmine jumped up and down on her toes before she wrapped Ember in a hug. Her sister-in-law teared up when she pulled away. "We've been trying for so long."

"I'm so happy for you. When did you find out?"

"The morning sickness hit hard this week. Joey has been up to his ears in work. I've been eating like crap because of the new patients we got in from the Argentina mission, and I thought maybe I ate something that upset my stomach. I took a pregnancy test this morning."

"I'm so happy for both of you."

Ember wiped the tears from her cheek. She pointed to Jasmine. "Sworn to secrecy."

Jasmine nodded, but she had a sinking feeling. She knew Joseph would be able to tell something was up if he spoke to her. They were done with their daily update from Jared and she needed to brief Chad on the developments. *Oh, well, that might work. Two or three birds with one stone.* "I'm crap with these kinds of secrets, but Chad is riding the fence line. I can pack a kit so we can spend the night out. That way I won't ruin any of your surprises, and I can talk privately with Chad, and we can see where things go."

"Perfect. Let me help you pack." Ember popped another cracker into her mouth.

CHAD LIFTED into the saddle of the line-backed dun gelding he favored. The horse, Tango by name, had speed and spirit, but was calm enough that Chad could relax and take off on long rides and think. He'd been doing that a lot the last couple of weeks. He'd announced to his management team that he'd be taking a hiatus. He hadn't had the satisfaction of firing Millicent yet, but when that day came, he'd be glad to see the back of that woman.

He lifted a hand and waved at some of the ranch hands as he left the barn. He'd started working with them in the mornings, helping to feed the animals and do odd jobs around the ranch. He had plenty of time to write music, but just sitting up at the ranch house doing nothing drove him insane. Jasmine spent most days at the training complex, either going through refresher training or working with Jared on his case. There hadn't been any movement on it yet. *That* frustrated him to no end. Since he'd been spirited from Nashville, two more people who had lawsuits against him had been found murdered. The press had put two and two together and discovered the link after the third person had died. Now? Well, now the press had strung him up—tried him and found him guilty without any evidence, only speculation. His record sales, however, had skyrocketed. He shook his head. People confused the hell out of him sometimes.

He checked on his mom daily by telephone. She and Zelda didn't watch too much television, so at least her exposure to the media circus that surrounded his hiatus and disappearance had been minimal. The last headline he'd read had him involuntarily committed to a mental institution somewhere in France. He chuckled and tickled his mount's ribs, sending it into a slow lope. He'd told John Smith, the ranch foreman, that he'd ride the eastern pasture and check the fence line before the cattle in the upper pastures were brought down. There was a nip in the air in the mornings now. The evenings required light jackets, and the leaves were starting to turn colors. He'd fallen in love with the simple life surrounding the ranch just as quickly as he'd fallen in love with Jasmine. He hadn't told her yet. The long-legged filly spooked easily, and getting her to open up and allow him in was a never-ending battle. She still kept a large portion of herself from him. He could feel it, but he wasn't sure where it was coming from.

Chad slowed his horse to a walk. The sun rose steadily as he followed the fence line from one pasture to the next. He stopped periodically to mend broken strands of barbed wire. His thoughts returned to Jasmine. They had chemistry in spades. Hot, explosive chemistry. They'd made love every night for the last three weeks, most nights more than once. Did he wonder what it would be like to dominate that woman? Hell yeah. Did he miss it?

Tango's ears shot up, his lungs filled with air, and he whinnied, shaking Chad out of his contemplation. He lifted the brow of his baseball cap and saw the rider coming over the small knoll behind him. A smile spread across his face at the sight of Jasmine on that dapple gray mare she always rode. He reined in and waited for her to catch up.

Did he miss doing scenes? In reality, no. He wasn't sadistic, and while he did enjoy giving the subs he did scenes with the pleasure they desired, pain wasn't his thing. He was a sensualist through and through. He could imagine Jasmine tied and writhing under his touch as he denied her orgasm only to build it back. He wanted to have her beg him for release and then choose whether or not to give it to her. The idea of finding and pushing her boundaries turned his crank with one hell of a lot of force, but if she never got to the point where that could happen? Her smile came into view as she rode closer. If that didn't happen, he'd be just fine as long as he still had her.

"Hey." She pulled up alongside him. He took in her pack, which included a sleeping bag.

"Hey, yourself. Whatcha got there?" He nodded to the filled saddle pack and sleeping bag.

"Well, I kinda have to be out of the house or I may spill Ember's big secret. I thought maybe you'd like to camp out with me tonight."

"I could be convinced." Chad avoided the half-hearted swat at his arm. "What is her big secret? Is she pregnant?"

"I didn't tell you that."

Chad chuckled at the wide-eyed look she turned on him.

"For future reference, sweetheart, anytime you tell a man a woman has a big secret, he will always assume she's pregnant."

"Why is that?"

Chad shrugged his shoulders. "Don't have a clue. May be ingrained into our DNA."

"Huh. Well, I have a big secret."

Chad's head whipped to the right. Jasmine nearly fell out of the saddle laughing at him. She pointed and laughed harder.

"Are you?"

"No! Oh... my... God... that was so funny! You freaked!"

"Woman, I should tan your ass for that." Chad couldn't help joining in on her laughter.

Jasmine stopped laughing suddenly and became silent. Yeah, he could have picked his words better. He saw the top strand of the fence line had snapped. He headed Tango in that direction and started the repair. He used pliers to form a loop from one of the two pieces. He wrapped it down and over on itself so it wouldn't release or unravel. Jasmine's silence while he worked bothered him. He'd obviously hit one of the things bothering her. She didn't like the idea of a spanking, and that was okay. Chad pulled out the wire stretcher and attached both pieces of the strand before he started cranking the lever and pulling the snapped wire together. Once he had enough slack, he threaded the second piece of the barbed wire through the loop he'd made and wrapped the tail around the stretched wire, securing the repair. Come spring, they'd need to check this patch again and replace the entire run if it failed. He put away his tools and swung up into Tango's saddle again.

"I'm sorry if what I said upset you." His mount moved forward down the fence line, and hers kept pace.

"You didn't upset me, but… I want to talk to you about that."

"I'd never hurt you, Jasmine. Pain isn't my thing."

"Okay. But what is your thing?" She glanced over at him and away again. He stopped his horse and waited for her to face him.

"My thing is you."

"But you want more." She kicked her horse, and he caught up.

"I want you."

"But am I enough? I don't understand what you did at the clubs, but I know that it was important, that you took risks to go there and that you were looking for something specific. Why won't you tell me what you want?"

Chad drew a breath and considered his answer. They'd gotten to know each other over the last three weeks. He knew every sensual spot on her body. He knew what kind of food she liked, the name of her first kitten and why her twin sister's hyperactivity drove her up a wall. She knew everything about him except this. It probably wasn't fair that he was keeping it from her.

"When I went to the clubs there were certain things that I enjoyed."

"Like what?"

He drew a deep breath and let it hiss out as he tried to think of words that wouldn't put her off completely. "I'm what is called a sensual dominant. I enjoy the lifestyle. But I don't need that to be happy."

"How would you do that?"

Jasmine's question cut to the chase, didn't it? "Do what?"

"What does it entail, being a sensual dominant?"

They reined to the right and followed the slowly sloping strands of barbed wire in silence. He'd much rather show her the pleasure he could bring her. Telling her might not advance his case. He searched the horizon.

"Why won't you tell me or… show me?"

Chad stopped Tango again and turned in the saddle. She was reaching out to him, and damned if he'd deny her. "Yes, I will, but to do that, you'd have to trust me to take care of you. Do you? Trust me?"

Jasmine's horse shifted. She pulled her eyes away from his momentarily. When she returned to his gaze, she nodded. "I... yes, I do. I want to try to be the woman you want me to be."

Chad shook his head, "Sweetheart, you *are* the woman I want you to be. If we never do a scene, I wouldn't regret it, because it means I have you."

"But you sought them out for years."

Chad nodded. He wouldn't deny it. He gave Tango some slack so he could rub his nose on Jasmine's horse.

"Do you have to have a dungeon?"

A bark of surprised laughter launched from him without a thought. "No, I'm not a sadist. I'm not into pain. How long have you been wondering that?"

Her blush rose quickly to her cheeks.

Chad reached over and touched her face with his leather-gloved fingertip. "I told you I wasn't into pain. Bondage has its place, but I don't need devices to limit your motions. Sometimes it's just a matter of telling you not to move... watching you struggle to do as I ask while I drive you insane with my touch." The tension drained from her shoulders. My God, the misinformation people were pummeled with about the BDSM community. Were there people who had a St. Andrew's cross in their basement? Hell yeah, but there were also people like him who sought the commitment and the connection more than anything else. He'd never found it with another. He had an opportunity with Jasmine. *If she'd just let go.*

"Will you show me?"

He stared at her. Her beautiful green eyes searched his. He nodded. "I will." He leaned over and kissed her quickly before Tango adjusted to his weight and shifted, pulling them apart. His cock pounded against his zipper. It was going to be one hell of a long afternoon.

CHAD WAS STRETCHED out on the sleeping bag. It was unzipped and flopped open over a waterproof tarp that would keep the dew from soaking into the bag. The horses were haltered and tied to a high-line they had strung between two trees near a large stock pond. The small fire they'd built was banked in a ring of rocks. Brilliant red glowed between black and gray cracks in the coals and crags of the charred wood not completely consumed. "The stars are beautiful tonight."

Jasmine looked up from where she sat near the fire.

Chad took off his baseball cap and hung it on his saddle, which he was using as a backrest. His eyes were on her, not the heavens.

She cocked her head and asked, "Are they?"

Chad nodded. "Come here."

Jasmine felt a bolt of unease but lifted to walk over to him. He stopped her before she lay down with him.

"Sit down next to me."

Jasmine blinked at the change in his voice. She looked around, although she knew they were alone.

"Jasmine, you asked me to show you. To do that, you have to trust that I won't let anyone or anything hurt you. I'm not into humiliation. I don't get off on suffering. I want you to feel pleasure and only pleasure. You have a decision to make. Do you trust me enough to take care of you, to ensure nothing happens to you when you are at your most vulnerable?"

She nodded and sat down with him. There was a cool breeze blowing, and the long pasture grasses bent subtly, sashaying back and forth to a concert only they could hear. Chad put his arm around her shoulders and pulled her back into him.

"Scenes aren't something a couple rushes into. In the clubs, they are negotiated. Safe words are decided upon, and limits are outlined. The Dom and sub rarely, if ever, play the night they meet."

"Why?" She felt like a child asking such basic questions, but she wanted to know, to understand him and what he wanted.

Chad drew a breath and looked up at the night sky. "Sex is an intimate act. Sex with a BDSM element is stripped raw, void of most of the armor a person wears on a normal day-to-day basis."

Jasmine leaned her head on his shoulder and gazed up at the tens of thousands of flickering pinpoints of light cast across the massive South Dakota sky. "Why would anyone want to feel that way?"

Chad dropped his gaze and took her hand in his. "When you're truly ready, you'll know, and I'll know." He lifted his arm and pulled her into his lap facing him. "But the one thing you must remember above anything else, if we never get to that point… if we never cross that line, I don't care."

Jasmine dropped her eyes. She knew that was a lie.

He chucked her under her chin, lifting her face up, forcing her to meet his intense gaze. "This is me being as honest as I know how to be. What we have together, right now, at this minute, is better in every way than the lackluster life I led before I met you. I'm happy for the first time in as long as I can remember."

"I never told you that I was engaged." The blurted confession hurt in places she didn't want to remember.

His gaze searched her face as if he wanted to be able to read her thoughts. "What happened?"

"He cheated on me. His lover got pregnant."

"He's a fucking fool."

His anger was misplaced. She had to explain. "No, when he asked me to marry him, I…" Jasmine raked a hand through her hair and blew out a long breath, gathering her nerves. "What we had wasn't like what is between you and me. He used me, and I think in a way I used him. I wanted to have someone who loved me. I wanted someone besides my brothers, sisters, and mom who cared whether or not I came back from assignments. Our relationship failed epically, because we didn't want the same thing. Hell, we didn't even like the same things. He would never sit and look at the stars with me. He would have considered it a waste of time." Jasmine glanced up at Chad and admitted, "I don't."

Chad leaned forward and kissed her softly. "Thank you."

Jasmine leaned into him and whispered, "That line you talked about crossing? I want that, someday. With you."

Chad caressed her cheek with his calloused fingertips. "Believe me, darling, *when,* and *if* the time is right, the stars will be as bright then as they are tonight."

"Promise?" She couldn't help replaying Evan's betrayal over and over in her mind. Couldn't help hearing his vicious words and knowing that he was right, that she had caused him to stray. Would she force Chad away too?

"I cross my heart." Chad leaned forward until she was on her back under him. He nuzzled her neck and licked the shell of her ear, sending a shiver through her. "Now the question is, how do we make love without getting ourselves eaten alive by mosquitoes?"

Jasmine laughed and pushed him off of her. She lunged toward the saddle bags and pulled out a can of mosquito repellant. "I say spray the outside of the bag, strip, get in and zip that puppy up."

The logistics of getting naked took less than thirty seconds after they coated the bag in bug juice.

Getting in and getting it zipped took considerably longer. Jasmine hadn't laughed so hard in years. When they finally got the bag zipped, Chad was on top of her. His long hard cock rested against her upper thigh and abdomen. Jasmine reached down to stroke the velvet soft skin as it moved over the hard contours of his shaft. She felt the wetness at the tip and swept it up in her palm as she lowered for another stroke.

Chad thrust his hips in time with her strokes. His lips sought out hers, and his tongue teased, coaxed and invited her response, taking as much as he was giving. Jasmine lost herself in his kiss and in his hands' caresses. The press of material around them limited their movements. Chad cradled her, his arms under her back, hands wrapped around her shoulders. Their body heat and the sleeping bag's warmth built a sheen of sweat between them. Chad entered her and buried himself deep.

"You feel so good," Chad whispered as he started to withdraw. He slowed when her body stiffened, and she gasped. Jasmine's eyes popped open, and she begged him, "Oh, my God, do that again!"

The wicked smile that blazed across his face held her eyes. He pushed forward and withdrew again, striking the same spot. Jasmine shivered at the combined sensation of his forward thrust against her clit and the slow drag of his hard cock against her channel. She closed her eyes and moaned, "Again." And he did, over and over again. Jasmine was so close. She raked her nails across his shoulders, arching, trying desperately to get him to move just a bit faster. To hit her clit a little harder, thrust back just a bit harsher.

'Please' became the only word she knew. She clawed Chad's back and shoulders, arched under him as far as his weight would allow. Chad's hand grabbed her hair and pulled it just hard enough to still her and make her look at him. "Just feel, baby. Don't fight it. Feel how good we are together."

Jasmine panted for air but didn't break the gaze they shared.

"That's it. So good together."

"Yes." Her world shrank to just Chad and the connection they shared.

"That's right. Just us."

Jasmine nodded, still caught in his hypnotic stare.

"So beautiful." Chad lowered for a kiss and his hips changed tempo. Jasmine didn't have time even to gasp for air before her orgasm tore through her. Every muscle in her body contracted and then expanded, sending her over into an avalanche of sensation that had been just out of reach for so long. She shuddered as he thrust deep and arched his back. His muscles bulged and his face transformed into a mask of pure bliss. He gasped for air before he slumped and dropped his head to her shoulder.

Jasmine floated on the wonderful sensations running through her body. She absentmindedly wove her fingers through Chad's hair. Sex with this man was transformative. If only she could believe that she made him happy enough to forget the lifestyle he'd lived for so many years. He rolled over and pulled her onto her side. They pulled the sleeping bag as high as it would go over their heads, then held each other, unaware of the cool night breezes, the rustle of the pasture grasses or the soft snorts of their horses.

CHAPTER 21

*C*had woke suddenly. The vibration of his cell phone hummed next to them. He pushed the sleeping bag off them and carefully reached over Jasmine to fish through his clothes before he located the phone. He palmed his Guardian-issued phone and glanced at the incoming number. Jared. Naturally, they'd issue him the only type of phone to get service out in the middle of nowhere. Dammit, *MIB, you're a pain in the ass.*

"'Lo." He cleared his throat and tried again. "Hello?"

"Sorry for waking you. I keep forgetting the time change." Jared's smart-ass, cocky voice let him know that last comment was an out-and-out lie.

"Sure you did. What's up?" Jasmine lifted off his

chest and cracked her eyes open long enough for him to kiss her forehead and push her head back down on his chest. He'd worn the woman out last night. She could rest a while longer.

"I thought you should be the first to know we caught up with Burns last night. He evaded apprehension, but we have his car and know where he was living."

Chad's body tensed, and Jasmine rose onto her elbow immediately. He knew she could probably hear, but he pulled the phone away from his ear more so she could hear everything. "You think he could lead us to the killer?" God, he hoped so. The murders had to stop. Once he was completely cleared of the situation, he was having his legal team reach out to all the families to see if there was anything he could do for them.

"We are hoping so... the crime scene techs have pulled partial prints off three of the scenes. There was some random DNA that has no profile attached in CODIS or NDIS. The same gun was used for all of the assassinations. We have a search warrant for this guy's home, car, and person. If it is him, we'll know soon."

Chad glanced up at Jasmine. "CODIS and NDIS?"

"CODIS stands for the Combined DNA Index

System. It is what the FBI uses for matching DNA profiles. NDIS, or the National DNA Index System, is the larger database system of DNA profiles of the US," Jasmine explained.

"A little early for my sister to be up," Jared taunted.

"She's not the one who's up." Chad gave as good as he got. The MIB had grown on him.

"Damn it, Nelson, too much information."

Jasmine laughed and snuggled back into him. "Thanks for calling. I like this ranch living, but..."

"I understand. We are still working it. The press hasn't let up, though your mom and Zelda aren't being harassed."

That was good. He'd been worried. His mom probably would tell him if they were being harassed, but damn, he'd like to be there for her. A damn good thing Guardian was helping. Speaking of which, he needed some of that too. "I keep putting off my management team, but there is paperwork I need to sign, deals that are falling through because I'm inaccessible. If it were just me, I wouldn't mind, but there are jobs and people's welfare to take into account."

"Understood. Have them send it to my office electronically. We will forward it. You can send it back to me, and we'll sanitize the thread before we get it back to them. What can't be done electronically, we'll courier to you."

"Cool. I've been working exclusively with my lawyer. I'll call him later and have him send the documents to you. Do I need to cancel my appearance at the CMAs?"

"When is that?"

"November. I have a performance, and I'm scheduled to present an award. My agent and manager are having a cow. My PR firm wants me to do an interview with *60 Minutes*. They said they could guarantee my privacy."

"No. No one goes to the ranch. That is our sanctuary, and yeah, it is locked down tighter than Fort Knox, but we aren't starting down that slippery slope. We could maybe do a video link interview. We have the ability to ensure the transmission can't be pinpointed. Offer that to your management team."

Jasmine nodded her head on his shoulder. He kissed her before he answered. "I'll run it by Jasmine and make sure my personal security doesn't have a problem with it."

Jared laughed, a carefree sound so at odds with the way he remembered the guy from their first meeting. "You do that. You have no idea how lucky you are to have her at your beck and call. The woman is one of the best PSOs I have, and you've got her all tied up."

"Not yet." Chad's mouth engaged before his brain. Jasmine slapped her hand over her mouth to stop the surprised sound she made.

Jared continued, "I don't want to know. Seriously. I'll work these issues and get back to you as soon as we have more information."

"Thanks!" Chad hit the end button and threw the phone on his clothes before he turned and pounced. He growled and tickled her with his hands while scraping her neck with his morning beard.

Her peals of laughter spooked the horses. They whinnied, but they both ignored them. Chad centered himself over her and leaned in for a kiss. The horses whinnied again. Chad could hear them stomping around along the line where they'd been tied. He didn't care, especially when Jasmine smiled, closed her mouth, and shook her head. "Morning breath," she mumbled through the fingers that flew to her face.

Chad pried at her hands. "It's like garlic. They cancel each other out."

"I'd heard that, but I don't believe it."

Chad jolted and swung his head at the comment.

He stared way up into the eyes of Jasmine's mother and stepfather. They sat on horseback and stared down at them. Jasmine wiggled further under him, damn near crawling down his chest. He lifted, basically doing a plank in the sleeping bag so she could hide.

"Umm... hi?" This was awkward—with a capital A.

Frank took a long glance around the campsite and then back at Chad. "So, I guess this is as good a time as any. What exactly are your intentions toward my stepdaughter, Mr. Nelson?"

Jasmine's head shot up and out of the bag. She looked at her parents around his bicep. "Mom! Frank! Really?" Her mortified gasp brought a flicker of a smile to Frank's face.

Amanda chuckled, leaned over her saddle and brushed her husband's arm with her hand. "Dear, you men can have this conversation later. Jasmine, you and Chad have a good day. Come on, Frank. Let's finish our ride."

Frank grunted before he turned his horse to follow Amanda. He glanced down at them once more before he left and shook his head. Chad felt the reprimand to his toes.

"Guess we should get dressed?" He waited until

the parents were out of hearing range before he asked.

Jasmine groaned. "What are your *intentions*? I'm so embarrassed. Honestly, I'm not a blushing virgin! Oh. My. God. He *didn't* just say that, did he?"

Chad pulled her up from her hiding place under him and kissed her hard. "He did. He cares about you. Come on, let's get some clothes on before someone else rides up."

JASMINE PULLED her hair back and put it into a messy bun before she mounted her horse. Chad had been quiet. She could barely look at him. She understood how mortified he might have been when his mother walked in on him at the beginning of his career. Lord, what she wouldn't give for some mind altering drugs right about now. She lifted into her saddle, and they headed back toward the ranch, following the fence line.

"What are we going to do when the dust settles?" Chad's question surprised her. She hadn't thought about it. Well, that was a lie. She'd thought about it a thousand times and then dismissed the situation because she didn't want to get her hopes up.

"With your case?" Jasmine asked just in case he was talking about the situation with Frank or something else.

He nodded. She shrugged her shoulders. "I don't know."

Chad reached over and grabbed her hand. They rode together like that for a while before he spoke again. "What we have is still new, but it's different... better. I don't want to lose this."

Jasmine felt the weight of his words in her soul. She knew he meant them. But there were so many reasons they would never last. Work being the primary reason. "Our schedules are insane. You'll go back to being you, appearing at the CMAs, writing hit songs, singing them. I travel the world for my job. I'm home maybe two months a year and not all at one time. I like what I do." She squeezed his hand and let it go when he pulled up at another broken strand of barbed wire. He dismounted and began working on the severed wire.

"I like what we have. I just want to know if it has an expiration date in your mind." Chad looked over his shoulder at her. He straightened and let Tango nudge him with his nose. "See, I'm of the opinion it doesn't if we don't want it to end. I've made up my mind. I'm done performing except for maybe special appearances that I choose. I love to write music, so that will be my focus." He looked across the rolling hills, and Jasmine followed his gaze. "I'm at peace here. I could see myself on a ranch, working... writing songs, being happy. Traveling for enjoyment, not business. Seems like a good life." He grabbed a pair of pliers and twisted the tightened wire together.

Jasmine leaned on her saddle horn with her forearm and ran her fingers through her horse's mane. The idea of them being together was a new one, one she'd just let herself start to think about. The tiny glimpses of hope she'd allowed herself to keep hadn't developed yet. She trusted Chad to understand her hesitance. They were new. She was more than a little skittish on talking about a future. The last time she'd planned on spending her life with someone, she'd been hurt. There were so many things tumbling through both of their worlds. Making a decision about anything now would be insane.

"It is good. Here and now. I don't have any answers for you. I don't know what the future will hold, but I do want to spend time with you. What we have? I know it is different, special. But it is still so new." Jasmine hoped he'd understand her caution.

Chad pulled off his baseball cap and wiped his brow before he started putting his tools away. "One day at a time, then?"

Jasmine waited until he mounted again. A sense of peace and contentment flooded her. She took his hand when he offered it. "Yeah, one day at a time."

CHAPTER 22

C had poured four three-finger glasses of Scotch and gripped the tops of the crystal tumblers, carrying them to the poker table. Dixon, Drake, and Adam were playing tonight. The four of them were more or less the regulars. Frank, Joseph and the ranch manager, John Smith, rotated in when one of them couldn't make it. This was the sixth week he'd sat in the same chair and played cards. He'd learned that Thursday night poker was a serious tradition, almost as serious as the ladies' *Supernatural* and wine night. It was a damn good show. He'd gotten sucked in and had been Netflicking one or two a day for the last six weeks. At this rate, it would take another year to catch up, but with Guardian no closer to the killer, he had time.

"Thanks." Dixon spoke around a mouthful of sandwich. Chad shook his head. The amount of food that the men around here consumed was astronomical. Of course, he'd also gotten roped into daily workouts with the Wonder Twins and Doc, as Chad had come to know the doctor. Doc had revealed the "Wonder Twins" moniker, and did that label pull a smile. The men ran the training complex and had designed the wind and solar farm in the next valley that powered the complex and kept it completely off the grid. They could throw the switch and use commercial power, but for the last year and a half, the complex hadn't needed it. An energy farm also powered the ranch. The men were freaking geniuses, and he'd never met two more down to earth guys.

"Let's start it easy with some five card draw." Drake shuffled and set the cards in front of Chad for a cut before he dealt them out.

"Any word this week on your case?" Dixon asked right before he took another huge bite of roast beef sandwich.

"Nah, Jared said they had another lead on the guy about a week ago. I'm not getting my hopes up again. This guy is like a ghost." Chad saw the look that passed between the other three. They did that often, and he'd gotten used to it. There was shit he couldn't know.

"Did they get the DNA back? Who didn't ante?" Doc tapped the table, and Dixon threw in his chips.

"They got the profile back, but there are no matches in the databases."

Dixon upped the bet, and the rest of them called. Chad looked at his hand again and pulled two to discard. He had three threes. Not bad for a first hand.

"Jasmine over with Keelee and Ember?" Drake asked as he dealt the remainder of the hand.

"Yeah, and Amanda. They don't miss a night of Dean and Sam." Chad looked up from his cards.

"Or wine." All four of them said at once, and laughed.

"How long you two worked for Guardian?" Chad asked the twins.

Dixon looked at Drake, and they both shrugged. "Seems like all our adult life. We did an enlisted hitch in the Marine Corps even though we both had master's degrees in engineering at the time."

"Told you we should have gone in as officers."

"Did you want to keep shoveling shit on that Kentucky horse farm until we got commissions? It could have been over a year before they had slots for both of us."

"True. Besides, we probably wouldn't have met Mike if we waited for the commissions."

"Mike?" Chad hadn't heard that name before.

"Yeah, Mike's a hell of a guy. He worked here for a while before he moved on. He's probably the only man who speaks less than Joseph."

Chad followed the latest bid. He hadn't drawn the other three, but he had drawn a pair of sixes. Full house. "No shit. He talks less than Joseph?"

"Yep, Chief uses words sparingly." Doc threw in his bet and called.

"Chief?"

"Nickname. He's of Native American descent."

"Do you know, he has yet to tell me what tribe he's from?" Dixon put his hand down. "Three fives."

"Hell, over the years, I've heard several guesses, but nothing from him." Drake laid his hand down as he spoke. "Nothing."

"Saw a picture of his mom and dad once. He got his looks from his mom and his stature from his dad. His dad was in a cop uniform, short hair, but even in the black and white picture it didn't look like his dad was Native American." Dixon spoke as Adam laid down his hand. "A pair of kings."

"What were you doing snooping in his shit?" Drake asked.

Chad laid his cards down. "Full house." He raked the pot in as the guys groaned.

"I wasn't, it was when he got shot at Joseph's place. I pulled his wallet out of his clothes that were torn to hell and the photo fell out. I put it back and let it be. And dammit, why does the rich guy win the pot?" Dixon took a pull of his drink.

Chad clucked his tongue and stacked his new chips. "You've won plenty off me, D-man."

"I think you have me confused with him." Dixon nodded toward Drake.

Chad shook his head. "Nope, since Doc told me about that scar, I've been able to tell the difference."

"Dammit, Doc, You can't be giving our secrets away like that!" Dixon whined.

Drake waved a hand in the air and replied, "He isn't bound by any Hippocratic scar oath, you oaf."

"Oaf? Seriously? If I'm an oaf what does that make you?"

Chad knew not to get in the middle of them. So did Doc. Adam leaned back in his chair and raised his eyebrow, waiting for the twins to remember they were playing a game. The man's patch made him look sinister, but he was probably one of the nicest guys Chad had ever met—for a former mercenary. He'd laugh, but it was true, and that freaked him out just a little bit. Doctors weren't supposed to be fighters… were they? In fact, most of the people at the ranch were either PSOs or elite team members, but there were several investigative types that rolled through to attend training. The hospital always seemed to have someone in it healing. Chad had gone over several times and had spent a couple of hours singing and chatting with those going through rehab or still in hospital beds.

They had played three more hands before Chad refilled the glasses. He gave up the pretense and brought the bottle over.

"You getting antsy to get out of here yet?" The doctor's question split the sudden silence.

Chad lifted his eyes from his cards and found all three men looking at him. "Nah, when this all blows over, I'm announcing my retirement."

"Seriously? You pulling a Garth?" Dixon passed a bag of chips to his brother.

"No, he isn't. Garth had a wife and two kids he was retiring to take care of… didn't he?" Drake looked at Chad.

"Dude, that was before my time. I've heard a lot of different stories, but yeah, he did walk away. I have enough money to last, and other business ventures to keep me busy. I love life on the ranch. Hell, I've written ten songs and have the melody for at least three more. I'm happy here." Chad grabbed a couple of kernels of popcorn and ate them.

"So, you could buy a spread around here." Doc concentrated on his cards as he spoke.

"Yeah? Where? I think Frank and the Hollisters have all the land around here sewn up, don't they?"

Dixon shook his head and looked at Drake. They both popped matching smiles. Doc shrugged and threw his discards into the pot. "The Koehlers had a ranch. It's run down, and the house needs to be torn down, but there's land, and it's not too far from here. Jared's husband Christian is one of the heirs. The boys asked Frank not to buy it because of the bad memories it holds for them and, well, no one else has that type of money to drop. You'd be out of the public eye. Hollister has learned *not* to be friendly to paparazzi. Hell, when it comes to protecting one of their own, those town folks can even be downright antisocial."

Chad turned that thought around in his head as much as the scotch would let him. He didn't see a downside. Close enough that he and Jasmine could... His thoughts hit a huge speed bump. Would Jasmine want to stay? He decided not to dwell on that question.

If he had enough land, he could build a studio, produce his records and tour when or if he wanted —streamline the number of appearances. The idea of being able to record here... that had merit. Jasmine could be close to her family. Close to the Guardian complex. But would she want to live in the middle of nowhere? As much as they'd talked, they'd studiously avoided speaking about the future.

He glanced up at the guys, realizing he'd spaced out on them. "Wouldn't hurt to take a look at the property. Should I ask someone to take me over?"

"We can, on Saturday." Dixon motioned to the three of them.

"Cool. Let me know when. I can go any time after the morning feeding." Chad worked with the hands feeding the horses and stock in the pastures closest to the house. Hell, he'd even spent two weeks mowing alfalfa and running the baler. Yeah, he loved music and the thrill of performing, but this place gave him a bone-deep contentment—a type of spiritual peace that he hadn't even found on the high he got from ten thousand fans singing his songs with him while he strummed. Oh, that was magical, but this... this was... home.

* * *

JASMINE WATCHED as Ember topped off everyone's wine glasses. She poured herself another cranberry juice. It was expected, because Adam was playing poker. One of the two doctors permanently assigned to the complex always refrained from drinking if the other was being social, but now that Ember was pregnant, Adam was off the hook for a few months. Besides, if Ember tried to eat or drink anything remotely unhealthy, Joseph growled and fumed. Overprotective to begin with, the man hovered now. Jasmine loved watching the couple, and even though Ember protested, the woman blossomed under her husband's intense adoration.

Their show had just ended, and Sam had been cast into purgatory. Again.

"If you were single and had a chance to date either Sam or Dean, who would it be?" Ember asked as she sank into the chair.

Keelee closed one eye and looked at Ember. "Sam, he's taller and so cute."

Ember scrunched her nose. "Definitely Dean. Have you seen those YouTube videos of him lip-syncing 'Eye of the Tiger' on the Impala? He's a hottie."

"Neither, both are too young for me." Amanda sniffed in an aristocratic manner and then bust out laughing. "Either, they are adorable!"

Jasmine laughed at the women. They all loved their husbands so much it was a tangible force, but they could be the ultimate fangirls too.

"What about you, Jazz? You're single." Ember asked. "Well, taken, but single."

Jasmine took a drink of her wine. "I think I have someone hotter than Sam or Dean, so neither."

All three women dropped their jaws and looked at her.

Amanda closed her mouth and shook her head. "She's a goner. Okay, ladies, bust out Keelee's wedding planner and we can start working on Jasmine's big day."

"Whoa! Hey, he's never, *ever* hinted at anything permanent!" Jasmine was half out of her seat when the three women started laughing.

"Oh, ha ha ha. That is so not funny!" Jasmine pushed back into Keelee's leather sofa and drank half of the wine remaining in her glass.

"Sweetheart, we've all been there—that point when you know in your heart that you love him, but you aren't sure of his feelings for you. It happens to everyone." Amanda patted Jasmine's leg.

Keelee almost choked on her wine. "Hell, I wish it was a moment of time. With Adam and I… well, let's just say I'm happy those years of my life are in the past."

Ember nodded solemnly and added, "Joseph and I had a rough time because of his profession." She blinked several times as if pulling herself out of the memories. Ember had gone through hell when she'd thought Joseph had died.

"Well, Frank and I had instant attractions. We're both too old to deal with the drama of it all. On our third, no, the fourth date, he told me he planned on marrying me, and I told him I thought that was a fine idea."

Jasmine leaned back and smiled at her mom. She deserved the happiness she'd found. "Chad and I are…" Jasmine searched for a term or a phrase to explain what they had together. "Hell, I don't know what we are."

"Then maybe you should ask?" Keelee ventured.

"I'm not sure I want to look behind that door, yet. I mean, once his case is settled, he's got to go back to his world and deal with the detritus that this situation has left in its wake. I'll go on to a new case. Honestly, I don't know why I haven't been reassigned already. He's safe here."

"You haven't been reassigned because Nelson refuses to stay unless you're here." Joseph's voice startled all of them.

"Dammit, Joey, you nearly scared the hell out of us!" Ember jumped up to fuss at him, but smiled as he stalked into the room. He hugged her to him and grabbed her ass, hoisting her up. She wrapped her legs around his waist, and he turned to walk out of the room. Ember peeked over his shoulder and waved. Her laughter prevented her from speaking.

Keelee, Amanda, and Jasmine sighed, looked at each other and burst out laughing. "I'm going to go peek in on Elizabeth and then grab us some nibbles to go with our wine and gossip."

Jasmine watched her leave and sighed. "I like him, Mom. I'm falling in love with him, and I'm scared to death. You've seen him perform here. You've heard him. He's too good to retire. His life is music, and I know he'll regret giving it up. And then there's me." She could feel her throat constrict under the emotions that pressed down on her. She'd tried to ignore the connection she felt to Chad. Tried to stop the waterfall of fear and insecurities.

"Oh, baby. You are so special and wonderful. I can tell by the way he looks at you, he cares about you."

Jasmine sniffed and wiped at the tears that fell. "But does he feel the same way? I mean, he's had his pick of women. He's Chad *freaking* Nelson, Mom. He's a superstar! You should see him perform. The night I was at his show there were tens of thousands of fans singing his songs back to him. What in the world can I give him that he doesn't already have?"

"Love, baby. Love."

Jasmine leaned into her mom and closed her eyes. "It wasn't enough for Evan."

"Evan didn't love you. He loved the connections he could obtain by being married to you. I think deep in your heart you knew that. Your brothers didn't like him."

Jasmine's laugh was more like a sob. She knew that. They had made their dislike for Evan obvious. She glanced up at her mom before she asked, "Did you?"

Her mom stroked her hair. "You loved him. It was enough for me."

"So you didn't like him?"

"Well… I *really* like Chad." Jasmine laughed at her mother's dancing around an answer and wiped her cheeks again. Her mom was an amazing woman.

"We all do." Keelee brought in a tray of cheese, meats, and crackers plus another bottle of wine.

"Why is it so hard? The emotions I'm dealing with, the uncertainty. Every time I start to think of a future with him, I have to remind myself he isn't like us. He's a superstar. I'm... so lost... I mean, with Evan it wasn't..."

"You can't compare what you had with Evan to what you have with Chad." Her mom kissed her on the top of the head as Keelee refilled everyone's wine glasses.

"Speaking from experience, if you let this man go without telling him what you feel, you'll regret it for the rest of your life. If he doesn't feel the same about you..."

Amanda interrupted Keelee. "With the looks I've seen him giving you when he thought no one was looking? He feels the same way."

Keelee nodded and continued, "Don't let this opportunity slip by. I almost lost Adam. When he was fighting for his life in that cave in Afghanistan, he didn't know I loved him and then his injuries... Just tell him, Jasmine. Don't wait."

CHAPTER 23

*C*had waited on their bed. They'd given up the pretense of sleeping in two separate rooms after that memorable morning when her parents caught them nude in the same sleeping bag. He listened to Jasmine moving in the bathroom while the myriad of possibilities presented by buying a ranch nearby floated through his mind. He needed to find the opportunity to talk to her.

The bathroom door opened, illuminating her silhouette. The woman was breathtakingly beautiful. He turned onto his side and pulled the bedcovers back. The light turned off, and he heard rather than saw her pad across the floor to the bed. He pulled her into his body. Her cold feet against his shins made him jolt.

"Shit, woman, what did you do? Put your feet in an ice bath?"

Jasmine snuggled closer, wrapping herself around him. "You're always so warm. My built-in furnace." Her low sultry laugh had his already semi-hard cock rock solid in two seconds flat.

He grabbed her ankle as her foot snaked to the back of his leg and started up toward his thigh. No shit, his woman was an ice cube tonight. "I think I'll buy you slippers for Christmas. Dammit, your feet are cold, woman!"

Jasmine suddenly stilled.

He rolled on top of her so he could see her face in the moonlight that filtered through the window. "What?"

"Nothing."

"No, that's not true. Something made you pull away from me. What is it?"

"You said you were going to buy me slippers for Christmas," she whispered.

"I did." He didn't know why that upset her.

"Are we going to be together then?"

Ahh... the question of the day, it seemed. He settled between her legs and propped himself on his elbows so he could concentrate on her. "I want to be."

She turned her head, avoiding his eyes.

He tucked a finger under her chin and lifted her face back toward him. "Do you?" Shit. The shimmer of tears filled her eyes. He caught one as it overflowed and fell down her temple toward her ear.

"I need to tell you something."

Chad closed his eyes at those whispered words. He lowered his head to her shoulder. The light perfume of her lotion drifted through his senses. The fear of losing her lanced his gut. He didn't want to hear the words, but he needed to know where he stood. He loved her. Bone-deep and oceans wide. He was so fucked if she didn't feel the same way. He kissed the swell of her breast and took a deep breath before he lifted his head. "What do you need to tell me?"

She lifted her fingers to his face and traced his lips. Her eyes glittered with unshed tears.

He grabbed her hand and kissed the palm. Good God, he was terrified right now.

"I... I love you."

Chad stared at her. Her tears fell unabated. He felt his heart beat for what seemed like the first time. She loved him. His heartbeat steadied into the tempo of the greatest love song he'd ever heard. She loved him.

"I love you, too." He lowered his lips to hers and consumed her through their kiss. Her arms wrapped around his neck and held him tight as he molded his body to her soft curves. Every thought, every dream, every hope he'd ever had focused on the passion of the kiss they shared. Her legs wrapped around him and his hips thrust, finding her core. He refused to break their connection, their shared breath. His body found hers and he thrust into her.

They were a perfect fit. She'd become the entity that filled the vacuum that had existed in the center of his soul. He moved in and out of her body. The intimacy of their connection reflected in the lingering kiss. They moved together, a perfect melody of beautiful notes. He drove them steadily toward the peak of their passion. He felt her clench around him, heard the catch of her breath. He lifted and drove into her as deep as he could, grinding against her, extending her release and launching his own. Chad lowered over her once again and stole her panted breaths. "I love you, sweetheart."

Jasmine ran her hands down his back. "I was afraid you didn't feel the same way."

Chad rolled to his side and pulled her into his chest. "You were?" He threaded his hands through her mass of hair, pulling it away from her body to help cool her flushed skin.

"I haven't thought about the future because I didn't want to consider the possibility you wouldn't be in it." She bent her head back and looked up at him. "I know your world is on its ear right now. You'll need to go back to Nashville, and I don't know where I fit in… if I fit in."

"I'm not going anywhere without you."

She drew random patterns on his chest with her fingertip. "I don't know your world."

"I don't want you to know it, and I don't want to go back to it. I want to create a new life with you." He'd been given the perfect opportunity to do that. Even if the little ranch didn't pan out, he liked the idea of going off the grid, controlling his life, writing and recording when he wanted, making appearances on his schedule, not the label's.

"How? What does that new life look like to you?"

Chad lifted up onto his elbow. He looked down at the woman he loved. He pushed a stray strand of hair over her ear. "You want the edited version, or are you awake enough for the whole damn dream?"

Jasmine mimicked his position. "I've got nowhere to be in the morning. Tell me the dream."

Chad leaned forward and kissed her before he flopped down onto his back and allowed her to settle in beside him. "So... I was talking to the twins and Doc..."

JASMINE YAWNED and sipped at the second cup of coffee of the morning. She sat in Dixon's office while he was out with one of the training cadre going over the newest course they had developed. She'd seen the outline on how to detect and counter the threat of 3D printed weapons. She shook her head and took another sip of coffee as she waited for Jared's call. He'd texted her at three this morning, six his time, that he would be calling. He was late, and that was rare. His secretary kept him on a tight schedule, so Jasmine knew something important had come up. She'd wait and drink her coffee.

She leaned back in Dixon's huge leather chair. The permanent smile on her face today had everything to do with the dreams Chad had shared with her. He'd asked for her input, wanted to know her opinions, and they had talked for hours and built the idea of a life together into a goal they would strive to reach. The Koehler ranch was small, but it would be perfect for what Chad and Jasmine had decided they wanted.

The phone rang, startling her from her daydream. She answered it on the second ring, putting it on speaker phone so she could wipe up the coffee that had spilled when she jumped.

"Training Complex, Office of the Wonder Twins, how may I direct your call?"

"Jazz, secure the line." Jasmine headed to the office door, shut it and hit the red button beside the cypher lock. The lights in the panel flashed from red to yellow and then to green.

"Secure, what's up?" She spoke as she walked back to the desk and her coffee.

"We finally got him last night. He was cornered. He knew it, and rather than giving himself up, he put a bullet through his chest." *No, no, no!* They needed answers.

"Is he dead?"

"He is now. Lasted for about four minutes before he bled out. Carlson got to him. He admitted to the killings." Jasmine drew a stuttered breath. The assassinations were only half the problem.

"Who hired him?"

"Carlson asked him. He said the guy faded fast, but he got one word. Millicent."

She dropped back into the chair. It fit. Millicent was at the house when the second threat had been delivered. "Is she talking?" Jasmine knew the woman had to be in custody.

"The FBI picked her up about thirty minutes after Burns died. She copped for a lawyer immediately and refuses to say a word."

"So she was the insider threatening Chad?"

"What? I didn't hear you."

Jasmine pulled her fingernail out of her mouth. She hadn't realized she was chewing on it until that second.

"Do you think she was the inside threat?" she repeated, and picked up her coffee cup, giving her hands something to do.

"It looks like it. The motive is what escapes me, though." Jared paused for a moment. Jasmine could hear someone speaking in the background.

"Jason just came in, Jazz."

"Hey, Jace." She acknowledged her brother.

"Hey. We've been over this six ways to Sunday. We don't have a motive, but we don't have any other suspects. I'd like to give Nelson the option of leaving the ranch. Guardian, and by that I mean Jared, will hold a press conference in thirty minutes. Chad will be wholly exonerated. The details of Ms. Wicker's involvement will not come to light until the investigation is over. I know Chad has the CMAs in two weeks. I'm sure he'll want to get in front of this mess."

Jasmine nodded her head even though her brothers couldn't see her. "I'm not leaving his side until we know for a fact Millicent was the inside threat."

"We figured." Jason's voice held a humorous undertone.

"Oh, and FYI, I'm giving you my two weeks' notice." Jasmine waited for a response, but nothing came. "Hello? Y'all still there?"

One of her brothers cleared his throat. Jared finally spoke. "May we ask why?"

Jasmine didn't stifle the bubbling joy she felt. "I'm taking a new position."

"What? With who?" That was Jason's roar.

"With Chad. I'm going to be his chief of security."

She didn't have to wait this time for the comments.

"Well, it's about time."

"Damn straight, about time Nelson acted." Her brothers spoke over each other.

Jasmine scoffed, "Like you knew what was happening!"

"Jazz, honey, the only two who didn't have a clue how perfect you two are together was... well, you two," Jason taunted.

"Whatever." Jasmine could feel the blush rising to her cheeks. "So can I ask a question?"

"Shoot," Jared responded.

"Do you guys like Chad?" *Silence*. Her thumbnail found its way between her teeth again.

"Yeah, we do. He is his own man. He faced this shit storm and dealt with it. Not many men would have been able to deal with the amount of crap that was flung at him." Jason's words brought a sheen of tears to her eyes.

"Thank you."

"Besides, now I have an in for concert tickets," Jared teased.

"Ass."

"Brat."

"I love you guys." She didn't try to disguise the tears in her voice.

"And we love you. Go tell your guy what's up. Give Dixon and/or Drake a heads up, and one or both of them will fly you to Nashville when you're ready to go."

"I will."

She hung up and wiped the tears from her eyes. She drew a deep breath and straightened her shoulders. She had some great news to deliver and the start of a new life to begin with Chad.

CHAPTER 24

he rush of the past two weeks seemed to meld together into one long interview. Chad's manager, Terry, had secured the services of another PR firm while his lawyers severed all relationships with Millicent's company. Just as he suspected, once he left her stables, all the other talent started jumping ship. Of course, the fact that the woman was being held without bond for the hired murder of five people may have had something to do with that too. The forensic accountants had found money transfers to Burns for the past four years. While there had been no spike in the accounts at the time of the murders, the money, the deathbed confession, and circumstantial evidence were enough to remand her until trial.

Chad and Jasmine cleaned house in Nashville. Everyone had been given notice to find other places to live when he first arrived in South Dakota, and Chad had provided financial assistance in locating other residences. Chad put Kirk in charge of ensuring everyone was settled. He hadn't seen Kirk since the day he'd walked out of his complex over two months ago.

At Jason's suggestion, Chad had met with his lawyers and management team away from his Nashville complex and conducted all meetings at his lawyer's offices. Jasmine's security teams made certain of their privacy. She'd been busy updating his security, getting a handle on his travel arrangements and his interview schedule, and working with the CMAs security on his performance and presentation. Chad spent hours behind closed doors with his legal team and pounded out a path forward. He worked through countless mountains of paperwork, started the process of divesting three companies, and initiated the groundwork for his own recording label.

He and Jasmine had put an offer on the Koehler place, which was accepted immediately. They had been meeting with architects in Nashville to draft the blueprints of their new home—a home, not the hotel that his Tennessee mansion had turned into. Jasmine was in charge of everything except the music room and the recording studios.

Chad stretched and pushed away from his desk in the office. The house was eerily quiet. He didn't realize how much noise had been in his life BG, or Before Guardian. Chad stood and cracked his back. They'd be leaving tomorrow morning after the awards ceremony. They were moving to South Dakota, permanently.

With a smile, Chad pulled the center drawer of his desk open, grabbed a small black velvet box and pocketed it. He hadn't found the exact right time to ask her... yet. A smile spread across his face. The song he was singing tonight was new. *I Am, With You,* was the song he'd written while traveling with Jasmine to South Dakota. He'd be singing it with his guitar as his only accompaniment. He glanced at the grandfather clock across the room. After placing all the documentation for his lawyers in a briefcase, he wandered out into the hall and down the stairs. He crossed through the massive entryway and headed back to the rooms where Jasmine's security team was headquartered.

"Hey, Chad, what can we do for you?"

Chad lifted the leather case. "The last of the

documents for the lawyers. You guys got everything you need to close up shop?"

"Yes, sir, we are good to go. We'll have a skeleton crew here. The rest will fly with you and Jasmine to the training complex. We'll leave from there and head home for Thanksgiving. After that? Who knows where we'll end up."

"Thank you for making these two weeks easier."

"Not a problem, it's what we do."

Chad shook the man's hand. He hadn't known any of the team long, but each and every one of them were good men.

He swung through the kitchen on the way back upstairs and grabbed a tray of cheese and fruit. From experience, he knew they needed to eat before the awards ceremony. The first time he went, he didn't eat and his stomach damn near ate through his backbone by the time he got to some food at one of the after-parties—if you could call the little bits of nothing they served food. He'd ended up going out with his crew. They invaded the closest McDonald's, ate and played an impromptu a cappella jam session. Bad idea. The cops had to respond due to the traffic jam they caused. Lord, he'd been fussed at by his manager and Millicent for that stunt. The smile slid from his face at the thought of the woman who was capable of hiring a killer to murder innocent people. He couldn't figure her motives. Why would she do something like that? What could she possibly stand to gain? And threatening him? It just didn't make sense. Talk about killing the golden goose.

He opened the music room door. "Jazz, where are you?" He heard a muffled thump from the bedroom. She'd been stressing over which dress to wear tonight. The woman was probably still trying to make a decision.

The door to the bedroom stood slightly ajar. He kicked it open and made a grand display of the tray he carried, only to drop the thing at the sight of what greeted him.

"Move, and she dies." Blood trickled from Jasmine's mouth and nose and soaked the gag Kirk had stuffed in her mouth. Crimson trickled down her chin, over her breast, and stained her white lace bra. Her right eye was swelling shut, and Kirk held a gun to her temple. Chad swallowed hard and looked up into Kirk's eyes. Jasmine had fought back. The man's eyebrow had been laid open, his cheek had a huge red welt, and his lip was split. *How the hell did he get the upper hand?*

"Kirk? Why?"

The man grabbed a handful of Jasmine's hair. She swayed on her knees, her eyes boring into Chad's.

"You were supposed to die, you son of a bitch! You were supposed to take the rap for the murders or die, so she'd see me!" Spittle spewed from the man's mouth and hung suspended from his lips. Kirk's hands shook. He pushed the gun into the side of Jasmine's head, forcing her sideways. That's when Chad realized blood was running down the back of her arm.

"Jasmine sees you, Kirk."

"Not *her*, you asshole! Millicent. Your precious bodyguard is the reason it all went to hell! I'm going to kill this bitch! She took Milli from me!"

Chad's mind whirred, trying to make connections. "She didn't do anything, Kirk. She was with me. Millicent went to jail for hiring a killer."

"No, you stupid motherfucker! *I* hired Burns! *I* told him who to kill! *I* was the one who left you death threats when the fucking FBI wouldn't investigate you for the murders! You were supposed to be blamed. She'd see you weren't what she needed in her life. Then she'd see she needed me!"

Chad's gut dropped as the puzzle pieces all locked into place. Kirk lifted Jasmine by the hair. She struggled to stand up with her arms tied behind her

KRIS MICHAELS

back. She shot a look toward the bed where she kept her gun. Chad followed her eyes and then looked at her again. She shot another hard look at the bed and crumpled, falling away from Kirk. The man's grasp of her hair prevented her from hitting the floor. The bastard raged at her action, kicking her back violently, tearing a scream from behind her gag.

Chad dove for the bed. He slid over the silk sheets, his hands diving beneath Jasmine's pillow. A sharp pain sliced through his arm. Chad rolled off the bed, falling to the floor, and pointed the gun. Kirk pulled Jasmine in front of him by her hair. "I'll kill you both!"

Jasmine's eyes darted down to the right before he saw her leg flash forward. Then she propelled it backward into Kirk's kneecap. He fell forward, the gun slipping from Jasmine's temple to in front of her face. Jasmine lurched and used her body to move his arm away from Chad. Kirk squeezed off a round that shattered the bedroom window. Jasmine fell to the ground, but Kirk remained standing. He took aim at the back of Jasmine's head. Chad opened fire and emptied the clip into the madman.

Kirk's body jerked with the force of each bullet. His arm flew up, the gun still gripped in his hand. He squeezed the trigger again in his macabre dance.

Kirk stumbled backward and slammed into the wall. The man's eyes traveled toward Chad. Blood frothed from his lips and down his chin. Small dark stains of blood spread slowly across the man's shirt before his body crumpled, sliding in a ragdoll fashion down the wall. Chad lunged toward Jasmine. His right arm was numb and useless. He used his left to remove the gag.

"Gun. Get his gun!" Jasmine gasped. Chad reached over and removed the gun from lifeless fingers. The pounding of footsteps up the stairs and the crashing in of his music room doors spiked his adrenaline again. He lifted Kirk's weapon and leveled it on the door. Jasmine rolled to her side and yelled, "Secure Tempest!" His security team charged into the room. Chad dropped the weapon and tried to untie Jasmine's hands. "Someone get me a fucking knife!" he yelled. A blade appeared and sliced through her bindings.

"Ambulance is on the way. We need to get the bleeding stopped, Mr. Nelson."

Chad nodded. "She's bleeding heavy. Down her back. Need to make sure she's okay."

"Yes, sir. We'll take care of her, too."

"Too?" Chad blinked up at the security specialist. He didn't understand. "Who else is hurt?"

Jasmine reached out and grabbed his hand from her prone position on the floor. He swung his head back to his beautiful woman. Her eye was swollen shut and blood smeared across her face, but she was the most beautiful woman in the world.

Her lips moved. Had she spoken? He blinked hard to clear his vision and peered down at her. He knew she'd said something. But things weren't making sense. He stared at her hand in his. Dammit, he was tired. Movements and voices jumbled into a cascade of noise that obliterated everything.

CHAPTER 25

*C*had woke up when his mom called his name. He felt like he'd drunk a whole bottle of scotch by himself. Lord, this couldn't be good. He hadn't gotten this drunk in years. His momma was going to whip his ever-loving hide. Chad peeled his eyes open and squinted in the direction of her voice.

"Mom?" He blinked, but the light was too bright to keep his eyes open.

"That's right, Teddy. Open your eyes for me. I want to make sure you're not brain damaged."

Chad licked his lips but kept his eyes closed. "Your fault. You dropped me one too many times."

A low rumble of laughter sounded to his right.

Chad tried to lift his hand to block the bright lights. "Oh, fuck me. That hurts!"

"Teddy, language."

He rolled his head toward his mom's voice. "Sorry. Turn off the lights, yeah?" He heard a click and blinked his eyes open without blistering pain searing his corneas to the back of his brain. *Hospital. Jasmine. Oh, fuck, Kirk!*

Chad launched upwards, only to have strong arms push him back into the bed. "No! Dammit! Jasmine! I have to help Jasmine!"

"You did, Chad. She's safe. She's safe."

Chad grabbed at the arms that pinned him to the bed.

Dixon smiled at him and repeated his words. "You saved her from Kirk. She's safe. They have her in a room down the hall. She's pretty banged up, but she'll be just fine."

"I want to see her. Man, you've got to get me to her room."

"Teddy, you just got out of surgery. Jasmine's momma and family are down there. These two boys have been here since they all flew in."

"Surgery?"

"A bullet tore through your inner arm and nicked an artery. You lost a shit-ton of blood. They repaired it. Don't worry. You'll still be able to play the harp, Martha."

"Damn, that's cool. I never could before. Seriously, though, Double D, y'all need to take me to Jasmine."

"Not right now, son." His mom answered for the guys. Hell, he saw the willingness in their eyes. He needed to get his mom occupied with something else, but she wasn't budging. Finally, he just shook his head. "You don't understand. I love her. I need to make sure she's okay."

"I know, baby. A momma always knows. She's resting. Like you should be."

Chad shook his head. He needed to see her. Kirk… Kirk… oh fuck, he'd killed Kirk. He grabbed at Dixon's hand. "I shot him. He was going to kill Jasmine. I killed Kirk."

Dixon squeezed his hand in return. "Yeah, Jasmine and the team gave their statement. The cops are going to want to talk to you, but it is just a formality. Guardian's people found a money trail that connects Kirk to Burns, and the deposits just before and after each murder substantiate his claim that he was responsible."

He loosened his grip and tried to control his breathing. "Millicent?"

"She's out of custody."

"He loved her."

"I think she knew. That's why she wouldn't say anything. Maybe in some messed up way, she loved him too. He was insane, Teddy. His obsession ate away at him for years." His momma ran her hand through his hair as she spoke. "As soon as the doctors clear it, we'll wheel you down to Jasmine's room, or if she can move before you, she can come down here."

"Where is she?" he asked Drake.

The guy smiled and lifted an eyebrow. "Two doors down the hall to your left as you exit."

Chad nodded. He took a deep breath and closed his eyes. He just needed a little rest before he got up out of bed.

Rest wasn't going to happen, though. First, the doctors came through, then the nurses, after them the detectives needed a statement, and then the MIB showed up along with Amanda and Frank. His mom hovered like a helicopter and Dixon and Drake hung out until the room got too crowded. Dammit. He wanted to see Jasmine, and he hurt. Hurt like a motherfucker, but he couldn't show it because he needed to get to Jasmine. Chad's nurse showed up, chased everyone out, put a syringe into his IV and hit the plunger. It was the last thing he remembered until something woke him. When he opened his eyes, it was dark. Sounds of a busy hospital filtered in from the hall. A noise drew his attention to the door. It opened, flooding the room with light. Doc wheeled Jasmine into his room.

Her face was mottled with bruises and swollen, but she was the most beautiful woman he'd ever seen.

"Chad, if you can slide over without too much discomfort we can make this transfer happen." Adam lowered his bedrail, and Chad scooched over, lifting his good arm to make room for her. Jasmine groaned as she lifted off the wheelchair with Adam's help. The small whimper when she lay down beside him told him how much pain she was in.

Adam covered them both and made sure Chad's IV wasn't tangled up.

"A deal is a deal, woman." He pulled two tablets out of his pocket and handed them to Jasmine. She took them and a drink of water he held for her. Jasmine carefully lowered herself onto Chad's shoulder.

"She refused to take any pain medication unless she was allowed to see you."

Chad rolled his head toward her and gently kissed her forehead. "Stubborn girl."

Doc put the rail back up and headed out of the room. "I'll see you both in the morning. Get some sleep."

Not likely, at least not right now. Chad had to get some answers to the questions that were racing through his mind. "How did he get to you?" He shivered when her hand ghosted over his chest.

"I was in the dressing room. I'd just tried on the Prada again. I thought I'd made a decision but wanted to see them both one more time. I'd just stepped out of the dress when he hit me on the back of the head with something. I didn't hear him come in. The next thing I know, he's dragging me around by the hair, and I'm tied up and gagged. I faded in and out a couple of times. I don't know how long he waited for you to come up. He was raving about Millicent. He told me how he was going to kill us. He wanted you to watch me die because you killed Millicent's love for him. I tried to get away a couple times, head butted him and ran, but the son of a bitch was quick and mean.

"I'm so sorry I didn't come up sooner."

"I'm not. If he hadn't been so worked up, my

distraction might not have worked." Jasmine sighed and settled a little deeper against him.

"I wonder if Millicent knew how much he cared for her. He'd play it off as it was him that wasn't interested, just having a good time. I assumed he was using her as much as she was using him."

"You couldn't have seen it. Don't blame yourself."

"You were bleeding, your back."

"He cut my scalp where he hit me. Every time he pulled my hair, it would bleed. It's nothing."

"I saw the way he kicked you. I see what he did to your face. It was something."

Jasmine yawned and hummed. "It's over."

"It is. Guess we missed the award ceremony." Chad was more than okay with that, except he had the perfect proposal worked out. Damn, he had the ring in his pocket... Where were his clothes?

"Yeah. Wonder if you won."

Chad kissed her forehead again. "Baby, they couldn't give me any award better than what I have in my arms right now."

Jasmine gave a small chuff of air that resembled a laugh. "Those comments will make me think you love me."

"I do love you." Chad was fading fast. He tried to

pry his eyelids open again, but her warmth and the medication they were giving him sucked him under.

"You going to marry me someday?" Her words tugged at his consciousness, pulling him back.

"I was going to ask you tonight."

"Oh... okay... the answer is yes."

"Good... go to sleep."

"Mmm..."

Chad took a deep breath and held her scent deep in his lungs before he released it slowly and drifted to sleep.

CHAPTER 26

Jasmine leaned against the window frame looking out at the moonlit bed of fresh snow. The view from Joseph and Ember's home was breathtaking. She and Chad had jumped at the chance to house-sit for the couple when they flew to Aruba for a two-week vacation.

The blue and silver tones of the full moon shimmered across the pastures, draping everything in a crystalline beauty. She toyed with the ring Chad had given her while they were both still in the hospital. The four-carat, marquis-cut diamond mounted above a bed of channel set diamonds on her left ring finger reminded her it wasn't a dream.

"The stars are beautiful tonight." The deep, sexy

timber of Chad's voice washed over her. She froze at the words that would forever be etched in her mind. Chad pulled her back into him. His large hand spread over her silk robe and pressed gently. Her body clenched, already anticipating Chad's attention. She released the breath caught in her lungs.

"Are they?" She shivered when he moved the hair from the base of her neck and his lips ghosted against her skin.

"Yes." He led her to the bed. The lights in the room were off. Only the moonlight illuminated their path. Chad turned and unfastened the tie of her robe. His hands fed through the material and slid the silk off her shoulders, leaving her naked to his touch. "So beautiful."

His lips trailed her collarbone as his fingers danced over her back with feather-light touches. "Do you trust me?" His mouth brushed over his shoulder.

"Yes." She panted her immediate response.

"Lay down on the center of the bed."

Jasmine watched as he moved around the bed and flicked the silk ties he'd attached to the four posts of the bed frame onto the mattress. Her body heated at the memory of what this man could do to her.

Chad tied her to the bed. The fabric was cool and soft, the restraints not uncomfortably tight, but restrictive enough that she couldn't move from the vulnerable position he placed her in. He lifted a black cloth from the nightstand and ran it through his hands. The movement and sound drew her eyes to his beautiful, talented hands. Hands that could play her as well as any instrument he'd ever mastered. Jasmine licked her dry lips. In the darkened room she couldn't see his eyes, but she could feel them. He lowered himself to the bed and moved next to her.

"I'm going to blindfold you. When we start, you will not be allowed to speak unless you need to stop. Any word you speak stops everything. Do you understand the rules?"

"Stops everything?"

"Yes." The black silk brushed her shoulder. She shivered again.

"So responsive. Do you understand the rules, Jasmine?"

"Yes."

"I'm going to walk out of the room to get a few items. We haven't started yet. Will you be all right?"

Jasmine drew a deep breath. She trusted Chad,

but the idea of being tied, naked, blindfolded and left alone... She felt her anxiety kick in. No, it was fear. Fear of what? Jasmine closed her eyes and tried to concentrate. He didn't move or demand an answer, almost as if he knew she was working through her feelings.

"I'm afraid." The admission tore from her but came out as a mere whisper of sound.

"I know."

Somehow those two words comforted her. He knew. He loved her, and he knew what he was asking her to do frightened her. "I'll be all right."

Chad leaned down and kissed her softly, just his lips pressed against hers, nothing else. "I know that, too."

He covered her eyes with the silk, tying it behind her head. He moved the knot to the side so she wasn't lying on it. "We are starting now. Any word stops the scene. I'll free you immediately."

Jasmine nodded. She felt him get off the bed and cocked her head as she heard him walk across the room and open, then close, the door. She took several deep breaths. She could do this. Her skin tightened, leaving goosebumps. The house creaked. She jumped. Dammit, she knew that sound. It was a normal nighttime sound. She shouldn't be hyperventilating like a teen at her first Freddie Kruger film. Jasmine drew a deep breath and let it out. Her world shrank as she listened intently. The central heating turned on. A wave of cool air pushed across her skin before the warm air from the system filtered through the room. She could smell the heated air. She heard the small pings of the metal in the air duct heating. Her breath steadied as she relaxed and let herself drift.

"Beautiful."

Chad's voice floated toward her. His calloused fingertip traced the length of her arm. Jasmine moaned. She focused on his touch. The touch disappeared, and she waited. The sensations were random —a caress on the arch of her foot before he swept his fingertips over her breasts. His light touch up the sensitive skin of her inner thigh ended before he reached her sex. She arched up, begging silently for more.

A harsh, sharp sensation on her right nipple lasted only a few seconds. Her cry of surprise echoed in the room. She felt water run down her breast. Ice. God, he'd used ice. Jasmine waited, acutely aware of any sound, but not able to determine where he was. She jumped at a soft brush of something against her armpit. It trailed down her side. A feather. Jasmine laid her head down on the bed.

"Stop trying to anticipate my touch. Just feel."

His tone hadn't changed, but she could sense he wanted more from her. Jasmine drew another deep breath and concentrated on relaxing her muscles.

"Good, sweetheart. So good."

Jasmine concentrated on the touches, sensations and soft words of praise. Slowly, his caresses became more sexual, drawing instead of teasing. His mouth, tongue, teeth, fingers, the feather, and ice all melded into a stream of moments. Her universe centered on his touch, not enough and yet too much. Time suspended. Nothing but Chad's touch and his voice existed. A mystic, wonderful sensation built inside her like a wave headed toward the shore. She heard his words, felt his touch, yet could feel herself drifting on that growing momentum. Jasmine felt her lover lift over and enter her. His body began pushing her the last few feet to the crest of whatever she was riding. It was there that her world floated in and around them. Chad's lips and fingers demanded responses as his shaft filled her. Jasmine somehow tethered onto his words, under-standing tones rather than meaning. His thrusts quickened. Her body shook with pleasure, and her world exploded into a million pieces of brilliant lights.

His soft caresses and whiskey smooth voice enticed her mind and body into a coherent, albeit exhausted, sense of peace.

"I love you." His whispered words completed her.

They surrounded her in safety. She snuggled closer and echoed the words of love he shared, her voice a mere whisper. She floated on the knowledge that Chad was her safety, her rock. A touchstone in the storm of her life. He'd risked everything for her. Jasmine sighed and smiled. She'd given him all of herself in return, trusting him to keep her and her heart safe.

CHAD WATCHED HIS STUBBORN, determined woman melt, then fly at his touch. He'd edged her for over an hour. When he finally gave in and pushed her over into the orgasm he'd been denying her, she shattered. His own release had threatened to consume him. Fucking perfect. He pulled out of her and untied her immediately. Her arms and legs wrapped around him and he pulled her into him. He took off the blindfold and covered them with a warm blanket, comforting her with reassuring words and touches. He'd seen subs fly before, and based on their previous lovemaking, Jasmine was capable if she ever let herself be vulnerable enough to trust him completely. She'd honored him with the gift of her total submission tonight. A thing of unmatchable beauty.

Chad held her long after she'd fallen asleep. Snow fell outside. The huge white flakes floating by the window across the room were hypnotic. He considered them, and his life, as he threaded his fingers through Jasmine's thick black hair. His world had been flipped upside down when she'd barged into his life and sent him flying back into the stack of chairs on the Georgia Dome stage.

He glanced at the dresser and the Entertainer of the Year award that had been delivered to the ranch several days ago. The wonderful things he'd achieved, the money he'd earned, and the lifestyle he led all paled in comparison to the love he held in his arms. They had a future together—one that included his music, but wasn't driven by it. He had finally found what he had been searching for all these years: a woman he loved more than life itself, and perhaps, one day, a family. They had a future with true friends and unlimited possibilities. A melody drifted across his thoughts. Words formed and wrapped around the melody. He smiled and reached for a pen and paper.

To read the next in the Kings of Guardian Series, Chief's story click here!

Guardian Defenders Series

Gabriel

Maliki

John

Jeremiah

Guardian Security Shadow World

Anubis (Guardian Shadow World Book 1)

Asp (Guardian Shadow World Book 2)

Lycos (Guardian Shadow World Book 3)

Thanatos (Guardian Shadow World Book 4)

Tempest (Guardian Shadow World Book 5)

Smoke (Guardian Shadow World Book 6)

Reaper (Guardian Shadow World Book 7)

Hope City

Hope City - Brock

HOPE CITY - Brody- Book 3

Hope City - Ryker - Book 5

Hope City - Killian - Book 8

STAND ALONE NOVELS

SEAL Forever - Silver SEALs

A Heart's Desire - Stand Alone

Hot SEAL, Single Malt (SEALs in Paradise)

Hot SEAL, Savannah Nights (SEALs in Paradise)

ABOUT THE AUTHOR

USA Today and Amazon Bestselling Author, Kris Michaels is the alter ego of a happily married wife and mother. She writes romance, usually with characters from military and law enforcement backgrounds.

Made in United States
Troutdale, OR
10/21/2023

13907266R00216